The End

of

May Road

Vol. II The Handover
Mysteries

D. L. Kung

EYES AND EARS

Eyes and Ears Publishers, Inc.
eyesandears.editions@gmail.com

ISBN paperback 978-2-9700748-2-3
1. Kung, D.L. 2 Mystery 3. Hong Kong 4. Suspense 5. China
I. Title

By the same author

To my husband, Peter,

chapter one

—Sunday—

'There are witches in this room.' Father Fresnay paused and looked down from his makeshift altar. Claire saw his eyes scan the hundreds of solemn, upturned Filipina faces. The soft chatter that always accompanied a Sunday Mass for domestic servants in Hong Kong—*amahs*—died away. The room was still. Slowly, the choir of ten white-robed women standing along one wall behind a portable electric piano stopped jingling their tambourines.

Fresnay's voice rumbled and his usually soft Scottish accent gave each word a threatening ferocity. 'You know who they are. Some of you have told the nuns of strange rituals involving the Host, the Body of Our Savior. We've also heard of someone taking money in exchange for casting secret spells, not for good, but for evil. None of this is approved by the Church!'

Claire had never seen her friend Fresnay look so severe, but then, she'd never attended one of his Masses at the Catholic Centre before. During the week, his ponytail of unruly black curls sprang away from his head in Hong Kong's humidity. Now it was tightly tied back. Instead of his weekday garb of pullover, baggy khaki shorts, and worn Chinese leather sandals, he wore livid purple and red vestments. Claire knew him Monday through Friday as a fellow China-watcher—a gentle, humorous 43-year-old Jesuit scholar in a tradition of Church Sinologists stretching back to the sixteenth century.

Even when he offered Mass on Friday nights out at his house in the New Territories for friends and hikers, he just threw on a faded cotton chasuble over his T-shirt and tatty running shoes. This morning she saw the traditional pastor in him, a guardian of faith and doctrine, unexpectedly roused.

She tried not to turn her head to look at Xavier or the Filipinas on all sides of her, but surely the others were just as surprised by Fresnay's outburst? Claire, her Swiss companion, and their newborn son were the only people there besides the priest who weren't from the Philippines; four white faces in a sea of light brown and yellow. The crush of women filled not just this floor, but four other stories of this harbor-front office building lent to the Church. Xavier and Fresnay were the only males in this room of more than two hundred souls, unless you counted tiny Caspar in her arms. She bounced her little bundle rhythmically, waiting for her friend's tirade to end, but the newborn slept soundly anyway, his tiny mouth making sucking movements as he smelled the milk in her breasts.

'Any of you who participates in these unholy practices puts your soul at risk. This is not religion,' Fresnay scoffed. 'It's something evil. It twists the teachings of Christ into the work of the Devil. Anyone tempted to play God is not welcome in this parish, and I hope those of you who know about this will confide in me or the other priests. Now,' Fresnay's expression softened, 'we come to the Words of today's Gospel.'

Finally, Claire stole a glance at her lover, but all she got was a view of Xavier's sharp profile, softening around the jawline with middle age. His narrow eyes, 'the legacy of some Magyar who stopped at our house a few hundred years ago,' were firmly focused on the altar. Xavier must have felt her gaze, for he crossed his right hand over to find her smaller hands clasped underneath Caspar's warm midriff. His grip was brief, but firm and reassuring. She had never said to him how important a man's hands were to her, but he seemed to know instinctively that his strong-muscled touch could calm or arouse her faster than any declarations.

He was a man of so few words, so unlike the American men she had known. Her last love, the CIA agent Jim McIntrye, had been a fast talker. Was it due to the vast language gap between his careful Swiss-German reflections and her American journalistic habit of snappy one-liners? Or would she find in the years to come that in any language he was less given than she to the obvious reactions and verbal navel-gazing of some of her reporter buddies? In the years to come . . . Again she caught herself assuming too much, but with Caspar in her arms and soft wool of Xavier's jacket rubbing her sleeve, she felt enveloped, almost overwhelmed with the comfort of love so recently acquired.

As for the Jesuit right now leading his congregation in Tagalog songs projected onto a white sheet in the corner of the room, Claire knew Fresnay well because she was a foreign correspondent covering China and Hong Kong for the American weekly *Business World*, and he was one of the two or three best Sinologists in Hong Kong—foreign or Chinese. The lanky priest holed up in his musty den with a team of monkish locals and regularly shared his analysis of mainland papers and radio broadcasts with a handful of journalists and diplomats. Claire and Robert shared a warm, but entirely professional relationship.

Her romance with Xavier had nothing to do with China. They'd met in Hong Kong, and dated whenever their paths crossed over the span of slightly more than a year—sometimes in Hong Kong, but just as often in Beijing, Canton or Taiwan. The formality their work schedules imposed had given their romance a courtliness that Claire still savored. There was an innate elegance to his attentiveness when he was with her that gave her confidence in his affection during the weeks they were out of contact. But affection was not passion. Xavier had certainly enjoyed her company, but he hadn't had children on his 48-year-old mind.

Things had turned out a little differently, Claire mused, no longer listening to Fresnay's thoughts on the three Magi. She'd tried to guess at the deeper longings beneath Xavier's cool Swiss exterior and understood they weren't to be discussed. A man his age didn't remain a bachelor through careless exhibition of his vulnerabilities.

And now—Caspar. Well, here he was, with reddish fuzz on his fragile scalp smelling of spit and Claire's perfume, a bit of rash on one cheek and a blister on his upper lip from sucking too hard.

She certainly hadn't planned on this baby. Her only recent experience with children was admiring her neighbor Vicky's little boy, Petey, over weekend coffees by the communal pool for a few minutes at a time. Claire had to admit to herself, if not to Vicky, that as a single career woman, she hadn't really felt much interest in other people's offspring. She hated the way kids interrupted conversations, nagged for snacks, and needed constant wiping and feeding. Vicky couldn't sustain an intelligent exchange for more than a few minutes, always listening with one ear while opening and closing little Tupperware containers of dry Cheerios and animal crackers at the same time.

Petey, always dragging his careworn, threadbare blue Sesame Street 'Grover' toy around the pool, was a clever and quiet child, wonderful in his way. But now Claire realized that the distance from Petey she had felt all along wasn't so unusual—that no child was as special as your own and then all children became more special by association with yours. Because of Caspar, her relationship with other women was now irrevocably changed. She'd joined a vast sisterhood of tired, overextended, bloat-bellied females—office-bound or not—who answered first and last to tiny, sticky tyrants of love and need.

Since Caspar's arrival, Claire and Xavier had arrived at a tentative happiness, although they weren't an official family yet, despite Fresnay's promise to preside over their vows, 'whenever.' Robert Fresnay, half-Scot, half-French, restricted his moral judgments to weekly duty in the confines of the confessional. Like many Jesuits over centuries of overseas missions, he preferred to work on his own, wearing what he liked and socializing with whomever he found interesting. Fresnay knew that neither Claire nor Xavier was a particularly devout Catholic and that they'd come to the Centre this Sunday ahead of Mass to post an advertisement for an *amah*. Fresnay hinted he understood Claire didn't want Xavier to marry her for the sake of propriety or Caspar. And Xavier might consider one proposal in his life just one proposal too many.

'Well, what did you think of my sermon?' Fresnay grinned at both of them wickedly as they later struggled through the flow of Filipinas along the narrow corridors and down by a creaky elevator to the sidewalk.

'Witches!' Xavier exclaimed over the deafening din of Tagalog. 'Claire promised me a sermon about three wise men searching for a baby, not a Halloween show.' Nearly a thousand Filipinas were pressing on all sides of them as they made their way out of the Centre and up the road to Statue Square, the heart of Hong Kong's downtown 'Central District.' It was a brilliant sunny morning, just one week before Christmas. The British colony's weekday commuters had deserted the main business area of Victoria Island but the feel of the week-day hustle for money lingered in the air and glistened down on them from the gold and silver-fronted high-rises. Garish Chinese holiday decorations in red, orange, gold and green dangled twenty stories high in the breeze.

'And they all go to Mass on Sunday!' sighed Fresnay, his towering frame protruding like a tent pole above the crush of women no higher than his elbow. It was a weird sight if you didn't realize that there were 128,000 Philippine nationals in Hong Kong, most of them domestics in kitchens and nurseries all over the territory. They were almost all Catholics of some variety, from the most sophisticated college graduates who earned more cleaning bathrooms in Hong Kong than teaching mathematics at home, to illiterate girls from the far reaches of the Philippines archipelago. From Luzon to the central Visayan Islands down to the southern island of Mindanao, long ravaged by the effects of civil war between the government and Muslim rebels, these women were their country's most lucrative, docile, and exploited export.

A block away, the trio entered a hotel coffee shop crowded with foreign tourists lingering over long breakfasts and local Chinese from advertising and film circles who liked the stylish anonymity of Hong Kong's many four-star hotels. Fresnay was still in a jocular mood as they ordered coffee for three and for the hardworking priest, a breakfast of sausages, tomatoes and omelet. He'd offered three Masses back to back and now he was hungry.

'But witchcraft?' pressed Claire. 'Aren't you exaggerating a little? I don't see any broomsticks or black cats out there.'

Through the plate glass windows looking onto Des Voeux Road, they saw thousands of Filipinas had camped out for the day—reading, eating, dancing to pop cassettes bootlegged from Manila, exchanging manicures, and selling each other jeans and makeup. Every Sunday, the government cordoned off two blocks just to accommodate the swarm of maids who had few other places on the island to relax *en masse*.

Fresnay nodded. 'We wondered too at first. Sister Iglesia heard some stories at the clinic about *amahs* laying out Chinese-style offerings of fruit and flowers at little home altars, muddling up Buddhist prayers to the Goddess of Mercy, Kwan Yin with the "Hail Mary." Or they'd tell each other to say prayers a certain number of times for guaranteed returns.' He smiled as he stretched the 'r' in 'guaranteed' with his Scottish tongue. 'We became more concerned when we caught some of the women putting the Host into their handbags instead of their mouths. Apparently, they took our sermon that the Host was the Body of Christ quite literally and thought they'd take Him home for a date!'

Fresnay's expression darkened. 'Last week we heard that someone in our parish here in Central has set herself up as a self-styled priestess. We have to find out who she is before she does some real harm. She's very clever—she has frightened the women who could identify her into silence. We suspect she's something of a spiritual vulture feeding off their loneliness. That certainly wouldn't be difficult to do, especially these days, when no one can say whether their lives will continue here as before once the Communists take over in June.'

'You think Beijing will change the labor policy? Force the Filipinas out?' Xavier asked.

'Not right away. But mainland China isn't exactly short of cheap labor, is it? As Hong Kong and China merge, would it make sense to continue seeing jobs and remittances drained away from China by the Philippines? And there's another, less political threat. You must have noticed that the Indonesian girls coming into Hong Kong are undercutting the Filipinas—not that those ladies outside are making a decent living,' Fresnay said.

Caspar woke up, his blue eyes staring solemnly as if he had just again entered the world for the first time. Xavier sniffed his backside playfully and then took him from Claire. 'I'd better change him before he empties the restaurant.'

'That big nose of yours is actually useful.' Claire gratefully handed him over. As Xavier headed for the men's room, she laughed to Fresnay, 'This is the man who said, when I told him I was pregnant, that he was very happy to be a father, but he would never, ever touch a diaper.'

Fresnay stared thoughtfully at Claire, certainly long enough for her to register an unusual glint of amusement in his eyes. 'You realize that man loves you?'

Claire shifted in her chair. 'Well, what I think is that he might not be sure about me as his dream partner—things have moved so quickly— but he can be sure that Caspar is his first-born son. He's converting all of his doubts about me into twice as much love for Caspar. He's gone from bachelor to devoted father overnight. I think it's natural. Things are good the way they are, at least so far. Don't worry. We're just digesting it all, bit by bit, day by day.'

Fresnay tamped down his pipe. 'Any woman in your situation would grab the first offer that came from the father of her newborn child, especially if he were as good-looking and intelligent as Xavier.'

'You know I'm too proud to settle for a mercy proposal. I've got a job, a housing allowance, and enough for a full-time, live-in babysitter.' Claire stretched her arms out wide, thankful to be freed of Caspar for a few minutes.

'That's not it. I think you're afraid he might be unhappy tied to you and you think you're putting his happiness before your own. That is real, generous love, but it's totally misguided in your case. But if you can't see it now,' he shook his head slightly, 'I wonder . . .'

Claire interrupted, 'Anyway, you say these Filipinas like to mix up other religions with Catholicism?'

Fresnay loved to display his scholarly talent for esoteric research into Asian politics and history. 'In the old days, I mean old, when the Franciscan Juan de Plasencia landed in the Philippines in 1577, he found the locals were animists, with a whole army of witches as part of their practices. The earth and sky were filled with spirits that had to be worshipped and placated. To make their gods happy, for example, the Filipinos killed slaves to accompany the master of the house to the world beyond—'

'Like Egyptians burying slaves with the mummies? Or Indians burning widows on the funeral pyre?'

'Exactly. Plasencia wrote that the Tagalogs of the hill country bound slaves to the corpse and buried them together. He wasn't the only eyewitness. A Spanish explorer, Diego de Artieda wrote to Philip II that he saw a Filipino captain buried at sea in his vessel with all his oarsman still alive on board!'

Fresnay paused to fiddle some more with his pipe and enjoy Claire's grimace. In over fifteen years in Asia, working her way up from stringer to staff correspondent and finally bureau chief, she had covered a deadly flood in Bangladesh, a train collision in Shanghai, and a horrific fire in a Thai toy factory that maimed dozens of young women. She'd seen dismembered limbs, interviewed lepers, and escorted refugees suffering gunshots wounds off sinking vessels in the China Sea. Still, she was capable of cringing at cold-blooded murder in the name of religion.

Fresnay warmed to his subject with his Jesuit's precision.

'More to the point now, the pre-Christian Filipinos used all kinds of sorcerers and quacks. The *mangagaway* healed the sick, or pretended to. The *manyisalat* bewitched lovers with potions. The *hokloban* killed people by magic, just by raising his hand. The *silagan* tore out the entrails of their victims—' Fresnay was happily ticking off voodoo men on his elegant fingers.

'You're kidding!'

'There's more. The *magtatangal* appeared headless at night. The *asuang*—not among the *Tagalogs*, but among the *Visayans*—flew around and ate people. The *pangatohojan* was a fortune teller, the *bayokin* was a man with a woman's nature, well, perhaps these days we would call him a transsexual, and the *mangagayoma* bewitched people with herbs, something like the *manyisalat*.

'My God, Robert, you're ready for another PhD, this time on Filipino magic! How do you remember all that?'

'Because oddly enough, in one form or another, these spirits aren't completely forgotten in some of the imaginations of the women who come to me in the confessional.'

Claire exclaimed as Xavier returned bearing Caspar. 'Xavier, you've just missed an encyclopedia of Asian ghouls!'

'I'm sorry I did, because I've always found the Filipino image today a bit too—what's the word, Claire—saccharine? You know, Robert, I spend so much time staying in hotels for my job, and no matter where I go in Asia, I hear these Filipino bands crooning sweetly in cocktail lounges, as if the whole of Filipino manhood was signed up for a five-year tour with a major hotel chain. Every time I go out to dinner at someone's house, there's another sweet-faced Filipina in a little white apron taking my coat and serving the dinner. It makes you wonder how the whole country was emasculated—'

The banging of drums and a crackling loudspeaker outside the windows drowned out their conversation. A megaphone blared the voice of a Filipina woman shouting in Tagalog It was hard to see what was happening on Des Voeux Road. Groups of Filipinas who had settled along the sidewalk in Statue Square around the corner and in the street right outside their window were hurriedly gathering up their picnic boxes, boom boxes and hawker stands. Squeals of excitement and argument filled the air. Scurrying off the street and onto the curb, female bodies of all ages and shapes pressed up against the coffee shop's plate glass windows..

The atmosphere around them changed. There had been more and more demonstrations in the last year, most by Chinese students and Democracy Party activists demanding more political dialogue and less threat of political retrenchment from the incoming masters in Beijing.

This time, it wasn't immediately obvious what the ruckus was about. Even though Fresnay was a Sinologist, he had had to master some Tagalog like all the other priests in Hong Kong serving the Filipina community. He strained to make out the speaker's words over the racket of the coffee shop.

'It's a labor protest. They want to raise their minimum wage to $3,500 Hong Kong a month. But I bet most of them are too scared to do anything but watch from the sidelines.'

That was less than $500 in American dollars, thought Claire. Not much for six- or even seven-day weeks working twelve to sixteen hours a day. And most of it had to be sent home to the islands to support the old and very young who couldn't work. Suddenly she heard screams as the bodies, including the wild-eyed faces, of women were squashed against the café's large window.

Claire looked with alarm at her two companions, gesturing at the windowpane to Xavier over the racket of women's hysteria. Now the screams competed with police sirens and whistles. 'I think the window could break!' she shouted. The three of them darted out of their chairs to move to the back of the dining room. Caspar started crying.

'Let's get out of here,' yelled Xavier, pushing some cash into the palm of a nearby waiter. They bid a hasty farewell to Fresnay who signaled that he felt needed out on the street among his parishioners. They fled out the back of the hotel and made for the high-rise parking lot at Beaconsfield House. They were driving the same old rusty Honda Claire had owned when she first met Xavier. They buckled the whimpering Caspar into his baby seat and headed up the steep incline of Cotton Tree Drive toward the island's Midlevels district.

Claire sighed, as much with regret as with relief. 'In the old days I would've been out there interviewing, taking pictures, running around with everybody else. God, Caspar's changed everything for me. All I thought about was getting him out of there.'

'A lot has happened very quickly for us, Claire.' Xavier stared ahead at the road. Glancing at his expression, Claire saw his mood had changed.

'What's on your mind all of a sudden? Not the Filipinas' protest? Don't worry, I'll find someone reliable to look after Caspar. I've got a list of recommendations from Vicky Sandford next door. You know, the mother of that little boy at the pool the other day?'

'You mean the one who dropped his toy in the pool and Mr Li fished it out with a basket?'

They both laughed at the memory of Petey's sorry, soggy 'Grover' dangling from the long end of the pool-keeper's sweeper. Petey had cried, 'Is he dead?' until Grover had dried out in the sun. Xavier had been attentive to Petey's distress, wiping tears off the three-year-old's cheeks as he waited for Grover's resuscitation. Claire had watched Xavier comfort Petey and from that moment on knew he was going to be an excellent father.

It was Xavier as husband she couldn't envisage. All the girlfriends tucked away back at headquarters in Geneva, not to mention the outposts of Xavier's past missions in the Middle East and Africa. What about them?

The *amah* question hung in the air. They'd borrowed a part-time *amah*, Consuela Barang, from friends of the Sandfords over the

Christmas holidays, but would have to give her up and hire someone full-time soon after the New Year. Claire's maternity leave was up in two weeks, and she had postponed the arduous chore of interviewing applicants while she recovered from childbirth. She wasn't looking forward to yet another expansion of her household.

In fact, she still missed living alone.

But Xavier's mind turned out to be on something else. He hesitated. 'Please don't get upset at what I'm going to say.'

Startled, Claire looked at him and laughed. 'Thanks. Now I'm upset.' She wasn't really, not yet, but Caspar started to whine.

'Please, just listen first. Can you get him to be quiet? Give him a cracker or something.'

'Xavier, he doesn't have any teeth. He can't eat crackers yet.'

'What about one of those plastic sucker things? A *nuggi*?'

'Xavier, nookie means something quite different in English from Swiss-German. You mean a pacifier. Anyway, it's bad for his teeth.'

'I thought he didn't have any.'

'Teeth formation. Xavier. . . '

'All right. Anyway, I got a phone call from Fabienne.'

Claire was unprepared for this news. '*The* Fabienne. The one you dated for a century or more?'

'Fabienne Jaccard. The photographer from Geneva. And she's forty. Only two years older than you. She has a project in Cambodia starting after Christmas and she thought she'd spend Christmas in Hong Kong.'

'With us.'

'Not exactly.' Xavier's eyes never left the road.

'With herself?' Claire deadpanned.

'No. Claire, I haven't had time to inform all my girlfriends, I mean my ex-girlfriends, that I met you and that we had Caspar so fast. I mean some of them had been going out with me for five or six years whenever we were working in Geneva at the same time or our paths crossed in the field. We didn't keep up a constant correspondence. It wasn't necessary. It was just nice whenever we met.'

'I see.' Claire saw precisely because it was the kind of relationship she had enjoyed with him herself. She hated this feeling, this heat of insecurity burning her throat. Now in addition to red hair, she had a red face. Say nothing, say nothing. She must love him, she hurt so much, and so suddenly without any warning.

'So I told her to stay at the Furama or the Conrad, or someplace else on the island, and that we'd show her around. At least we shouldn't let her be alone on Christmas Day.'

'Great. Our first family Christmas. Let's start our own special traditions without delay.'

They drove on in a cloud of tension. Xavier turned off May Road onto Tregunter Path and slammed on the brakes. A police sergeant, a tall Westerner, stood smack in the middle of the road.

'Please show me some kind of identification, sir' he said. 'Where are you going?'

'We live at number three, Branksome Towers,' said Xavier.

The officer spoke into a walkie-talkie. '*Sam ho, Honda lai-a.*'

Claire forgot Fabienne and studied the policeman intently. He looked a bit like an old-fashioned movie idol of the forties, dark-haired with expressive eyes—over-polished somehow. Not a typical English look. He was relaying their destination and car type to another officer ahead in Cantonese, but after all her years in Hong Kong, Claire recognized his Cantonese as freshly acquired from language school. He waved them on, but they had to drive slowly to navigate past three police vans partly blocking the curve of the narrow two-lane 'path.' For another hundred or so feet, they were waved ahead by young Chinese officers, silver numbers shining from their epaulets, walkie-talkie bursts squawking at their hips.

'Slow down Xavier. I see John Slaughter. He can tell us what's going on.'

The Chief Inspector saw their car approaching and was about to usher them peremptorily into their building's parking lot when he recognized Claire and nodded. His weather-beaten skin and heavily freckled hands would have given away his long years in colonial Asia even before you were close enough to catch his fluent Cantonese. But Claire knew his past anyway, having worked with him over the years on stories involving fraud, triads, kidnappings, even crimes across the border in China.

'Hello, Claire, my dear. Good morning, sir. I'm afraid there's been an accident. Very sad business indeed. We've found a body in the *nullah* near your building. We're examining the scene now and want to keep the traffic to a minimum.'

'I see,' Xavier answered. He was not so much younger than Slaughter, who was in his early fifties, and not the sort of person to rubberneck into another man's official responsibilities. Claire was more curious by nature than Xavier. Fifteen years of reporting in Asia had made her feel proprietary about excitement in her own backyard, but for Xavier's sake, she said nothing.

In a moment her curiosity was painfully, awfully answered. She strained to see more of the ambulance in the curve of the road just before Xavier turned into the lot. She could make out two Chinese ambulance workers and a Chinese policeman gently easing a stretcher into the back of the van.

'Oh, God, it's Petey. It's Petey,' she cried out. Xavier braked hard to a screeching stop.

'It's Petey!' Claire cried again, looking desperately at Xavier, as if he could magically fly from the car to change the terrible scene lying before them. The small limp blond, doll-like form of Vicky's only child Peter Sandford lay still in the middle of the long canvas. He made no protest as a rough blanket was drawn up over his face.

'Sorry, Sir! You have to move on.' A Chinese constable, polite but firm was leaning gently into Xavier's window.

chapter two

—Monday morning—

The police cars had finally gone. There wasn't much of a breeze and the sun had already burnt off the dawn mists from Victoria Peak above Tregunter Path. It was still jacket weather, something of a treat in a semi-tropical city. An excellent morning for golf out at Fanling's eighteen holes near the Chinese border, if you could get away from the office for a few hours. A pleasure to open the windows of the 9:07 Branksome Towers' residential shuttle bus and feel the fresh air brushing your cheeks, as you thundered away with the other commuters from Midlevels to Central's office towers seven minutes down Garden Road.

Claire walked across Branksome's parking lot and dodged the shuttle bus as it departed without her. In thirteen days—and she was counting—she would be back on it and headed down to the bureau, Caspar entrusted to someone else's care for the day. She craved a return to her normal life, and in the same instant, wondered how she would manage to leave her son for more than a few hours.

She headed up the Path's fifty feet to the next apartment block. A phone call yesterday had been enough to learn that no one could see Vicky until this morning. Claire knew her own face was still puffy from tears of shock and sympathy but she resolved to be as strong as she could for her friend's sake.

From the outside, the Sandford's building, 'Tavistock,' was just another number on Tregunter Path, a stark high-rise residence poised vertiginously on the slope of Victoria Peak in one of Hong Kong's 'better' neighborhoods. The swimming pool lay glistening blue, but unused, next to the entrance. The slapping and thumping from squash courts beneath the asphalt hinted at a regular Monday morning game for two full-time housewives.

Claire was so immersed in her own worries about how to comfort Vicky that she almost overlooked a note pasted on the floor-length mirror inside the elevator. It was written in Chinese and Tagalog and addressed to the maids working in the building. 'Please do not disturb us any more. Take the service lift where you belong. If you don't like it, go back to the Philippines. Don't forget that you are employed here as servants! Don't ruin the reputation of your own kind who disagrees with your attitudes and actions. This applies to the use of the shuttle buses also.'

No English version, Claire remarked. She'd studied Chinese and music with equal fervor some twenty years before at U.C. Berkeley and unlike many residents, could see this was intended as a nasty secret penned by Chinese tenants. Middle-class Chinese families were relatively new to this neighborhood. The *Economist* had tagged such Hong Kongers as 'the new yellow sahibs.' In their heyday, the British might have felt the same about servants using the front 'lift' but would have handled the problem much more discreetly. But then ten years ago the maids would have stuck to the servants' entrance without question, Claire reminded herself. Lines weren't drawn so clearly now as they were even in the late seventies when she'd first arrived in the British colony.

Tensions were rising. With the takeover by Beijing in less than a year, where was Hong Kong heading? Of course, everyone loved a colony as long as they could be top dog, or as Connie was already calling Xavier, 'Master.' And the families that had been *nouveau riche* Chinese industrialists in the seventies—the Foks, the Paos, the Kwoks—why they were more elite these days than any faded colonial bureaucrat.

Who was running the show during these final days of the countdown: the incoming mainland Communist Party officials or the billionaires with their Cantonese forebears and Canadian passports? The elected legislature, now almost a lame duck body or the freshly minted 'provisional legislature' of Beijing-appointed toadies? The American Chamber of Commerce controlling eight billion American dollars of investment in the territory or some yet-to-be-named Cantonese sock puppet acting as Beijing's 'chief executive?'

Certainly it was no longer the British.

Claire hesitated in front of the Sandford's apartment. She felt yesterday afternoon's hole of horror open up inside her stomach all over again. The front door looked as if no tragedy had occurred. The door buzzer burred in the usual way. The Angel of Death had painted no Biblical sign on the door. Fate could land on your doorstep, Claire thought, and look as mundane as the daily paper waiting on the mat.

But when the front door opened and an exhausted Filipina maid admitted Claire into the living room, she saw Victoria Sandford flopped on the sofa like a collapsed marionette, legs akimbo, arms hanging between her knees. Claire couldn't see her face from the doorway but already she knew that the chirpy, precise, athletic young Englishwoman had vanished.

'Who is it, Manny?'

'It's Claire, Vicky. Are you alone?'

Vicky nodded wearily. Claire walked straight over to the young woman's side and sat down. Vicky's short brown hair was a mess, her delicate features swollen with crying, her sweater and woolen skirt looking slept in. It was clear that at nine in the morning, the bereaved and shocked mother was very alone indeed.

'Ian's flight arrives back from Sydney this afternoon. They found another pilot to take over his routes. I spoke to my father last night. He and Mother will arrive tomorrow from Wyverstone. The doctor gave me a sedative. I'm still feeling rather numb. I'm sorry. Would you like something, some tea or . . ?'

'Some tea would be nice,' Claire said directly to the *amah* Manny standing mutely at the edge of the large living room in her blue and white striped uniform.

Claire couldn't think of any words of comfort that would not sound like bad television dialogue, especially since she had only just come to know maternal passion herself. In those early weeks of new motherhood, it was not unusual for Claire to wake suddenly, apparently for no reason. While Xavier slept, some animal instinct would lift and carry her into Caspar's little room.

She'd find the pale face, the heavy awkward head and the red wisps sticking to his skull, damp with hot sleep. She would check his breathing, and then, like some lioness alone with her cub in a dark cave, lick his cheek, move close to his soft mouth and smell the milky sweetness. Did every mother feel this sensual tie to flesh that had so recently been her own, and yet was never hers from the moment of conception? Was losing a child like losing your arm? Would Vicky feel Petey's loss every single day for the rest of her life, like the twinges of a phantom limb?

'John Slaughter stayed with me until I felt ready to rest last night. I didn't want to see Manny—I think I was quite hysterical. But I have to believe it wasn't her fault, it all happened so suddenly,' Vicky said softly.

Then she forced herself to carry on. 'Did you know John and Daddy fought in Malaya together? They were both very young then. It was practically the first posting for both of them. Now there's Daddy sitting back in the pub near the Old Rectory House and here's Uncle John holding my hand, telling me Petey is dead.'

'At least it was someone who knew your family.'

Vicky sighed almost cynically and sat up straighter, tugging her skirt back down to her knees, and fiddling with a gilt button on her cardigan.

'Yes. Not likely next summer, hmmm? At least it wasn't some PAP or PLA soldier shouting at me through some foul interpreter. But it's not much comfort, is it? You and I have talked about it so many times. We've known he had epilepsy since he was about nine months old. Before this, there was always some warning that he was going to have an attack. He'd say, 'Mummy, I don't feel good. The singing is in my head again'.' Vicky paused. 'Last night all I could imagine was how he must have suffered in those few minutes before Manny got to him, wanting someone to come and help him, and I wasn't there.'

She looks wretched, thought Claire. Imagine, there were moments when I got pregnant that I didn't even want Caspar. Wasn't sure.

Vicky turned her tortured face towards Claire. 'Did you see him, Claire? John said Xavier and you drove past on the road. John identified the body for the family and they've still got him. I just don't think I'm up to seeing him today.'

'Yes, I saw him just as he was put into the ambulance. I felt just . . . ' Claire caught herself verging on tears, the last thing Vicky needed to keep herself going. She started over. 'You know, they say sometimes, "He looked just like he was asleep," but Petey looked more peaceful than that. I can't believe he suffered long.'

'Ian's going to want to fly the body back to England.' Vicky was staring away from Claire, out towards the harbor, so it wasn't obvious how she felt about this. Ian Sandford was a Cathay Pacific pilot, a decent man in his late thirties, but inclined to dominate his efficient and dutiful young wife.

'And what do *you* want, Vicky?'

Vicky turned, almost incredulous, her eyes welling up with pain. 'Want? I want my baby back. I want to hold him. God, Petey, why—' Claire took the young woman in her arms and held her sobbing friend for endless minutes. Tears coursed down her face. Manny brought in the tea tray stiffly. When no instruction came, she placed it, gleaming on top of starched embroidered linen on the table at their knees, and then disappeared back into the kitchen.

Finally, as Vicky collected herself, Claire poured the tea. For a while, the two women sat in silence. Claire took in the utter Englishness of the room. If you forgot the bright sunlight reflecting off the white ferries in the harbor at the foot of the steep slope, and just scanned the chintz-covered easy chair, silver-framed photos on the side tables, the clumsy watercolor seascape by Vicky's mother, and the ceramic dog guarding the front door, you'd think you were in Putney or Hampstead.

Then you might notice that the seascape was of a beach in Penang, the fishermen wearing sarongs as they gathered their nets at dusk. The chintz upholstery of the large reading chair in the corner pictured orchids and parrots, not roses or sparrows. The throw cushions were covered in contrasting Indonesian batik, not needlepoint. The ceramic dog faced a cheap foot-high porcelain elephant from Thailand. Claire could never forget an old New Zealand news hack nicknaming these ubiquitous doorstoppers, 'Buffies.' 'Tripped over the buffie again,' he would exclaim drunkenly at parties. Finally Claire demanded to know why 'buffie,' and he had shouted, 'B-U-F-E, Bloody Useless Fucking Elephants!' at the top of his lungs while his hostess blushed.

A large Korean chest in the dining room dwarfed Vicky's side tables. Ten chairs, each carved on its back with *ming*, the Chinese character for 'brightness,' flanked a polished rosewood dining table. And the tea set wasn't silver but Selangor pewter. The whole picture was painfully neat and unoriginal. A blandly tasteful, timeless room of the fading British Empire readied for the constant flow of adults, not children. Vicky had trained Manny well, with a colonial rigor learnt at her mother's knee, thought Claire.

Vicky seemed to read Claire's mind. 'Mother's already saying she wants me to come home for good. But England's not my home. Never was. Even during school days, I wanted to be here.' Vicky wiped her eyes carefully. 'Got to pull myself together. That policeman, you know, the sergeant with John, Anthony Crowley? He's coming back at ten to ask me some questions to file his report.'

'He'll be here soon, then.' Claire gave her another hug. 'I'll come back tomorrow.'

But Vicky didn't let her go. 'No, please stay. You know, hold my hand a bit.' Vicky seemed almost embarrassed by her very human need for support. 'I'm sure he's going to be terribly nice, but I just need someone here. Please stay. I mean it.'

It was the same inspector Claire had seen on the street yesterday. Crowley was on time, ready with a notebook and a comforting expression on his face. He reminded Claire of an young undertaker she had once met, professionally pleasant, pleasing to look at during difficult times and a better actor than anyone in the party of genuine mourners when it came to expressing grief. He made Claire strangely uncomfortable and glad she could stay for Vicky's sake.

'Hello, sir.' Manny's voice was hardly even a whisper as she opened the door to him. Claire glimpsed a strange expression—distrust or fear of his authority—on Manny's wide, almost Chinese face.

'Hello, Manuela, good morning, Mrs Sandford.' Crowley paused, looking at Claire expectantly.

'How do you do, Inspector Crowley. We met on the street yesterday. I was in the Honda. I'm Claire Raymond, a neighbor.' Claire stepped forward to shake his hand while explaining. 'Mrs Sandford asked me to stay a bit longer. I hope that's all right?'

'Well, I have to ask some questions as part of the official record. I'm not sure you—'

'I'd like her to stay very much.' Vicky's face looked stricken, but her voice was firm. She didn't say 'Please.' Claire thought again of Vicky's upbringing. If her father had retired from the Colonial Services at the top of the ranks, Crowley was a mere nobody to a daughter whose life was still lived in the receding shadows of the old era. Crowley nodded as if to say he had no further objections.

'Mrs Sandford, we know, of course, that your son died of a sudden epileptic attack while playing on the other side of the Path near the *nullah*. Your servant Manuela said yesterday he liked to play in a favorite spot of his in the woods there, very close to where she and a group of friends were picnicking. Was this routine, that your amah would watch the boy on Sundays?'

His tone betrayed something. Do you make your help work even on Sundays?

Vicky had heard it too. 'Well, officially it's her one day off,' she admitted. 'But when Ian is flying, she takes him along with her friends for an hour or so to give me a rest. I'm expecting another child. I'm in my ninth week.'

Claire took Vicky's hand. 'Oh, Vicky, I didn't know.'

Vicky managed a wan smile and murmured to Claire. 'We haven't even told my parents, Claire. We were going to keep it quiet for a few months until we knew everything was, you know, well on its way. Now I almost hate this life inside me. I can't explain it. How dare this new baby be so safe and healthy inside me, as if nothing had happened to Petey? I don't want another child if this is what it leads to, all the love and the happiness just ends, like some, some,' Vicky was determined not to crumble into sobs again, 'some massive great thing landing on top of you, and you can't breathe, you can't believe you'll survive one more minute knowing what has happened.'

Claire held Vicky's shoulder tightly, until she felt her calm down.

'Excuse me, Inspector, but is this the really right time to interview Mrs Sandford? Couldn't we wait for her husband to return home?'

Claire found Crowley a strange combination—good looking, but somehow too eager and a little pompous all at the same time.

'I'll only need another few minutes. Then I'll confirm the report of the *amah*, and we'll be finished. Mrs Sandford, how serious was his illness? I recall you telling me a bit about it few months ago, when I bumped into you at the bus stop while I was on duty. You were on your way to the doctor, weren't you? Didn't you tell me his illness was under control? Did he have these attacks often?'

'Just a few at first. And as soon as we got him on the medication, the seizures were much less frequent. But lately, say over the last year or so, they started getting worse. The threshold, as Dr Trythall at Matilda Hospital calls it, that threshold was lowering. We all found it strange, including the doctor, because we caught it early enough and we thought the outlook was quite good. Usually the threshold gets higher the older a child gets, and as long as they get lots of sleep and not too much excitement, and you keep the anticonvulsants like Dilantrin on hand, you worry less and less. There are the side effects to watch out for, of course, sometimes nausea, anemia, and other things, but we didn't have any problems with those. You can talk to Dr Trythall . . . '

'Yes, I suppose we should have a word with him. I, um . . . It must have been very hard for you and Mr Sandford to watch him suffer, I'm sure. I once read about these *grand mal* seizures.'

He was unctuous, Claire thought. Vicky was on the defensive. 'They don't use that terminology any more, Inspector Crowley. Petey had partial seizures, he stayed conscious, but they were 'complex' partial seizures. Something inside his brain, his temporal lobe, would misfire. He might start to talk nonsense or not quite nonsense, but not quite sense, if you see what I mean. Sometimes, as he was so little anyway, it was hard to tell. As the seizure spread, he would hear songs, or voices, recall previous places or people. He'd say, 'Mummy, I feel funny and . . . '

Vicky stopped and sighed. Then she drew herself up again and seemed determined to finish. Crowley was taking notes and nodding sympathetically. 'We tried to remove Petey from anything that we noticed might trigger an attack. It could be certain songs, loud sounds, a lot of stress. It wasn't easy in a city like this with all the construction work, the traffic, just constant noise. I tried to keep the house as restful as possible.'

But never really relaxed, thought Claire, remembering Ian's demanding personality and the airline's constantly expanding schedules, the stewardess strikes, the safety rows with the Chinese staff, the budget worries, the localization policies. No, Ian never rested. It was unlikely Vicky relaxed.

'Did you consider removing Petey from Hong Kong?'

'He was still too young to go away to school. I take him to England, of course, to visit my mother every summer,' she stopped, realizing she'd forgotten that Petey was dead.

'I am so sorry, Mrs Sandford. Please convey my condolences to your husband as well. You know, I walk the Path as part of my rounds some mornings with Constable Yueng. I used to see Petey regularly with Manuela buying vegetables at the truck that stops along the road. He was an absolutely delightful child.' There he goes again, thought Claire. Vicky was looking at him almost resentfully.

He returned to business. 'Well, yes. Um, we'll get back later if we have any further questions. In the meantime, I'd like to interview your *amah* just to complete the routine.' He slapped his notebook shut and Claire noticed his smooth, well-manicured hands. He was such a strange combination of slick manners offset by an unfashionable northern accent, the working class vowels muffled by effort and probably some years in London.

'Thank you.' Vicky sat upright as if she were holding her breath until he left. Claire, would you show him back to Manny's room? Thanks so much for stopping by. It was good of you, really.'

Claire kissed her friend gently on the cheek. 'Then I'll slip out the servant's door. Get some rest. Only a few more hours until Ian gets here. Try and hold on.'

She led Inspector Crowley through the heavy door connecting the dining room to the long, pristine, tiled kitchen and pushed open the equally heavy door leading to the servant's corridor. Manuela opened the door of her own room just two inches, enough to see who was knocking. She was crying now and her face was flushed a deep magenta. She looked shocked when she saw Crowley waiting outside her door. Still, shuddering, she took in Claire's presence, too.

She gestured sobbing to the Inspector to sit on a folding metal chair next to the bed, but he declined, so she remained standing in front of her two visitors. 'Please stay with me, ma'am,' she pleaded. Claire turned for consent to Crowley, who nodded his okay. Relieved a bit, Manuela wiped her brows and eyes with a large white handkerchief.

Claire had lived in Hong Kong since her early twenties. Looking around the small space barely large enough for three adults to stand in, she could see Manny was relatively lucky. She'd seen the inside of enough Hong Kong homes to know how many Filipinas slept under the dinner table every night, or shared the bed of the youngest child in the family. Some slept in kitchen pantries or closets converted into bedrooms, their clothes hanging directly over their heads in a long suffocating row, the television set attached somewhere near the ceiling, if they were lucky enough to get one. The unlucky ones were expected to sleep on mattresses next to the washing machine in the laundry room.

Most old Hong Kong apartments didn't have western toilets for the servants, only Chinese-style holes in the floor for squatting over. Many servants' rooms didn't have baths or even proper showers. Landlords installed garden hoses or showerheads on pipes over the toilet. Most ate their meals from a rice cooker next to their beds. The kitchen was for the master's family.

Manny lived in privacy in a whitewashed room with its own separate bathroom with a shower, sink and toilet. Her single bed had fitted sheets. There was a plywood standing closet and a small television. On her bedside table was a statue of the Virgin Mary strung with tiny necklaces of plastic flowers. Leaning against the statue was a snapshot of a small boy sitting on the back of a jitney in Manila, one of the ubiquitous jeeps bedecked in garlands, neon paint and wild slogans that served as the city's fastest form of public transportation.

Crowley waited for Manuela to stop her sobbing, but the woman showed no signs of calming down, so he plowed on, a bit too loudly.

'Please tell us, Manuela, everything that happened yesterday up to the time you came running up to me on the sidewalk and took me to see Petey's body?'

Manuela gasped for breath, wiped her eyes and her shaking slowed down enough to talk. Claire tried hard to suppress the thought that came into her mind—the typical colonial daughter maintaining a stiff upper lip in the living room matched by a Filipina's Hispanic sense of melodrama. Yes, these were clichés come to life, perhaps. But damned if she hadn't seen in her years of reporting the same things again and again. Maybe she'd been in Hong Kong too long.

Manuela was talking between taking deep breaths. 'Yes, sir. In the morning I went to Mass at St. Joseph's with some of the other Filipinas who work in this building. We took the shuttle bus from the parking lot and came back by the Peak tram to the May Road station. It was after eleven. When I came home I made lunch—egg mayonnaise salad—for Mrs Sandford. I got Petey and took him downstairs to meet my friends for a picnic. Mrs Sandford was going to have a rest.'

'How did Petey seem to you? Did he appear to be sick? Were there any warning signs of an attack?'

'Nothing, sir.' Manny's shoulders were heaving up and down.

'Where did you have your picnic? Who was with you?'

'There were three of us. Usually there are more, but this time it was only Narcisa and Aurora. We usually have our meetings—'

'Meetings? Or picnic?'

'Well, both, sir. First we have the meeting of the Charismatic Society and we pray at the clearing above the Path just past the footbridge.'

'Where Tregunter Path meets May Road on the other side of the bridge?'

'Yes, sir. The building construction workers eat lunch there during the week. That is where they pile up their working materials for the building next door they are working on. We usually meet there about one o'clock.'

'And where was Petey?'

'He went up the path to a little place where he likes to play.'

'By the *nullah*?'

'Yes,' Manuela seemed suddenly eager to make a point. 'But this time of year, there is no rain, sir. There is no water. It is not dangerous. And sometimes he goes to play with the gardener on the slope next to the clearing, where they grow the plants. But the gardener knows where we are.'

Crowley nodded sympathetically to Manuela as he took notes. There was no backyard or park for kids to play in along the Path, except for an old mini-tennis court that had fallen into disuse and stayed locked up all year. But a footpath led up from the road, cutting gently across the slope through the brush and trees. Sunday walkers used the footpath to descend from the top of Victoria Peak all the time. It was reasonable of Manny to let Petey potter around nearby, safer, in fact, than trying to play closer to the road where speeding cars were a hazard.

'There, there,' said Crowley awkwardly. 'Nobody is blaming you. Did Petey go over to the nursery to see the gardener yesterday?'

Was Manny hesitating? She answered quietly, 'No, sir. He did not go near the nursery yesterday.'

Claire leaned quietly in the doorway, watching Crowley ask the questions, just doing his job. As a journalist, she would have let Manuela do more talking.

Crowley probed again. 'So what happened?'

'We had finished our prayers, and we were dancing to some music, sir, and eating some *adobo*, singing and laughing, just having a good time. Every ten or fifteen minutes I would check on Petey. I knew where he was because I could always see his red sweatshirt through the trees, and I was watching where he was sitting on the ground. Suddenly I noticed he was very quiet. I told my friends I am going to look at Petey. When I got to the place where he was, he was lying on the ground, sir. He was very quiet, but his mouth was full of saliva and his face was blue.'

Manuela's expression turned inward as she relived the panic all over again. 'So I say to myself, Oh, my God, my God, and I call out to my friends to come help me. He didn't close his eyes or say anything, and I was shaking him and crying and shouting to him, but he didn't answer.

I was very, very frightened, sir. I had been watching him all the time, when we were praying, through the trees.'

Manny's head sunk, her shoulders heaved and a deep wailing came out of her chest. 'My God, my God,' she repeated, shaking her head in her hands. 'I am so sorry, sir. I knew Petey could get sick very fast and needed his medicine. But I gave him his medicine and it did him no good. It always protected him before this. God has cursed him with this sickness.'

'So that's when you came running down to the road below and saw me?'

Manny wiped her eyes carefully and recited slowly, reliving the order of events as accurately as she could. 'First, I saw that neighbor lady, Mrs Reynolds, Imelda's employer, driving past and I tried to stop her, but she ignored me, even though I was waving and shouting from the sidewalk. But she does not like the Filipinas. Then I saw you. Yes, sir, I was very happy to see you.'

'But by then, of course, it was too late. How long did you stay by the body before you came for help?'

'Only one or two minutes, sir. My friends, they were crying and crying and I had to make sure they wouldn't touch him if I left him even for a minute. They were hysterical and didn't go for help when I told them to. Just stood in one place screaming and crying. It was very hard to think what should I do. I was afraid. My little boy Ramon died in Bontoc last year. This is Ramon's picture. He got sick and he died, too.' Manuela took the photo of the little boy in the jitney in her hand. Claire realized Manuela might be on the verge of a long story. 'He needed some medicine, but he didn't get it in time. I miss him every day.'

'We're very sorry, Manuela, but I'm afraid we have to go now. There may be more questions later, and you're going to have to stay here with the Sandfords, even though it might be uncomfortable for you.'

Manuela starting sobbing more loudly. 'I have a big pain in my heart for my Ramon. If only I could talk to him once again, but now I will never talk to him, never again, and he wonders where I am. I feel a very big, big pain in my heart now for Mrs Sandford, too.'

Crowley looked at Claire and muttered curtly, 'You might recommend Mrs Sandford pass on some of those sedatives to her *amah* here. I'm very sorry to hear that, thank you, Manuela. We'll go now. Please take good care of Mrs Sandford. Do everything you can to help her, and try to be kind if she loses her temper or is short with you. She would have to be a saint not to hate anyone connected with this tragedy right now.' Crowley put his notes away.

'Yes, sir, I will, sir. Thank you.' Manny gathered herself shakily to show them out through the kitchen. But Crowley said, 'Thanks, that won't be necessary. We'll go out this way.' He opened the back entrance's heavy door to lead Claire out to the steel and cement landing that served the servants' elevator. It was a sharp contrast to the front entrance with its beveled mirrors, tropical plants and gold handrails.

'We'll speak to the gardener, and Mrs Reynolds to confirm what Manny says, but it seems fairly straightforward. I hope I didn't seem brusque, but I've interviewed Filipinas before. They can be a terribly emotional lot.'

'It worries me. Oh, not the crying, I mean, the whole thing of leaving your children with someone else, all day, every day,' said Claire, half to herself. 'I'm just about to hire an *amah* for my own newborn this week. This kind of thing makes you think twice about giving your children five days a week to anyone, no matter how well meaning they are. I wonder if there was anything that could have been done? Can anyone take care of your own child as well as you can? Was she really watching, I mean *really* watching?'

Crowley spoke coolly. 'Am I right in thinking you're a journalist? Yes? The name rang a bell. No, I don't have much time to read, but I think I saw you on a talk show discussing the crisis between the Chinese army and the American navy last March in the Taiwan Straits.'

'Yes, that was me.'

Well, in my short tour of duty here in Hong Kong, I've learned that there are some questions that are very dangerous to ask. All middle-class women hire working-class women to look after their children, who in turn give their own children to their mothers to raise. And all this money earned goes in circles, and the children? From what I've seen, the Filipinas are as careful and kind as any sort of nanny you'll find anywhere in the world. If a mother has to work, well, she could do worse.'

'But,' he gestured dismissively back at the Sandford flat, 'these women aren't working. And if I had a child, I would want his own mother to be at his side, not someone with a Third World primary school education and half-baked English. But then,' Crowley smiled wryly, 'I wasn't brought up in one of these colonial families with hot-and-cold running servants. My mother raised me, by herself, in Leicester, with no thanks or apologies to anyone. She cleaned other people's houses during the day and worked a second job on Friday and Saturday nights. Left me those nights with an auntie.'

He was obviously quite proud of his mother, but stopped there, as if embarrassed by the direction their chat had followed. Claire wondered to herself what had brought him to Hong Kong, especially with the handover imminent. There was no future in the force, no possible promotion opportunities for a good-looking Englishman with ambition, and if he didn't have the education and push to make it in banking or commercial circles, it was a strange dead end.

It was policy to make sure that the upper ranks—at one time almost all British—were increasingly filled with talented Chinese as the colonial administration came to a close. Crowley would certainly never see himself made Senior Superintendent in the service of the Special Administration Region of Hong Kong to come. The Hong Kong government had stopped actively recruiting in London many years ago. Even the Hong Kong Governor's deputies were Chinese, save one Australian-born press spokesman.

They said goodbye politely at the gate of Claire's building. It was only ten-twenty in the morning. Claire's first interview with a candidate to be Caspar's *amah* would be arriving at ten-thirty. She felt momentarily like calling the whole thing off. She opened her front door heavily, filled with misgivings. Did she really have to work? For her sake? For whose sake? Until a year ago, work had been all she had besides her music, studying the piano having been a way of life from the age of eight. There had been a time when she had even considered making music her career. Instead the lure of travel, with journalism paying her way, had won out. She'd earned this job the hard way, by sticking out long years of free-lancing in the field, rather than joining the corporate race for overseas postings back in the States.

Maybe it was hard for a man like Crowley to understand that her identity as Claire Raymond, the byline, was more than a persona; it was her source of financial, social and emotional support. What was it her ex-lover Jim had said to her that amazing night when they both admitted their feelings? 'I can't believe the famous Claire Raymond is with me tonight.' Well, even if Jim was gone—or disappeared rather—in a mystifyingly abrupt departure on US government business somewhere else, her identity as Hong Kong's longest serving resident American correspondent was immutable.

Now for Xavier she was just Claire. Bylines and ten-day assignments in Shanghai wouldn't impress little Caspar. Those two men, large and tiny, had offered her hope of being other things, maybe simpler or better things? Was she giving those other choices a fair shot?

Claire felt depleted by the emotions of the morning. Letting herself into their apartment, she thought again of Petey's laughter, then tears, at the swimming pool the last time she'd seen him alive.

As she entered her living room, strong cigarette smoke assaulted her nostrils. Neither she nor Xavier smoked. A small figure lounging on the shaded balcony was silhouetted against the bright morning light beyond. The woman turned at the sound of the front door slamming behind Claire. She rose sinuously and came in from the balcony wearing a tentative smile framed by dark brunette hair cut into a perfect fringe. As she came into the room, hand outstretched to greet Claire; the other hand pulled a cigarette from full, deep red lips. '*Salut, Claire. Je suis Fabienne.* I'm so sorry. I hope you don't mind. Your girl let me in. I don't know which hotel Xavier booked for me. So I thought I will just come here until I will reach him.'

Fabienne paused, taking in Claire with large eyes. One gamine hip was cocked upwards in well-cut jeans, barely topped by a soft oatmeal-colored sweater and finished with small suede boots. Still recovering from childbirth, Claire knew that her black trousers stretched obviously across her slack stomach, and the white cotton shirt she had thought chic was already more than fashionably wrinkled.

Fabienne smiled again, almost too knowingly. 'What a beautiful baby you have, but so unlike Xavier. I would never have guessed he was the father.'

Claire fumbled a recovery and managed a perfunctory handshake. She decided to let the slur on Caspar's illegitimacy slide past her, and having regained composure sufficiently to ask if the flight to Hong Kong had been comfortable, she asked Connie to get the woman a cold drink and settled her guest on one of the sofas in the living room.

They chatted about the weather, life and liberty, sitting opposite each other, marking time while Claire waited for Xavier to return her quick alert by phone.

'I have my career and my personal life, and that is enough for me,' said Fabienne.

Claire wasn't idiot enough to ask Fabienne to detail what or whom she reckoned her personal life included. 'I have my career too, and then Caspar came along. He's changed a lot of my ideas just by being here,' Claire admitted, 'You never wanted children yourself?' She wondered if they could, after all, strike a sympathetic chord somewhere.

'I wasn't meant to play the cow,' snapped Fabienne, lighting another cigarette.

Claire wondered what face Fabienne showed to Xavier, because it was hard to picture these two together. There was nothing left to do, but wait for Fabienne's speedy departure for the hotel, and moo goodbye, she thought ruefully.

chapter three

To be fair, Fabienne could have recited the day's weather report and it would have sounded to Claire like a recital of intended barbs. It only needed a few more comments from the Genevan and the taxi might not have been necessary. Fabienne was welcome to take the quicker route over the wall of the Vonalps' balcony, roll down the hillside and plunge into the harbor's polluted waters. Worse, Fabienne exuded an air of satisfaction, even patronizing approval, at having gained entrance to the apartment thanks to Connie in order to inspect Xavier's offspring alone.

Her tiny hands cupped gracefully around a mug of mint tea, the Swiss-French woman had rattled off all the places she'd seen, 'except Hong Kong, of course, and Cambodia, this is the first time,' but it didn't take Claire long to realize that she was actually listing, carefully, all the places she had visited *with Xavier.* Was it her imagination or was Fabienne watching for a sign of recognition from Claire of familiarity with Xavier's past?

And for someone so spare and light, she was remarkably immovable. She sat for a full five minutes while Claire stood, she stood in the middle of the room chatting for another five while Claire waited patiently, hand on the doorknob. And when Claire finally did open the front door to bundle Fabienne, her camera bags, and expensive black calf leather carryall downstairs for a taxi bound for the Excelsior Hotel, there was Leo standing right in their path.

Leo Franklin was the three and a half year old Eurasian child who lived in the only other apartment on their floor. Since moving in next to the Franklins, Claire had not felt much warmth from his parents, the

Australian financier Giles or his well-groomed Chinese socialite wife, Lily. But Claire had loved Leo immediately for his light laughter trailing from under the front door, for the infectious games he played with Petey Sandford in the swimming pool shared by three buildings along Tregunter Path, for his toys left strewn along the stairwell and for his ribald 'I-can-see-your-butt' humor.

Today Leo was wearing his latest Disney promotional T-shirt over tiny jockey briefs. But no matter what his current video passion, Claire had nicknamed him 'Little Boo-Boo,' after Yogi Bear's sidekick, the first time they met. Not understanding the affectionate reference, it had offended Lily, sensitive to any imagined interracial slur.

'You are so sweet! You are so cute! What is your name?' Fabienne had dropped to her knees. So Leo had dropped to his.

'Poo-poo,' mugged Leo.

'That's Boo-Boo,' corrected Claire. 'He's a little cartoon bear I loved when I was his age. But in real life . .?' she prompted him.

'Where is Real Life?'

'Good question, Leo. Actually, his name is Leo Franklin.'

Fabienne was rubbing his cheeks and ruffling his hair ferociously. 'Where do you live, *mon cheri? Mon petit homme!*' Fabienne was pouring verbal syrup on the boy's head so thick it would glue them both to the foyer marble for weeks, thought Claire.

'In the zoo,' Leo's eyes were narrowing.

'And you are an animal. What kind? What kind of animal?'

'A bumposaurus. They go like this.' And Leo went down on all fours and hopped around, his thumbs and two fingers making raptor-like grasping gestures. To Claire's delight, he then sunk his teeth into the suede-covered ankle of her guest.

'Now you're dead,' he said, shaking his head with sympathy.

Claire instructed the taxi driver to take Fabienne to The Excelsior with ill-disguised haste. The hotel was not offensively distant from their apartment, being on the same side of the harbor as Tregunter Path, nor was it smack under their noses in Central. How Swiss of Xavier, thought Claire sourly, to be so neutral and diplomatic.

The morning had already had its fill of emotions—grief, resentment, jealousy, and indecision—and it was still early in the day. She sighed and leaned back against the dining room wall and surveyed her living room.

What had Fabienne inspected? And what impression would it make on a Filipina applying to work for her? It was a room not very different in proportion from the Sandfords', but certainly a world away in taste and history. The walls were lined with a hastily unpacked jumble of her own books: Chinese poetry, literary biographies, murder mysteries. In the corner, where the light was pouring onto the unpolished surfaces, stood her German grand piano, dragged to Hong Kong from Shanghai by some émigré family and unloaded on a small Chinese music store in Wan Chai to be discovered by Claire one Saturday afternoon. There were her piles of yellow Schirmer music scores and her cherished map of China drawn by 16th century Jesuits, bought under the appraising eye of Father Fresnay at an auction downtown. The rest of the room was a sorry collection of battered whitewashed rattan, its cushions covered in faded salmon linen.

Six months ago it had all been unceremoniously thrown together with the help of a team of sweating Sichuanese moving men alongside Xavier's Corbusier chair, Balinese masks, wall hangings, stereo and CD's. The final chaotic decorator touch was the collection of hurriedly-purchased baby gear: a stuffed lion from Narita Airport, a hand-me-down baby walker from *The Time of London* family in Beijing, a shiny British stroller from friends at the Hong Kong and Shanghai Bank, and a bouncer hanging in the kitchen doorway from Claire's bachelor State Department friend, Harris Hillward.

No wonder *Architectural Digest* hasn't called, she sighed. She slid the balcony doors as wide open as possible to air out the room. When she went to the nursery to check on Caspar, he wasn't there, and startled, she discovered him instead in a Moses basket in the center of the kitchen floor. Consuela was ironing a shapeless velour item about ten inches long.

'Connie, what are you doing?'

'Ironing the baby suits, ma'am.'

'Connie, you don't have to press a baby's stretch suit. I appreciate your thoroughness, but I don't think it's going to make much difference. That's like ironing towels. It's just not necessary.'

'I already ironed the towels, ma'am.'

'I see. Thank you.' Claire suppressed a smile. Connie's expression was a mix of pride and fear of a reprimand. Claire had no intention of going through such a scene every day. She would have to overcome her initial instinct to virtually cower from her domestic help in the assumption they would know better than she how to run a family home. The whole idea of some poor girl working six days a week from breakfast until after dinner left her feeling a mixture of gratitude and embarrassment. This lifestyle was a given for working mothers in Hong Kong, but Claire came to it desperately in need of relief and yet uncomfortable.

No, there was no avoiding her responsibilities, even if she was backing into them so reluctantly. She saw she was going to have to establish priorities with the permanent *amah*. For years she'd done her own laundry and shopping in between assignments in Taiwan, Bangkok, and Beijing. Saturdays had meant a quick swipe at the bathroom, a vacuum over the worn Chinese carpets and a spritz of Windex on the mirrors.

She had realized in the last few weeks that Xavier's job required a certain preparedness as agency people arrived with little warning from Geneva, Washington, New York or the field, and expected drinks on short notice, if not dinner. Caspar, too, wasn't just a bit of housework she could catch up with between assignments. For a brief second, she stood motionless in the corridor of her own home and realizing that every room of her home was shared with another presence, hated the new burdens of home and motherhood, the very burdens that triggered the ill-contained resentment of the tired, virginal Filipinas all around her.

Connie had gone to answer the door to Ysidra Pangilanan. Ysidra looked about twenty and wore her hair down the back of her neck in a braid. She was dressed in a black skirt and red shirt and smiled tentatively at Claire. They sat in the living room; Ysidra perched on the edge of the long rattan sofa.

'Connie says you are a relative of hers?'

'Yes ma'am.'

Claire smiled warmly. 'What kind of relative?'

The two Filipinas exchange mumbled consultations.

'A cousin, ma'am.'

'Can you tell me something about your work experience?'

'Yes, ma'am.' Nothing followed. Claire looked at Ysidra, who smiled politely back, fiddling patiently with the end of her braid.

Consuela, pretending to polish the dining table behind them, started an urgent Cebuyan exchange.

'Connie, does your cousin really speak English?'

Connie smiled helpfully. 'She is very, very shy, ma'am. She works for a Chinese family now in Mongkok. That man is very bad man and he is always making trouble for my cousin because she is so pretty. He climbs into her bed while she is sleeping. She beat him away many times. Anyway, my cousin wants to work for you very much, ma'am.'

'So you said, and I appreciate her eagerness, but you promised she spoke good English.'

'She learns very quickly ma'am. And she loves children very much.'

'I see.'

In the negative sense, Claire thought, this might be easier than she thought. She could do nothing for Ysidra, and having compared Ysidra's features with Connie's, suspected they were more closely related by bus lines than bloodlines. For the moment there seemed to be nothing she could do but send Ysidra back to the Mongkok bed hopper.

The next candidate, 'Teddy' Agrava, was anxious for the job, but wasn't available until her current employers emigrated to Canada in three months' time. She'd seen the advertisement at the Catholic Centre's bulletin board asking for applicants with experience with newborns. Actually, she had no experience with children, although she was a trained nurse. Someday, she would like to emigrate to the US where her half-sister was a nurse in Washington D.C. Check.

The third candidate, Luisa Tarlac, had forgotten her references, then admitted she was breaking her contract because her employers were 'very picky about everything, changing sheets, watering the plants. Always very tough on me. They show me no consideration, and the employer's wife is not healthy in her mind.' Check.

The fourth candidate, Arellina Santos, didn't show up.

Claire retreated to the bedroom with a wad of tissues and emptied herself of grief over Petey and frustration with the morning. A cold beer and cheese sandwich now sat half-consumed on her desk. Guiltily, she wished to be removed from all these intimacies. Life in the office was so impersonal, so safe by comparison. You wrote about other people's tragedies, bankruptcies, wars, and divorces with equanimity. You polished off people's successes and failures with a white wine and soda at the Foreign Correspondents' Club.

She looked up to see Xavier standing in the doorway of her office, a particular look of amused and loving disgust in his eyes.

'I see you and my child have shared a San Miguel for lunch.'

Claire straightened up. 'Oh, you should have called. You've missed lunch. He's sleeping soundly.'

'I'm not surprised, although you keep telling me beer is good for the baby. Anyway,' he sat down on the end of the chair, 'I didn't come home to see him. I was a little worried about you. It's only ten minutes from town and I couldn't think of anything I wanted to eat and the secretaries ordered all these smelly takeout noodles in fish sauce.' He sighed, 'I just felt like clearing my head.'

He sat down and leaned over her, stroking the long stray red curls that hung over her shoulder. While he played with her hair, she reciprocated by straightening the collar of his lightweight wool sports jacket. He never had to dress too formally for his agency job. He wasn't even wearing a tie for work, just a turtleneck sweater. She loved the way he wore his clothes, thoughtlessly, perfectly, 'decontracté.'

As she brushed off his shoulders, she thought to herself, 'This is how monkeys in love must groom each other. They don't make promises or take vows. They bark until the rival monkeys retreat into the bushes. Then they sit quietly in the midday shade and pick out lice.' The back of his hair curled over the cashmere, so she played with his hair, too, and smiled.

Possibly it was a little too brave a smile, because he sat back and asked pointedly, 'Did everything go all right with Fabienne?'

'Of course,' Claire shrugged. 'I've been airing the house out for the last couple of hours.'

'Yes, well, she's always smoked. I used to smoke heavily too, remember.'

'I wasn't referring to her cigarettes. She also implied the baby wasn't yours.'

Xavier sighed. He kissed her softly and murmured, 'I'm with you. You . . . remember? You have no reason to be nervous about her little comments.'

Claire turned away slightly embarrassed. Xavier pulled back at her small rejection.

'Remember, you're a little shock for her, too. But she means well, so don't worry. Anyway, she called me from the hotel and suggested lunch, but I told her—'

'So that's why you're here in the middle of the day'

'Well, maybe I'm not ready to see her. It's strange the idea of you both in the same city. As it turns out, she has friends here in town besides me. I don't think it's going to be a problem for us, and Claire, it shouldn't become a problem, okay?'

Was she being scolded or loved, or both?

'Did you spend some time with your friend next door?'

'Vicky, yes. Nobody realized Petey's epilepsy was so bad. And there's nothing you can say in such a situation. I wish I could have checked back with her, but I've been interviewing *amahs* all morning.'

'I hope you didn't hire someone without my meeting her,' Xavier protested playfully. 'I want someone beautiful, who calls me 'Master,' cooks me *rösti*, has a warm bath waiting when I come home every night and folds the dinner napkins into little orchid shapes on the plate.'

'I think you're joking, but the pathetic thing is, I can't be totally sure. Is that really what you expect in a servant?'

'No, I was talking about you, not the *amah*.'

Claire laughed. 'Right. You've spent so much of your life in hotels and tents, I'm not sure how you expect me to run your first real home.'

'You should know me better.'

'I say that to myself every morning now that I wake up with a man in my bed and a baby next door yelling for my body.'

'You'll get used to it. You haven't got a choice. You're stuck with two new men in your life.'

Claire was about to say, 'Is that a promise?' But Xavier reacted badly to Claire's insecurities. She could look at her cards every day and still not know if she was playing a weak hand or a straight flush. Why was that?

Dovie Ocampo came on time, but she just missed meeting Xavier. She was a woman in her fifties, wearing no makeup, her short hair tucked behind her ears. Claire was surprised to see she was wearing a wool bouclé suit, the sort Englishwomen of a certain type would wear to tea.

'I learned about the job from Mrs Sandford, ma'am. Only on Saturday.'

'I've just seen her. She's holding up incredibly well. We're all shocked by what happened,' Claire replied.

But Dovie knew what she was there for. 'I have worked for Mr and Mrs Evans-Smith since 1973.' She handed Claire her typed references in a business envelope. Claire immediately recognized the government letterhead.

'As you probably know, Mr Evans-Smith is retiring from the post of Secretary for the New Territories. He'll join his wife in England in a month's time. Mrs Evans-Smith had already made arrangements for me to work in Sha Tin, near my daughter and her family. But then my daughter decided to return to Manila next year, so I thought I would like to work on Hong Kong side again, closer to other friends who work for families in government.'

Claire took in Dovie's introduction, privately absorbing the surprise of her introduction. So old Evans-Smith's time was up, she remarked to herself. Of course, all the old colonials, the men she'd interviewed in her first heady days of local reporting in Hong Kong fifteen years before, they were going now. Those who had stuck it out were just eking out their contracts until the handover for the sake of bigger pensions. But were they as sad as the younger men in their forties and fifties who were retiring early from the Hong Kong government to the shires, men who in another era would have had another good twenty years of colonial service ahead?

She was thrown momentarily back in time to her days starting out at the South China Morning Post as a local reporter. What confidence men like Evans-Smith had enjoyed then, shuttling between their offices in Government House, the Murray Building and Beaconsfield House. At the end of the day, they would ease over to the Hilton Hotel's Dragonboat Bar for a few drinks, then mosey by diesel taxi back up to their government-subsidized flats with ceiling fans and large portico'ed balconies overlooking the harbor. The weeks were punctuated by Sundays in shared ownership of a little Chinese junk. At the sound of the Noonday Gun back in the harbor, the boat boy would pull out the metal tins of curry tiffin and cold San Miguel. Things seemed so much more straightforward then, well before 1984, when they signed away Hong Kong's future away in a deal with Beijing.

And such men had been, for the most part, kind to her, the lanky red-headed and raw-boned American newcomer, brashly tackling the stodgy colonial hierarchy with her blunt questions and tart articles in the local English-language paper. Evans-Smith had been particularly courteous, she recalled, although she had seen much less of him in recent years. Her assignments for *Business World* were regional now, big-picture stuff for American readers.

With nostalgia, she recalled her own strangely carefree ways, if that was the right word for working eleven-hour days, ten days at a stretch without a day off. Her wardrobe had consisted of denim mini-skirts and black cotton Chinese sandals, T-shirts, and for full effect, cheap Chinese '555' cigarettes. She'd worked hard without union protection until late into the evening shift, then finished her evenings in the club for local journalists—Australians and northern Englishman as well as Chinese—the poor journo's version of the more glamorous Foreign Correspondent's Club, a haven for well-paid network cameramen and PR hacks.

When had she first seen Alistair Evans-Smith, with his wacky, unruly hair that sprang away from his forehead like a rooster? He'd been one of the old Governor MacLehose's point men in pioneering relations with the powerful clan families living near the Chinese border back in the late sixties and seventies . . .

Dovie's cough drew Claire back sharply.

'How is Mr Evans-Smith?' she asked the older woman. 'I haven't interviewed him in almost ten years, although we've brushed shoulders socially every few years since. You know how Hong Kong is.'

'He's very well, ma'am, except, you know, a lot quieter since his daughter died five years ago. He never talked about how he missed her, but we all knew how sad they both felt. You know, he used to sing a lot around the house on the weekends, but after Viola's death, he never sang another note.'

'I'm not surprised.'

In fact, Claire had read about it one day, picking up an abandoned South Chinese Morning Post while she waited for some faxes to come through to her in the business center of a Shanghai hotel. The Post was two days old, and five minutes after reading the item, Claire had pushed it to the back of her mind. In the seventies, she'd met the daughter once, but it was hardly a formal introduction. Viola had been a noisy young child romping on the balcony of a government flat through one of her parent's curry lunches for young members of the local press during Evan-Smith's stint with the Government Information Offices. She had totally forgotten. Totally. She chastised herself; single career-bound reporters on deadline were rarely the most sensitive people. It had been downright callous of her not even to send a note of condolence.

'Well, the inquest was so quiet. I remember reading it had something to do with the swimming pool at the residence,' Claire said.

'Yes, ma'am. She drowned.'

Dovie fell silent. Nice to know she was discreet. The death of Viola Evans-Smith had never been explained publicly in great detail, and there were hints of something hidden, but who knew? Probably Dovie.

'Mrs Evans-Smith has already gone back to the U.K. to prepare their home there. They asked me if I wanted to go with them, but I would like to stay nearer to my daughter. I'm really too old to emigrate.'

'Actually, I'm wondering if the care of a newborn doesn't need a younger woman. Do you mind if I have a word with Mr Evans-Smith?'

'No, of course not. That's why I brought my references. As far as pay is concerned, I am looking for the same level I was earning before this, and also, ma'am, I would like to continue to have my Sundays off, not Saturdays.'

'You speak excellent English.'

'I taught English as a young woman. But servants' pay in Hong Kong was much higher than teachers' salaries in Manila. And the Marcos days were very difficult for my family. My late husband was a newspaperman. We all left the country after martial law was imposed.'

'Do you like working with children?'

'Yes, and I like to keep house. I make fresh bread every morning, I can mend, cook Chinese and Western and Mrs Evans-Smith sent me on a Thai cooking course. I can do dinner parties, although I am not so good now at staying up past midnight to clean up. I feel it the next day.
'

'We all do,' Claire joked, 'and besides, we don't give many state dinners, Dovie. In fact, if I have any worries, it is that this household won't be anything like as grand to work in as the Evans-Smiths.'

Dovie looked clearly disappointed. 'I thought your husband was a government official with the United Nations?'

'Yes, well, he's not my, I mean he is with a development agency connected to the UN, but our style is not what you might imagine from your past experience. I mean, we don't have a lot of formal dinners or receptions. At least, not right now.'

Claire realized that she didn't even know what she was talking about. They had hardly shared a house before Caspar was with them. Nothing was 'normal' yet.

'I see.' This might be a comedown for Dovie, who was putting her handbag back on her lap in readiness to go.

Claire was fearful of losing this candidate so soon. 'On the other hand, you might find the location is good for you, since there are many government families along Tregunter Path, and of course, you'll have Sundays off to go to Mass, and we won't intrude on your private life at all. The hours will be as regular as a baby's schedule allows.'

'I see,' she said again. Clearly, she was not impressed. The telephone rang and Claire went into the television nook to answer it.

It was Fabienne. This woman didn't talk, she trilled. ' 'ello, Claire, I spoke to Xavier this morning, just to tell him the room is absolutely perfect, with a view of the water, and so many boats, I really want to do some photographs of the harbor, during the night as well as during the day. This is just the way he described it. And I want so much to see the town, and thought perhaps we could all go out tomorrow night, for dinner, you know nothing fancy, just the real Hong Kong. Would you like that?'

Caspar was crying in the kitchen. The ring of the extension had wakened him. Where was Connie? Probably sulking in the servant's quarters over her 'cousin's' failed interview.

'Fabienne, I'm afraid I have to go see what's the matter with the baby.'

'Oh, of course, I'm so sorry. Yes, I'll discuss the plans for tomorrow night with Xavier. He's so good at organizing things. Meanwhile, could I just ask you, do you know a good place to have my camera repaired? The little door that holds the battery at the bottom has come off. It's a Nikon, and I need it to be fixed very, very quickly, for my work, not just for my holiday here, and—'

'Fabienne, could we talk about it later?' Dovie was rising from the sofa to go.

'Well, it's something that I have to do right away, in case, you know, they don't have the tiny, tiny part I need,'

Dovie had headed down the corridor without her handbag.

'—and I know that if I bring the camera in right away, that way they will be certain to have it repaired before I go to Cambodia. Otherwise . . .'

Dovie had returned with Caspar in her arms. The boy was pulling on Dovie's short hair, his face creased from sleeping on a toy left in his basket. Dovie was swinging and bouncing him almost violently from side to side, but despite Claire's alarm, Caspar was starting to close his eyes, whether from relief or motion sickness, Claire couldn't tell.

'Fabienne, I'll see you later.' Claire slammed down the phone and took in the scene before her with a sigh.

Dovie was still swaying, more gently now, and she smiled at Claire over the baby's shoulder. He was cooing slowly, his sobs subsiding with huge heaves, his little hands holding tightly onto her collar. Dovie's smile was no longer polite, but truly warm, directed totally at

Caspar rather than Claire. Claire felt her shoulders, until now gripped by nervous tension, drop about two inches with relief. Caspar was making little 'uh-uh,' sounds of contentment and his mouth made little kisses full of hope for milk.

Dovie handed him over to Claire without ceremony, saying, 'I'm sure he'd like a little meal. He's not used to the smell of me, but he'll be more comfortable in a few days. Perhaps you would like to talk to Mr Evans-Smith about my references?'

'Yes, I would. Thank you, Dovie. Thank you very much.'

chapter four

—Monday—

Claire offered to drive Dovie all the way home to the New Territories. The forty-five minute trip gave them a better chance to know each other. Dovie had her opinions—no question about that—and she was anxious to explain how developments in the New Territories had come to obscure what had been, not so long ago, low-brushed countryside perfect for hiking on a Sunday with friends.

Well, now, first Claire should know that those new towns were full of Chinese teenage gangs these days, Dovie said, mainland kids who lived an unruly existence straddling Hong Kong's border with China. They harassed the Filipinas travelling in and out of town on the mass transit railway, making lewd remarks at the young women, and showing no respect for the older ones.

'When I was young, it was the Chinese who worked in our homes as servants, not the other way around,' she said plaintively.

But in the end, Dovie had had a good life, although she'd always wished she could have stayed in the Philippines and used her university degree to teach. Now that she was older, Dovie didn't feel so comfortable working alone in a large old house, all but one of the staff—old Ah Lok—let go with the death of Miss Evans-Smith, followed by Freddy's departure, and now the move of Mrs Evans-Smith to England.

Dovie was very proud of Freddy. She'd taught Freddy to read, in fact. Mrs Evans-Smith was always very busy with charity work, so Dovie had coached him from the age of six, and of course, he had done his A-levels with flying colors and gone on to university. Dovie showed Claire a picture of the gawky Evans-Smith junior on an English lawn in front of what looked impressively like Oxford.

Claire realized after some twenty minutes of this that she was getting qualms about Dovie's motherly affection for Freddy. Claire hadn't planned Caspar, that was true, but now that she had him, she wanted to enjoy her motherhood, not hand him over to a substitute bosom that would claim him as her own.

This prompted another fear on the heels of the first. As Claire listened to Dovie's affectionate description of Freddy's rowing prowess, Claire wondered, would Dovie see Caspar as some kind of leftover, an also-ran to Freddy, after her long tenure with the Evans-Smith family?

It would not be the last time Claire would find herself reciting an unspoken Working Mother's Prayer: Love my son, but not too much. Teach him to love you, but not too much. Help me in every possible way, but don't take over. Be more perfect than I could ever be, more patient, wiser, but never let him see your superiority over me, because I am his mother, the Queendom and the Glory, forever and ever, Amen.

The driveway up to the old Secretarial residence was a shock to Claire who hadn't seen it in a decade or more. On that long ago summer day, visiting one of Evans-Smith's predecessors, she recalled, the curb had been lined with bougainvillea, a long promenade of fuchsia and green, the rest of the grounds protected from the beating sun by a lush carpet of elephantine ivy leaves.

The ivy was still there, but had overgrown the flowers and spread across the gravel drive in greedy patches. The white house looked almost the same, but as Claire parked her car in front of the porch, she could see that the paint had broken off the bases of the columns near the steps, and that the window trim was broken off in places.

The Hong Kong government had never been poor; in fact, it was sixty billion US dollars rich these days, but recently the allocations were going in different directions. There were two legislatures, the outgoing one broadly elected under the last British governor and Beijing's puppet appointees waiting for their turn after the handover. It was hard to know where the public works money was going to go, should go, or would go, once the Communists took over. The Brits had only shown the Communists the colony's accounts for the first time this year. Even an optimist had to expect a comedy—or tragedy—of mismanagement, at least for a while.

The government had once held up the Secretary for the New Territories as the man on the front line, juggling the delicate relationship between the colonial government—safe and snug back on the island south of the harbor—with the clans that ran the rural areas to the north, bordering China. Many of the villages still adhered to the inheritance and property laws of the Ch'ing dynasty. Visiting Father Fresnay's weekend house in Ham Tin village in Sai Kung was to return to the final decade of the 19th century. But not far away, expressways plowed through the New Territories past walled villages, clan shrines and traditional cemeteries like laser lines of the future cutting through time.

The border the Brits had so vigorously patrolled all those years was now fast becoming a historical artifact, as thousands of trucks, ferries, buses and trains surged up and down the land and sea corridors that connected Hong Kong's commuters and traders to the industrial boomtowns of Guangdong province. That border was dissolving, and now the man, who as a talented young deputy Secretary had more than once singlehandedly cowed the clannish Heung I Kuk elders in fluent Chiu Chow dialect, his sun-bleached cox's comb bobbing with political determination, that man was now sitting in his garden looking out across the bluff toward the distant seacoast, patiently waiting for his tea tray.

'Lovely winter weather for a bite outside,' he said as a welcome, with hand outstretched, rising out of his garden chair. Claire noticed one of his knees seemed a little undependable so they both sat down rather quickly. Dovie had slipped discreetly into the house by the servants' entrance off the garage.

Even in the sunshine it was chilly, and Claire kept her green wool coat belted around her. Evans-Smith wore an old tweed sporting jacket over one of those hand-knitted sweaters mainland Chinese had always worn before they started getting Hong Kong fashion shows by satellite TV.

Now Dovie reappeared, half-supporting an old Chinese servant in white shirt and black pants, a woman so bald only three or four strands of hair crossed her scalp before winding into a tiny bun at the nape of her neck. Claire recognized her as one of the dying breed of famous 'black and white *amahs*,' a highly regarded sisterhood of Guangdong women who took vows of chastity and served families from young womanhood until death.

'A mother now,' Evans-Smith said looking over Claire. 'Finally!'

'Hmmm, rather late, but what the hell, why not?' Claire answered cheerfully.

'Got your hair? Yes? Well, let's hope he has your spunk.'

'He's got his father's bellow, that's for certain,' Claire said, helping Evans-Smith arrange the tea things.

'Haven't met the father, have I? Well, you're the mother, at any rate, and I bet he's a devil, your little fellow. Well, they all are, and then, just when you've humanized them, got them to stop bunging their food all over the Tibetan, they're off, like Freddy. Ta, ta, and that's it!'

They laughed together for a moment and then fell quiet. Claire sighed. The view stretching beyond the garden and across the hills had once been an uninterrupted, magnificent stretch of Chinese farmland. Now to one side, there was an expressway heading northward, thundering with huge trucks headed for Shenzhen and Guangzhou.

'This is a great lookout point for seeing how the 'New Towns' are now the old New Towns,' commented Claire, pointing to the aging estates crumbling in a welter of hanging laundry and peeling painted numbers on the water-washed concrete walls.'

'Yes, and over there, are the new New Towns,' he rose and gestured to a couple of steely towers catching the late afternoon sun some miles away. His finger moved again to a slope overrun with Mediterranean-style villas, 'and there are the newest of the new, at a million-plus for what we used to call a two-up-two-down back in England. I thought it was a speculator's folly when it first went up, but I guess the world isn't going to run out of upwardly-mobile middle-class Chinese any day soon.' He chuckled, more to himself, than to Claire. They sat down again to enjoy their tea.

'Tell me a little about Dovie,' asked Claire.

'Well, I'll say it straight out.' He thrust both hands into his jacket pockets. 'She may not be right for you. She's used to the government lifestyle, you know, and she hasn't handled an infant in more years than she'll admit. I'm not sure you could expect her to do the night feeding on a regular basis, not the way Althea handed Freddy and Viola over during those first couple of months.'

'Well, given I'm going back to work soon, that's the one feed I'm sure to be around for. It's the others that are a problem.'

'I'm always careful with women in your generation, but I must ask anyway. Do you have to go back to work?'

'Well, you know better than others, it's been my life for more than a decade. I love this city, and things are really getting interesting now up in Beijing with the changes in government. By this year next time, I'll bet you Deng has died and we're watching a real power struggle behind the scenes.'

'Oh, they'll never change up there, whatever they call themselves down here. It's the corruption you have to watch, not the Fifteenth Party Congress or who they finally make a scapegoat for Tiananmen once the old man goes. Their imperial tendencies go back centuries, but—' His brow furrowed and he drew himself upright, 'we're talking about childcare, not the Communists, my dear! No, I only asked whether you had to return to work because the time with your children is very short, however you look at it. Very precious years indeed.'

He glanced across the lawn almost despite himself. His gaze lingered in the middle distance, where the empty swimming pool, a rudimentary, old-fashioned cement hole lay accusingly, full of cracks and browned stands of vine leaves. Claire imagined the ghost of Viola, walking across the grass, and glanced back at Evans-Smith, who was suddenly complacently sipping his tea.

Had she imagined such a disconcerting moment? No, the lines on his face were deep-set and no humor could erase his profound pain. Claire realized with a jolt that when they had first met, his most outstanding feature, apart from his hair, had been his freckled, sunburnt complexion. The deep crevices were riddled with dark brown and stark white patches now, as if the skin had given up trying to make sense of its melanin over too many years in Hong Kong's blistering sun.

She spoke as soon as she had regained her composure. 'I'd like to give Dovie a try, but I feel so responsible taking her. I gather the usual thing is to do a one month tryout to see if it works, but you'll be gone by then, and I couldn't just let someone with her experience wander the job market like a newcomer.'

'That's not likely to happen. It's true I'm supposed to join Althea in a month, but I've got a lot to clear away. My departure may have to be delayed. Between the two of us, I expect we could make sure Dovie is happy one way or another. Have a go.'

'All right, I will. Now I'll ask you a separate question.'

'Well,' he laughed, 'it'll hardly be the first time you've put me on the spot!'

'Do you really want to leave Hong Kong?'

The white flip of hair flew up with a thrust of his chin. 'No. No! It's been my life! First studying languages at Cambridge, then the people here, and now the handover. And they need us, God damn it! If only these arrogant little yuppie businessmen realized it, with their venture capital in Shenzhen, golf courses in Changan, and housing developments in Zhuhai. And their loyalties! 'Marched'em straight from Whitehall to Jongnanhai without so much as a nod to the interests of the average man on the street.' He laughed unconvincingly but even an alert glance from Claire didn't deter him.

'Do they think they're so much cleverer than Shanghai's bankers in 1949? And suppose it all works? Suppose they do manage to turn southern China into one huge Hong Kong? Who ran Hong Kong so successfully for them all those decades they were making millions on plastic flowers in Hung Hom? We did, our hundreds of nice boring bureaucrats in their summer knee socks and white shorts! But no, now the British administration has to go, and God knows what's taking its place.'

'Well, since last week we've known our fearless leader is going to be C.H. Tung.'

'Of course it was always going to be C.H. Ever since the Communists bailed his shipping operations out of the red in '85—'

'$120 million US is more than bailing him out. They bought him outright!'

'Well, let's just say we've suspected they've had their eyes on him for a plum job ever since. Six months ago an old friend of mine saw him dining up in Beijing, but his hosts weren't northerners. They were his father's age, old friends of C.Y.'s from Shanghai, no doubt telling junior how loyal dad cleverly used his fleet to play both sides of the fence during the war. Yes, they can count on C.H. even though he's made such an obvious show of slanting towards Taiwanese interests. All part of the theatrics . . . well planned, I must say, ' Evans-Smith sniffed and bit emphatically into a piece of cake.

Claire smiled at him. 'We need men like you to stick around and pass on those tidbits of news we can use, the lore that puts it into context.'

He scoffed. 'No one wants us around, not even you journalists. Always looking for a new angle, not an old one. Well, that's what they always said about Hong Kong—borrowed place, borrowed time, and so I guess that means we led borrowed lives? I hope they'll be happy with the bunch that takes our place—a bunch of rubber-stampers prattling on about understanding Asian values? Do Asian values make you feel better when you get tossed in prison for complaining about corruption or calling Li Peng the butcher he is? They haven't a clue of what's coming as soon as CNN and ITN leave town.'

A fresh breeze ruffled his hair and he drew his jacket more closely around him. Claire was snug in her coat, but her tea had turned cold. She served herself another piece of lemon poppy seed cake and asked him, 'But what about barristers like Max Pereira, or Rebe Wing? Won't people like them continue the traditions of judicial independence, accountability? After all, it's the rule of law that counts.' These were two of Claire's friends, both popular advocates of constitutional law in local legal circles.

Evan-Smith shrugged. 'Pereira's half Chinese, half Portuguese. He's a marvelous barrister, first rate. But he owns a house in England and has an English wife. You watch and see how the Party marginalizes him with racial innuendo. And Rebe? Well, maybe there's some hope there. Her uncle's an important intellectual up at Fudan University, and that'll hold water with the Shanghainese working down here. After all, Jiang Zeming will probably be in charge, and he's the core of the

Shanghai mafia running the country. But look at it the other way. It's one more bit of leverage Beijing has over people like her. Call it sour grapes, my dear, but the signs aren't healthy. God, things looked a bit different in '84.'

'But your friends in the Foreign Office got angry when we questioned you so hard about the agreement.'

'We said then it was the best we could do. I'll tell you a secret, my dear. I wish we'd tried a whole lot bloody harder. It's too late now. Too bloody late.'

It seemed a lonely night to be driving, and Claire indulged herself with the still-novel pleasure of anticipating warm bodies at home to welcome her. By the time she reached Midlevels an hour later, the sun had long ago set in the gray waters to the west and the lights of the city stretched below. A slow-motion camera could have woven the ferry routes into bright yellow strings linking the two sides of the harbor, the neon signs of garish blues and yellows and red blinking off the water, and on toward the Kowloon hills.

Connie answered the door but to Claire's surprise, Xavier was not yet home. He'd left a message on her answering machine saying that he was stopping to have a quick drink with Fabienne before coming home, 'Just to get her schedule for her visit settled.'

If his purpose was to settle one woman, it had only unsettled another. It had never occurred to Claire that in making it clear Fabienne wasn't welcome as a house guest, she was encouraging Xavier to see Fabienne separately as an alternative.

She waited for him for almost an hour, and getting famished, accepted an omelet from Connie before excusing her for bed. Dovie had already retired after a long day of unpacking in the second half of the servants' room, conveniently partitionable by design.

Claire lay in bed, waiting for the sound of a car below. The 'drink' must have started at the end of his working day, if not earlier, and it was now nearly half past nine. She put her head underneath the pillow to suffocate her anxiety. It was impossible to sleep, as tired as she was. Finally, just as she was dozing off, she heard the little 'eh-uh, eh-uh,' that signaled Caspar's hunger for the last feed of the night. She went to his crib and sitting on the daybed underneath a moonlit window, guided his mouth to the breast. It was calming and she ran through her mind again for any reason to doubt Xavier. She could find none. The telephone rang and she leapt up, answering as reasonably as she could.

'Oh, good, you're still up. I was afraid you'd gone to sleep. I'm sorry. This drink has dragged on and on. She really needs to talk, and the best thing is to just listen.'

'I was worried about you,' Claire lied.

'I wish I were home. I'll be back soon,' Xavier said. Was he lying as well? 'Do I hear the little sausage?'

'That's him. But he'll be asleep again by the time you get back.' Claire couldn't help but feel the warmth of their child in her arms and the love in Xavier's voice. She curled up with a dozing infant in her arms on their bed, pulling a mohair throw over her shoulders and fell asleep within a few minutes.

She awoke to a woman's screaming like a shrill alarm coming from the foyer outside the front door. Claire rolled away from Caspar, who stirred, and put him safely in his crib. He didn't wake. She grabbed her bathrobe. She ran through the darkened living room, the bars of the bamboo playpen shining in the cool blue moonlight near the balcony door. She threw aside the bolts of the front door, as she saw Dovie and Connie emerging in nightgowns from the kitchen.

The three women stared into the landing outside the front door. Leo Franklin's *amah*, Narcisa, from the other apartment immediately opposite Claire's, was pulling at her hair and pounding on the elevator button, hysterically screeching, 'The Devil took him. The Devil! Help me, please.'

Seeing Connie and Dovie, the frenzied young Filipina started shrieking in Tagalog and both Connie and Dovie firmly seized her shoulders and head to calm her down through her sobs. Claire stood helplessly with them, towering over all three women. Nothing would stop the screeching.

'Dovie! What happened?' Claire yelled over the hysteria.

'Ms Raymond, Leo is gone!' Dovie was struggling to contain Narcisa's flailing limbs.

'Leo, LEEEOO!' Narcisa shrieked, her face a mask of fear. The three women half-carried her back into the Franklin's apartment. Claire quickly ran through the rooms, double-checking to see if Leo had wandered. His little bed was mussed, but there was no trace of him. She dashed back through the dining room and into the kitchen in her bare feet and opened the heavy door leading to the servants' rooms, a short corridor just like the one in her own apartment with a bedroom door, a bathroom door and a heavy steel-braced door leading to the servants' landing and facing the exit used by Dovie and Connie.

To Claire's surprise, the back door opened easily and Claire realized that Narcisa had first gone out to that landing for help and only afterwards decided to rouse the tenants at the front instead.

She returned to find Narcisa jabbering hysterically in Tagalog at the kitchen table.

'Has she called the police?' Claire demanded breathlessly, her heart pounding.

The answer came quickly from Narcisa herself, 'No, ma'am.'

'All right. I'll take care of it. Where are the Franklins?' Claire asked.

This time Dovie answered. 'They're still out to dinner, ma'am.'

'Get her something, some milk, tea, anything, Dovie.'

Narcisa had thrust her hand out at a number written on a post-it and stuck to the kitchen wall. Claire didn't recognize the host's name, but that wasn't surprising. Giles Franklin was an Australian stockbroker who worked all hours, as far as Claire could judge from their short acquaintance. On the weekends, he left early for the Aberdeen Boat Club leaving Lily to look after Leo. Lily spent a lot of time watching Leo play with Petey at the pool, but she didn't mingle very much with other wives, Chinese or Western. While most of the women got a bit of a tan, Lily was careful to protect her skin. The Franklins moved in financial, not government circles, and in recent years, there had been a big influx of new talent in banking and brokering.

Claire wavered, wondering whom to call first. She called the police. They would know how to handle breaking the bad news to the Franklins. She asked for the officer on duty, and using John Slaughter's name as a reference, reported a missing boy.

Within the hour what had seemed to Claire like a tranquil night of private jealousies had become a nightmarish carnival of public fear.

Xavier found his front door standing open and his own child sleeping peacefully untended, while Claire called to him from the Franklins' living room where she was holding vigil with Connie and Dovie over Narcisa. After twenty minutes of Narcisa's uncontrollable hysteria, the Franklins had arrived in the parking lot in their Lexus escorted by a police car.

With barely a nod to Claire, they locked themselves in the master bedroom with a Chinese inspector. Claire heard Lily crying and Giles' excited, angry baritone. More junior officers came and went from the bedroom while an unseen inspector on duty named Quek issued orders in terse Cantonese.

'What exactly happened?' Claire pressed Connie, who knew Narcisa, a delicate and beautiful brown nymph, better than Dovie could after less than a day on the job. She was worried an intruder had assaulted Narcisa, but that theory turned out to be wrong.

'Narcisa came to check on Leo before she went to bed and he was gone,' said Connie.

'But how? How could anybody get past her bedroom through the servants' corridor without her realizing it?'

'She was watching television. She says she didn't hear anything.'

'But why? It isn't possible,' Claire said, aghast at the simple idea that someone could enter a flat and take a child without discovery.

'It's happened,' said Xavier somberly. 'Wasn't there a case in America where a girl was taken during a slumber party, while other people in the house were awake?'

'Yes, of course. But how, here, with Mr Liu on duty at the gatehouse, and all the *amahs* knowing each other?'

'Actually, it was probably criminally easy,' Xavier said uncomfortably. He glanced back at their own apartment, and Dovie, reading his thoughts, said, 'I'm going, sir. Come on, Connie.' They muttered a few more words in Tagalog as they left to cross the carpeted foyer back to their rooms. Dovie looked exhausted by the drama of the evening. Suddenly Claire wondered again if she hadn't hired someone who was too old to take on the responsibility of Caspar.

Xavier was in his raincoat and standing by the sofa. There was an awkward pause between them now that they were alone. The discomfort was tangible but for a moment, Claire couldn't remember why she was annoyed with him. She'd completely forgotten Fabienne. Xavier turned his back to look out the balcony doors at the harbor. Perhaps he feared a private interrogation from Claire but she had no energy to consider his long absence with the other woman.

The sounds of Lily Franklin weeping as Inspector Quek and Giles Franklin emerged in conference at the end of the corridor broke the tension between the two lovers.

'The police asked me to wait here and give them a statement about the time I arrived and what I found,' Claire explained. 'Why don't you go ahead?'

Clearly tired and relieved, Xavier nodded and kissed her on the cheek.

While Claire waited for Quek to take her statement, she went to the Franklins' dining room window and looked at the blackness of the hill reaching up the back of the Branksome apartments. There were no more buildings above them until you came to the Peak Tram station shining brightly at the pinnacle of the small mountain. There was no road behind them either, no streetlights—just low trees, thick undergrowth and one narrow walking path that meandered up the hill to the Peak Café, the same little trail at the end of May Road where Manny and her Filipina friends had picnicked.

Through the darkness, she saw flashlights playing among the trees, flickering and disappearing, like sinister fireflies. Cantonese shouts echoed against the back of the building. The police were searching the semi-tropical jungle growth.

She murmured to herself, so as not to frighten Narcisa, who was sobbing more quietly now on the sofa alone. 'Strange . . . first Petey and then . . . But that was an illness, so this is different.'

Suddenly she turned to Narcisa. 'Tell me something. Why was the back door unlocked?'

Narcisa looked at her in shock, enough shock to stop her tears. Claire went to a side table where a box of tissues stood and handed one to the maid.

'The police are going to ask that first. Why didn't you lock the back door when you retired for the night?'

Narcisa's looked panicked, but then gathered the strength to answer, 'But I hadn't gone to bed yet, ma'am. I told you, I was watching television. I usually lock the door when I go to brush my teeth just before I turn out the lights.'

'Yes, of course, I'm sorry.' Claire knew she had sounded as though she were accusing Narcisa of negligence.

'I am sorry,' she repeated.

Her thoughts turned back to Xavier and Caspar waiting for her in their beds. The sight of him standing there had been such a relief after the long jarring evening. She felt a wonderful strength coming from him, this near stranger she had flung her future at. But she was too old to tuck her fears under the pillow of a strong man, even one ten years her senior. Not even he could claim to guess what evil thread of coincidence had brought not one, but two dramas to Tregunter Path in the space of two days.

She glanced at a framed photo of Leo with his father on the deck of a pleasure boat, at laughing "Little Boo-Boo," and she felt maternal terror clutch at her throat.

chapter five

A few weeks before, Claire had stumbled across some Christmas CDs in the discount bin of a music store. Feeling a mix of childlike enthusiasm and self-consciousness, she scooped up "Jingle Bells" and other standards by Frank Sinatra, Elvis Presley, Leontyne Price and Luciano Pavarotti, and handed over her credit card too late for sense to check her sentimental impulses. For years she had virtually ignored Christmas, apart from dispatching presents to her elderly parents in California on December first. There had been the obligatory phone call back to the States on the day itself and then on to the next news assignment.

She wasn't sure now what Xavier expected of their first Christmas together, especially with a newborn suddenly in their midst as if tailor-made for their high-rise manger. Passing by a factory outlet in Wan Chai specializing in tinselly exports, she'd loaded up on their first family ornaments. But buying reindeer, music, and a new red felt stocking to hold Caspar's gifts couldn't disguise their lack of a shared history together.

The imported fir had been delivered this morning, a forgotten apparition of hope and good cheer that startled them all after the previous night's horror. It stood expectantly, reproachfully bare, in the morning sun. Claire spread out her piles of new Yuletide junk, hoping Consuela and Dovie weren't watching this virgin effort through the small window of the kitchen door.

There weren't nearly enough shiny balls, she saw that now. Other families grew naturally, and their trees accumulated a history alongside, layer-by-layer, drummer by nutcracker. A family and its Christmas tree needed time. She was still so shy of Xavier's possible European coolness for her corny American yearnings, that she hadn't suggested they trim the tree together. She would surprise him.

Instead, he had certainly surprised her. Fabienne was far worse than anything her jealous imagination could have conjured up—kittenish, intelligent, and chic. She and Xavier had spent many such holidays together in the years past. A few vacations at a spa in Saturnia, Italy, a motorbike sojourn along the southern coast of France, and even a 'fabulous' Christmas on a Greek island. No mistletoe, no Elvis singing "Jinglebell Rock" or Harry Connick Jr boogying up "Winter Wonderland."

Images of Xavier and Fabienne together, lurid sexual snapshots, flipped through Claire's vulnerable imagination. She fought them off valiantly, but was flung back again and again by her own appetite for confronting and surmounting the worst. Supposing they had done *that* together, and *that* and *that*. Supposing he had wanted Fabienne more hungrily each time, that he had written love letters he had never penned for Claire, lingered over possible gifts for her, compared her favorably with every other woman he met. He had gone back to Fabienne many times. With each reconciliation, his partner grew stronger, more independent, and more equal to him in every way.

Claire realized now how much she would have liked more of a courtship. After all, what little time they had spent dating before her pregnancy had been wonderful. She remembered that first night they met, an evening almost two years ago. She'd rushed pell-mell—long, dark, red hair in the wind—to a hotel reception, but had gone to the wrong function room. The host was Xavier's UN development agency, not the Shanghai Stock Exchange authorities she was looking for.

It was typical of Claire's hectic days as bureau chief that it took her a few minutes to realize she was in the wrong room. By then it was too late. Xavier had seen her across the crowd, mentally met her, bedded her, and consigned her to his long list of global conquests. Or so he later confessed.

When exactly, during all those early, carefully orchestrated months, had Claire realized he was looking at her more intently than before? Not after their first night together, nor the first time they went out as a couple for a rather stilted junk outing with reporter friends of Claire's.

Through all their sporadic lunches and dinners, coordinated painstakingly according to their deadlines and travels around Asia, Xavier had kept his emotional discretion.

It must have been that moment in Bali. They'd 'stolen' a springtime week together in Indonesia. Xavier was driving their rented jeep along the dirt road into the brilliant green hills around Tenganan. Heavy rains had come and gone before they ventured out after lunch into the refreshingly cool jungle. Just before they reached the picturesque village, he had to navigate their jeep under a waterfall that had sprung out of the terraced fields checker-boarding the slopes that rose above the one-lane dirt track

Xavier maneuvered the jeep left to the edge of the other side of the precipitous path, but even then, Claire was drenched by the spray as the jeep jounced through the torrential stream pouring down from overhead. Xavier braked and looked at her anxiously and tried not to laugh, she was so suddenly bedraggled. She glanced in the side mirror and saw a soggy red mop. She had tried hard on this holiday to straighten out her hair into a more sophisticated look, but now it hung wavy and matted on her shoulders. She burst into laughter and tenderly he touched the thin, wet cotton of her dress. He cupped her breast and kissed her deeply, then reached beneath her cotton skirt and ran his hands up her thighs. Everyone working those fields was still indoors, finishing their tropical siestas. He licked the rainwater off her neck and shoulders, all the time his hand caressing her underneath her skirt. Their lips and tongues entwined, they forgot themselves as he hoisted her on top of his lap and plunged himself deep, deep inside her.

Since then, she hadn't bothered to try any new hairstyles. The expression on his face that day had told her they weren't needed.

Claire could not have felt uglier this morning if she had grown claws and warts overnight. She tried to talk herself out of this evil funk, imagining the Christmas tree as a hostile witness to her distress. Claire's hair would be combed, her bathrobe clean and her son bathed for Christmas morning. But the tree would stand in the middle of the room, every branch screaming, 'Jealous, mean-minded, obsessive bitch! Right there, the one with the red hair!' Like those talking trees in Oz pelting Dorothy with apples.

There were so many serious, sad things going on around her, what a waste of energy to be scrutinizing the navel of Xavier's old sex life. She hadn't felt this kind of cancerous jealousy since high school. It had to be hormones, she concluded.

She wondered if it was too soon to look in on Vicky again, and then remembered that Vicky's parents had arrived by now and wouldn't want a near stranger around. From reading the morning papers, Claire knew that the disappearance of Leo Franklin had cast a new and even darker shadow over Petey's death. Claire felt immediately outraged by the implication, and wondered what new suffering it was going to cause Vicky unnecessarily. What had been treated routinely as a tragic accident now had to be re-examined, the articles claimed, from every angle. So on top of houseguests, the police would be back at Tavistock to interview everyone once again.

Maybe she could be of some help, by getting herself out of the apartment and putting her journalist's investigative skills to good use. She was feeling rather under-occupied, an unusual sensation for a woman who had spent her whole life studying, then working nonstop, and always doing her own chores. Maternity leave was dragging on her and the murmurs of Connie showing Dovie around the kitchen hinted she would be *de trop* there too. Claire's habitual fallback during idle moments was to lose herself at the piano, but she realized that there, too, lay a new irony in her life. Her freest time was when Caspar was napping and because he was asleep, the last thing she could do was ripple up a few noisy Bach fugues.

So, to get out and clear her brain, but how? She wondered if perhaps she could find out more from Mr Ip, the gardener working a small plot on the hill above Tregunter path. Chinese gardeners worked seven days a week. Had he seen anything that day that Petey died? Maybe Crowley's Chinese was too poor to earn the older man's confidence. The presence of a translating constable might have only created more distance. Claire's work at the *South China Morning Post* had put her into daily partnership with the Cantonese-speaking staff photographers and her Mandarin dialect training had been the base to which she added some working Cantonese. The mix of dialects made those same photographers groan at her accent, but it was worth a try.

She told the two *amahs* she was going out for a stroll and caught their expressions of mutual relief. On her way to the front door, she wondered if she should remind them to lock up, then hesitated at the thought of over-reacting, then thought again. Two children were gone. That was a fact, even if it was a tragic coincidence. One missing was one too many. She went back into the kitchen and instructed them to check the back door entrance as they came and went. She made sure they double-locked the front door as she departed. Of course, they would. They didn't need to tell her they were shaken up themselves by Narcisa's fate.

She paused outside the front door for a moment, remembering the scene of last night, and stood again on the very spot where they'd tried to calm Narcisa. Instinctively, she reached down and gently tested her own doorknob. It didn't turn. She was tempted to ring her bell just to make sure the *amahs* didn't open the door, but this was laughable paranoia, she told herself.

She recalled one of her deepest experiences of irrational fear from her childhood. Visiting her grandparents one Thanksgiving in Detroit, the five-year-old Claire had listened from under the dining room table in the dark to the adults gathered in the soft light of the living room just through the arch between the two rooms. She heard them talking about cyclones that had swept away parts of houses and whole cars in Michigan. And as she listened, she had wondered if a cyclone might come up right as they were complacently winding down a pleasant evening and snatch that part of the house that was dark where she squatted under the heavy oak table, leaving the brightly lit room intact and the grown-ups safe.

To the little girl, filled with her first conscious sense of separateness from her parents' embrace, it had seemed imperative that she reach the light of the living room in the few remaining seconds before a storm could strike. Just a few feet and she would no longer be alone and vulnerable, but surrounded by their comforting arms. Just a few inches to go . . .

That was fear, and it returned suddenly with its primitive irrational power. It made no sense now, with Caspar under the care of two loving women. She braced herself and went downstairs. Just feeling the bright sun hit her cheeks made the morning better. She crossed the parking lot, wondering how she would approach Ip, when something caught her eye. In front of the gatehouse, three Filipina maids in their crisp cotton blue and white striped uniforms stood under the community bulletin board. They weren't gossiping or waiting for the shuttle bus, but chanting or praying, their heads bowed underneath the handwritten notices on the board. The girl in the center was sobbing as she mumbled her prayers.

Claire moved more slowly, trying to make out their words. She glanced up at Mr Ho, the morning watchman. He shrugged indifferently to the scene beneath his glass window and kept on smoking his cigarette and chatting with a Chinese policeman on duty.

The weeping girl turned out to be Narcisa.

'Narcisa?' Claire ventured. Narcisa turned her tear-streaked brown eyes to Claire and nodded hello. Claire had forgotten how pretty she was, even without any makeup and in a boxy shirtwaist. 'Narcisa, is there anything I can do?'

Narcisa hesitated, but walked slowly towards Claire, composing herself. 'Hello, ma'am. You know, I am going to lose my job. I am advertising for a new one.'

'No one talked to me this morning. I'm sorry to hear that. In fact, I'm just trying out a new *amah*. But if she doesn't work out, perhaps we can talk. Is it because of Leo, of course? Has there been any news?'

'Not yet, ma'am.'

'Will you come and sit down and talk to me?' Claire's first instinct was to comfort the girl, who couldn't have been more than eighteen years old. But her second thought, as she helped the distraught Narcisa to a cement bench to one side of the squash court entrance, was to keep her wits and ask questions that might help bring Leo back. Could it be the police knew some reason to connect Leo's disappearance and Petey's unexpectedly fatal attack?

Narcisa clearly needed someone to hear her side of the story. 'It's my fault, all my fault, but I never thought it would hurt Leo.'

'Why is it your fault? What happened?'

'Now I will get no references from Mrs Franklin and the law is that I have to leave Hong Kong within two weeks of the end of my contract. I will have to go back to Banaue. My family there is going to suffer so much hardship because they won't have the remittances I send them.'

'Narcisa, start at the beginning.'

'I can't tell anything, ma'am. I still need a reference from my employer.'

'You mean the Franklins don't know the whole story?'

Narcisa sobbed and hid her face in her hands. Claire put her arm around Narcisa's small shoulders, a physical kindness so overwhelming that Narcisa burst into heaving wails that nearly choked her. Claire sat her down on the bench and Narcisa poured out her heart.

'Please don't tell the Franklins, ma'am. I lied to you last night.'

'About what?'

'About the back door, ma'am. I will tell you the truth. A few weeks ago I met a nice man, a Filipino gardener up on Lugard Road on the Peak, and he wanted to see me at night. He has to work as a houseboy on Sunday because his employer entertains every Sunday lunchtime, and I can only go out during the day on Sunday because I work all the other days, and I have to be back by the evening to prepare the breakfast.' She looked up at Claire for sympathy.

'So this man, he asked me many times if he could come and see me in the evenings, but of course, I said to him the Franklins don't let me go out in the evenings.'

'Did you ever ask Mr Franklin for an evening off?'

Narcisa looked at Claire with her beautiful, wide eyes. 'You know, ma'am, none of the *amahs* are allowed out at night, except sometimes Saturday night, but I work Saturday nights too. Mrs Franklin wants me to serve at her dinner parties.'

Of course Claire noticed that whenever she visited a friend in Hong Kong, the Filipina domestic was on duty. She had never really asked herself how the Filipinas managed a private life of their own. They were, in fact, unacknowledged slaves, paid the minimum to do the maximum. She was impressed that Narcisa had even discovered there was an available Filipino man in the entire British colony. The competition to catch his eye must have been Olympian, even for a beauty like Narcisa.

'So he pressed me many times to let him come to my room, but not tell the Franklins. Of course I knew it was very wrong, but I was tempted very hard, even though I know such a thing is a mortal sin. After the first time, I went to confession and after the second time, I went to confession again, but now I don't feel it is so wrong because this man is very kind to me. He says someday we can get married. And then . . .'

'You left the back door unlocked for him, is that what happened?'

'Yes, ma'am, but how did anybody know? Who would do such a thing? The Franklins were out for the evening. I was taking a shower. I was not watching television. But now I am telling you the truth. It's true that even if I were watching the television, I would have seen someone coming past the door, but I was in the shower. That is the truth.'

'Yes, yes, I believe you.'

'I thought Jun might come while I was in the shower. I didn't hear anything. '

'Jun?'

'Junior—my friend. But he didn't come. And I haven't heard from him today. There's no way I can make a phone call in private. Right now Mrs Franklin thinks I'm buying vegetables at the truck down the road. I didn't tell her I had to put up the notice today, and we were planning to say prayers for blessing.'

Claire squeezed her shoulder. 'Then what really happened last night, after you finished your shower?'

'Well, I decided to go to sleep. It was about eight o'clock. I get up at five-thirty every morning, but I set up the coffeemaker the night before. About a quarter past ten, I woke up. I realized I had been thinking so much about Jun, about getting ready and how he didn't come, and then feeling so sad—I had forgotten to set up the breakfast things. While I did that, I realized that I had forgotten to check on Leo and that's when I found his crib was empty. He was gone. I was so frightened.'

'And that's when you came screaming out into the foyer?'

'Yes, ma'am, and I lied to the police, but I think they knew I was lying because they asked me what television program I was watching and I think I lied about the wrong one. I tried to check the program listing this morning, but the newspapers of yesterday were thrown out already. And then, Mr Franklin, he told me after the police went away last night to start looking for another job.'

'Did you tell him about Junior? Does he blame you for Leo's being missing?'

'I don't know about that, ma'am, but I think he has a bad conscience, because I have already have some trouble with him, so he knows that I wanted to go a long time ago. But until now Mrs Franklin was very good to me, better than my previous Chinese employers.'

'Mr Franklin also seems all right to me. What kind of trouble?'

Narcisa took a deep breath and whispered to Claire, 'Twice he came into my room at night and said if I'm not nice to him, he will fire me without references. And my brother's family has many children to feed. But after the first time, I told him I would never let him come into my room again, or I would tell Mrs Franklin and get her to write my reference for a new job. I don't belong to him, I don't have to do his dirty things.' Narcisa was crying again, harder than before.

'Narcisa, that's a very serious charge to make about your employer.'

'And now he leaves me alone, but he watches me all the time. Maybe he knows I have a boyfriend. One day he said I looked "too pretty" and asked "who was I flirting with these days" right in front of Mrs Franklin. So I feel really bad for her, and I don't want to leave her alone. I want to help her, help her until the police find our Leo. He is such a good little boy, ma'am.'

Narcisa was trembling. She looked up at Claire with a wild look in her eyes—a mix of desperation and shame. Claire could see how the teen-ager's guilt tormented her.

She waited a few moments for Narcisa to calm down.

'So the police really don't have any idea? Lots of people might get the television program mixed up when they've been through such a shock.'

'Yes, ma'am. I told them I forgot to lock the door on time, only that.'

'Did you tell anyone before last night you were leaving the back door unlocked for Jun?'

'I don't trust all the other *amahs*, only some. They are full of envy. I told Regina that Jun was visiting me and maybe Aurora. I didn't tell Manny or Imelda because they are much older, already over thirty, and Manny's husband is a no-good back in the Philippines, living with another woman and having other children with her, and Imelda never got married. So they try to boss the younger girls around because they are jealous.'

'But perhaps Regina or Aurora gossiped?'

'It is possible.' Narcisa turned thoughtful. 'So anybody could know.'

'Last night I thought I heard you say, 'The Devil took him"?'

Narcisa looked at Claire with alarm. 'You heard me?'

'Of course. That's what you were screaming at first. Before we came out of the front door, I think, or maybe just after we opened the door.'

'Yes, ma'am. I was very upset. You must forget that.'

'Did you really mean the Devil? Or did you suspect someone, a real human being, of being as evil as the devil?'

'No, ma'am.' Narcisa fell silent for a moment. 'I don't know who would want to take my Leo. Only the Devil would do such an evil thing.'

'You believe in the Devil?'

'Yes, ma'am, all Catholics do. I am a Catholic.'

Claire, who had been raised Catholic in California, hadn't imagined the Devil per se roaming the earth since before her First Communion. Even at seven years old, she suspected he would leave his pitchfork and red Union suit at home when he visited suburban California, but she didn't contradict Narcisa.

'Do you think the Devil could take a human form?'

'Yes, ma'am, in fact, I know it is true.' To imply otherwise seemed to offend Narcisa's sense of faith and the world. Her two friends still stood under the community notice board waiting for her. Claire said she would tell Narcisa if she heard of any jobs and left them taking out their rosaries for a hail of Hail Mary's.

Narcisa's story had been more sordid than Claire had anticipated. As sympathetic as she might feel toward Narcisa as a human being, she would never knowingly employ a girl who entertained men by the back door. Nor would anyone else in Hong Kong.

The maid's story about Giles Franklin was even more disturbing. Once before she had heard through friends that an acquaintance of theirs, a Financial Times reporter in the midst of a divorce, had been propositioning his *amah*. No doubt these things happened. Monday morning's account of the Mongkok Romeo sprang to mind.

Still, Narcisa's version was open to a wide variety of interpretations; it was possible that Franklin had actually raped her or that Narcisa had cold-bloodedly seduced him before she befriended Jun. Anyway one looked at it, it was a mess.

Claire started off for Ip's potted terraces overlooking Vicky's building next door. Another woman was marching toward her along the sidewalk, strangling a handbag under one arm, her head looking back over her shoulder in hope of a possible taxi. It was the wife of the Deputy Secretary of the Public Works Department, Fiona Reynolds. Claire had met her only a few times before her move with Xavier to Tregunter Path and only to rub shoulders at cocktail parties.

'Mrs Reynolds? I'm Claire Raymond, we met at the National Day reception for Macau?'

Mrs Reynolds turned straight to face Claire, her eyes invisible behind large black sunglasses with a little gold fish perched on each corner. She was dressed expensively in a fuchsia linen suit, her golden bouffant hair-sprayed off her forehead, which glinted in the sunlight with sweat and powder.

Fiona squinted at Claire. 'Yes, I remember, you were chatting with Sunny Kwok? Reporter, aren't you?'

'On maternity leave. I'm taking a walk to get fit again.'

'I never walk if I can help it.' She spat out the words.

'Don't you have a car? Someone said yesterday that you were driving past on Sunday near where they found little Petey Sandford?'

'Car's been stolen. Right out of the car park last night. With all this terrible news about the little boys, nobody has time to chase another missing car. That's the third this month from Tavistock, smack out from under the nose of our watchman. I told Barrie last night, the management along Tregunter Path has just gone downhill since they sold the building to that new company—'

'Pacific Profits.'

'Yes, that's the one. I believe our watchman must be part of some racket. I mean how can these triads just drive our cars out of the gate without being seen? Two Benz's and a Daimler that belonged to the Bank man, what's his name . . . '

'Patrick White?'

'Yes. Listen, I absolutely must get a taxi. I'm late for the Club.'

Claire had the distinct impression that Mrs Reynolds had already warmed up her morning with a breakfast sherry. A taxi whizzed past them, a red blur already carrying passengers. He came worryingly close to Mrs Reynolds who was teetering on her white high heels a few feet into the Path, her free arm wagging vaguely in the breeze.

'Bloody man, he could have struck us!'

Claire waited for Mrs Reynolds to join her back on the sidewalk. 'There'll be another one soon. Did the police ask you if you saw anything on Sunday when you were driving past the *nullah*?'

'God, yes, question after question from that Office Crowley. Dreadful person, a sort of wide boy in uniform. Have you seen the types turning up at Kai Tak these days? Barrie tells me that the other day he went into the loo off the Mandarin Grill and he couldn't believe his eyes. The attendant was a boy from Watford. From *Watford*, would you believe, standing there in one of those little Chinese outfits with a little black cap and red tassel on top—the exact same outfit they put their Chinese boys in.'

'Shocking.'

'Absolutely. Anyway, this detective Crowley kept insinuating things, as though I should have stopped, as though I would have even noticed one of the *amahs* waving at me. I was in a frightful hurry that day to pick up Barrie at the Aberdeen Boat Club. Driver was off. Between you and me and the gatepost, I can't remember seeing any girl on the road.'

As Fiona Reynolds sputtered out her excuses, Claire realized that she had less than a decade on Claire, but certainly it felt as though they were separated by a generation. Claire thought of Vicky and reflected; here were two different versions of colonial females, Vicky so direct and clearheaded even under the greatest duress and Fiona in a humorless fluster because she had to take a taxi.

'Anyway, it's an appalling story, this disappearance of the little boy right on the heels of the Sandford child. Something is terribly amiss around here. We've lost out sense of order, of control, and there's nothing worse than that. I blame the police in the end. They should keep a better eye on things. The whole place is going to go to the dogs anyway, once we leave. Barrie's got to stay for the handover ceremony, of course, but we've already booted out our lodgers back home in Sussex. Thank God our son is in public school back in England. As far as we were concerned, there was no question of his staying on here after he turned seven. The Island School, the International School, even the Swiss-German school, well, a lot of those kids use drugs. This Ectasy rubbish. Read about it in the *Post* the other day.'

'You must miss him a lot, though,' Claire sympathized.

'Terribly. But it's really better for him, you know. We see him during the summer. I'm used to it. Here's another one.'

And like a hunter in hot pink bagging a diesel tiger, Fiona pounced on an empty taxi and tumbled in, shouting, '*Hoi joong wan*,' to Central.

As the driver shifted into gear, Fiona leaned out the window. 'Better to have them in a proper school back home, especially as there's no real future for them out here anyway. By the time they reach ten, they're bored.'

Claire hadn't taken the time yet to reflect on the life she was offering Caspar. Would Xavier want to send his son to the monastery school in Switzerland that had educated him forty years before? The thought clutched at her. They'd never talked about where they would live after Hong Kong, provided there was an 'after Hong Kong' for them as a couple. If she didn't marry Xavier, would he leave this posting for the next without her and Caspar? She realized that in the rush of work at the bureau, the strain of pregnancy and the move to Branksome, there were profound uncertainties she hadn't broached with him.

A hundred feet above where she stood, Ip emerged from his hut on the slope and started hoeing along a bed of small flowered plants. From behind, with a cloth around his head protecting him from the sun, he looked almost like an old woman. At the sound of Claire's footfall, he turned and watched her, almost indifferently curious, leaning on his hoe. She realized he was waiting for her to finish her ascent. He watched her as she pulled herself up off the road onto the hill, then skirted irrigation ditches and rows of knee-high snake plants, then passed a few rows of strange, low herbaceous borders, to reach a footpath cluttered with hoses and fertilizer bags.

She wished him good morning in Cantonese, '*Jo sann*.' He grunted and waited expressionless. Of course he had no idea who she was, unless he had noticed her new habit of taking daily walks with Caspar in a baby harness.

She started again in Cantonese, 'My name is *Lei Mun Ch'ing*.' Claire's Chinese name was a mix of sounds and meaning. 'Raymond' became '*Lei Mun*,' and the meaning of Claire, clarity, became the Chinese word for clear, '*Ch'ing*.' She continued, 'I heard you were here on the day Petey Sandford, that little boy died.'

He nodded and went back to re-potting a fern, answering in strangely slow Cantonese, the eight tones of the dialect riding high and low as if in spoken opera, '*Pei-tei*. A good little boy. He liked to visit my garden. He was sick.'

'I'm a friend of his mother. She's suffering so much.' Claire used the Chinese term—so resonant—'eating bitterness.'

Ip nodded and looked up at her from where he was squatting. His face was deeply tanned and furrowed, and his hair cut short, like a stiff brush. But oddly for a Chinese who worked all day with the earth, he wore new gloves.

He stood up and stared at her, 'Have you come to ask me questions? I told the police, I didn't see *Pei-tei*. He didn't come play here.'

'Did you see the *amahs* eating over there?' Claire gestured in the direction of the picnic site about fifty feet across the slope. A clearing nestled at the foot of a grove of trees that shaded Tregunter Path.

'I heard them.' Ip nodded. 'When they discovered trouble, they made loud noises.'

'You didn't help?'

'I didn't know it was the boy. Then I saw the police and ambulance. Every week, they dance, they shout, they cry. I don't pay attention to them. It's their crazy religious custom. *Meng cha-cha, chi hsin-a*.'

Claire could well imagine that the sight of a Charismatics' prayer meeting, especially with *amahs* speaking in tongues, would strike any Cantonese as 'crossed wires crazy.'

Ip lost his patience. 'I've finished. *Tso-ah.*' Claire realized he was now shooing her off with a dismissive flick of his hand. Certainly he had the right but she'd done nothing to offend him. She stood her ground.

Her stillness angered him. He shouted, '*Ma Faan ah.*' Hassle. '*Tsuo-bah . . .*' Get going, this time in the accent of northern China. Perhaps he had switched to Mandarin because he noticed her Cantonese betrayed traces of Mandarin training.

'But—'

Then Ip exploded into a string of curses Claire could only partially understand. His inexplicable temper shook her. '*Deng-i-deng,*' wait, wait, she pleaded, but she was getting nowhere.

She stumbled a little, backing down the slope. But he was still irritated and kept rattling out phrases too fast for her simple Cantonese. He'd said what he had to say. Claire was humbled to think she had presumed she could do any better than Crowley with his constable. Ip might be just another irascible old man who wanted to be left to himself. But if Claire had detected a trace of affection for Petey underneath Ip's gruff exterior, it had also crossed her mind that Ip's interest in Petey might not be as innocent as he played. There were those pristine new gloves. And there was no doubt in her mind that, despite what he claimed, from where Ip lived and worked seven days a week, he had enjoyed a clear view of almost everything that had happened the day Petey died.

chapter six

The police were streaming all over Branksome, moving floor by floor, door by door, their walkie-talkies screeching up and down the elevators, as they interrogated every single one of Claire's neighbors about Leo Franklin.

They carried copies of Leo's picture for the residents who weren't familiar with his curly hair and elfin face. They asked everyone, whether they'd seen Leo, where they'd seen him last—here in the parking lot, or there, by the swimming pool last summer. Excuse me. Pardon me. I'm sorry, sir . . . Who had been seen talking to him in the last week? Did you ever see any stranger initiating play or conversation with the boy by the poolside or in the car park? Who knew the Franklins had gone out for the evening? Had anyone seen them driving away?

The officers were polite, but there was a new aggression to their interrogation, a tone that was only partly to do with the new aspects of the case. Older colonials noticed a new assertiveness and less deference than in the old days. No doubt about it, the handover had happened already behind the scenes, in the dressing rooms, somewhere backstage when the *guay-los* weren't watching.

Moreover, the standard of their English was noticeably low. In the old days, good English had been a prerequisite of promotion. Now it was Mandarin that kept the ambitious attending evening classes. This morning, the questions were clearly stated, the answers cooperatively given, but the comprehension of some of the policemen was incomplete. The investigation was lumbered down with misunderstandings.

Nonetheless, the questions were straightforward. What time that evening did you go out, sir? When did you return, miss? Did you see anyone in the corridor? In the lift? In the servants' stairwell? In the lobby? Behind the building? In fluent Cantonese, uncertain English, broken Tagalog. All morning and all afternoon. It seemed like the whole of the Hong Kong Police Force was on Tregunter Path, putting all its public strength, and visible support behind apprehension of the culprit.

So why did Claire feel no comfort? Why did she feel like no longer witnessing this inevitable failure in slow motion? She knew that superb police work had just located a violent criminal who had carried out three bank robberies in less than a year. They'd found his arsenal of bomb equipment, remote control devices and AK 47's, all hinting at expert training as a soldier in the People's Liberation Army. That was the kind of crime they could solve by paying off informers, tracing weapons, and twisting arms attached to the underbelly of the territory.

Tregunter Path was not their territory. The nastiness here was somewhere hidden, neither in closets nor in the backs of trunks, but in the recesses of someone's mind. And that diabolical mind could hide behind an all-pervading hysteria and neurotic atmosphere that increased with each week leading to the handover.

She had retreated to her bedroom to try on work clothes. Nothing fit. On her bed lay the discarded reminders of her pre-baby figure: the lithe silk flowered dress cut on the bias, the natty black linen cigarette pants with the matching sleeveless vest, the rose chemise in light-weight wool crepe with the halter neck. Either her hips strained the seams of the skirt or her milk-laden bosom, once so girlish, pressed against her bodice like that of a middle-aged matron.

She sighed, realizing there were horrifying hints of her mother's figure reflected in the mirror. Even some of the red shine had faded from her hair. How she had anticipated her first real evening out again with Xavier. She'd imagined wearing something casual, but seductive. He would be wearing the same black cords and cashmere turtleneck she had admired on a date shortly after they met.

In her fantasy, they would stop first for a drink at the Foreign Correspondents' Club, long enough to show friends that she'd come back to life from the strange and unfamiliar world of maternity to the old gang. Ah, but unlike many of them, she wasn't stuck at the bar for the night with the lost and lonely; she was going to move on in every sense of the word.

Maybe they would head then to the Café de Paris, where Maurice would hang over their table for a minute or two recommending the walnut, Roquefort, and endive salad. And Xavier would pull out a picture of Caspar, all purple-skinned, puffy-eyed and beautiful, and Maurice would exclaim in professional admiration, 'But who would guess that Madame just had a baby!'

She had to continue this courtship for her own satisfaction, to know not only how she felt about Xavier as a partner for life, but also to reassure herself that Claire Raymond still prevailed over that tiny *dominus* called, to lull an unsuspecting world, 'baby.'

In fact, she was in a rotten mood, angry with herself and the innocent redheaded 'peanut' in the Mickey Mouse pajamas for her dilemma. She didn't really have a clear idea of what she wanted more: to drag herself back to her safe routines as much as possible of China reading, watching, analyzing, leaving Caspar and Xavier in the margins, or to let professional life take a backseat to her relationship with Xavier—make it work, go the whole bristle-bearing hog.

She wasn't used to feeling unkindly toward her child. How could this quotidian anger have survived the sadness and terrors of the past three days? She blamed Fabienne and the ugly fears her arrival provoked. Claire didn't have all the time in the world to make up her mind about Xavier. Because Nature, in the form of a sexy, heterosexual single woman, abhors a bachelor.

Fabienne even had prior claim. What did Fabienne want? In fact, why was she here, *really*? Claire didn't give much credence to Fabienne's assignment in wherever, whenever, Cambodia, sure, sure, that led to this 'stopover' in Hong Kong.

Now, on top of everything, Fabienne was the occasion of their first evening out on the town. It wasn't even worth leaving the baby for.

And that was hard enough, without Xavier and Fabienne standing at the front door of the apartment looking—was it Claire's imagination?—as if *they* were the couple heading out for a night of fun. She reviewed the evening drill with Connie for the third time.

'You understand that the bottle of my milk in the freezer is only in case I call you and can't get back in time for the eleven o'clock feeding.'

'Yes, ma'am.' Connie smiled obligingly. Perhaps the other *amahs* had warned her about the panic of the first real evening out for a new mother.

'And I will get back in time. Don't let anyone in the apartment for any reason. And if you feel like laying down, leave all the doors open so you can hear him crying.'

'Yes, ma'am. I always do that.' Connie's answer was irreproachably patient. But she was clearly counting the seconds until they all left and she could watch a soap opera on the little black and white TV in her room behind the kitchen.

'Come on, Claire, it's going to be all right,' Xavier's tone was at its most Teutonic, but he hadn't learned yet that authority rubbed Claire the wrong way.

'I'll try to call from the restaurant around nine-thirty.'

Connie hesitated. 'That might wake the baby, ma'am.'

'She's right, Claire. Please, come, everything is going to be all right.' And now she felt Xavier taking her by the shoulders and moving her gently but firmly out the door.

'The number of the doctor is above the telephone, with the telephone number of the police—'

'Claire! Half the police force is on duty inside this very building for the entire night!' Xavier seemed in a hurry to get the evening started.

Fabienne stood waiting behind him in the foyer in a short red knit mini shift with wide cowl neckline, a skinny, shiny black patent belt and chic black sling-backs. It all went well with her dark, Louise Brooks-sort of charm, offset only a tad by her largish shoulder bag. Claire had settled on a straight black dress and covered up the bursting seams with a short antique Japanese kimono tied in front over her still-round tummy with a gold embroidered cord that matched the gold threads woven through the silk.

They paid off the taxi at the top of Lan Kwai Fong Street, the L-shaped alley that had become the epicenter of nightlife on the Hong Kong side of the harbor in a wave of Yuppie development in the late '80s. The short foot of the 'L' was highest on the steep hill that backed the business district of Central. It was noisy, but dark; some kitchens and small cafés operated along this quieter stretch. Fabienne's heels clicked perkily on the street, and once or twice, when she tripped in the semi-darkness of the uneven asphalt, she instinctively reached for Xavier's arm for support.

They reached the turn of the 'L,' and paused before navigating the steep decline between two rows of blazing clubs and restaurants.

'There was a huge street fair here five years ago, and so many drunks carousing in beer foam—they started a landslide and a panic, and twenty-one people were crushed to death,' Claire told Fabienne.

'How morbid! That explains the police, I suppose?'

Claire too had noticed the patrol striding purposefully uphill to pass them two abreast on one and three on the other.

'You see the two men squatting down by that nightclub, 'California,' the two Chinese leaning against the wall?' Claire gestured farther down the street.

'They're probably point men for drug suppliers to the kids around here.'

'It's not all that nasty,' chided Xavier. 'C'mon, Claire, you're just feeling bad because of Petey and Leo, I know. Everything looks a little dark to you tonight. Try and cheer up.'

'Oh, Xavier, don't be so tough on her. She's right to be feeling so low. It's the hormones, right?'

Claire felt like some grandma being taken for a walk. Don't coddle me, chick, she thought, I'm post-partum, not senile.

'Here's the place I was thinking of,' Xavier stopped triumphantly outside a small doorway under a sign, 'The East is Red and the Blues is Here! Hong Kong's best spot for jazz!' He did a little shimmy and grabbed Claire's hand affectionately for a two-step on the curb.

'Jazz! I don't believe it, Xavier. You promised me something exotic! I can hear jazz in Zurich or Paris any night of the week!' Fabienne pouted, the shine of gloss on the lower lip reflecting neon colors hanging overhead.

Claire interrupted. 'This is the place we always planned to check out, but never got a chance, Fabienne. Let's try it.'

'Nooo, Xavier, you didn't used to be so square, so straight.'

The small shoulders had completely turned away from Claire and the cowl neck of Fabienne's top was slipping slightly off to one side. Xavier's strong hand moved protectively to cover the bare neck so vulnerable in the night air. Claire felt her gorge rise.

'I haven't changed that much, you may remember I always loved jazz. You should know, you're the one who stole my valuable collection of Coleman Hawkins.'

'Borrowed. You never said you weren't coming back. I've also got your racing bike, your collection of Asterix and Obelix books, your espresso machine, and—'

'I consider we've got a fair trade,' Claire interrupted, putting her arm around Xavier with the cutest and meanest smile she could muster.

'*Ca va, ca va*, girls, the jazz was just an idea. Claire and I will go there another time. He kissed Claire's temple, gently.

'He wasn't such a bore in the old days,' Fabienne tried to joke with Claire. She wasn't giving up.

'What's she talking about?' Xavier joked apologetically to Claire.

'That's what I don't want to know,' Claire said dolefully. If *her* ex-lover Jim had come along to finish the quartet—not that Claire knew where he was or why he'd even disappeared—he would have surely taken care of this bitch twenty minutes ago.

'OK, Fabienne, what did you picture when I said something exotic?'

Fabienne smiled like a child who is unashamedly satisfied to see she can make trouble.

'Let's see!' She clacked away, maneuvering the steep, long steps sideways on her little heels and waved to them to follow her. About fifty feet ahead was a turning off Lan Kwai Fong where newer clubs were sprouting up. Claire felt a certain rush of adventure, despite herself, as they started to follow the woman in this new direction. The street narrowed and took another sharp turn uphill past a Vietnamese noodle stall and many small hardware and tool-die shops, their roll-down metal frontages pad-locked firmly against the night crowd. Narrow, rust-stain pre-war buildings standing four or five stories high in this part of Central's backyard muffled the raucous music of Lan Kwai Fong only a few blocks away.

'*Voilà!*' Fabienne stretched out one arm dramatically, like the doorman of a four-star hotel and bowed, then winked knowingly at Xavier, 'Maybe something a little kinky, *monsieur?*'

Claire had to admit Fabienne had good eyesight. There was little immediately visible from a distance, but next to a darkened doorway was a small glass cabinet displaying a few photos. Over the showcase were Chinese characters advertising a proctologist's specialization in hemorrhoids, but Claire decided to let this information go unexplained to her companions who didn't share her knowledge of the language. The photos themselves were, at first glance, of famous western film stars, although there was so little light, it was hard to make out much more. From the top of the narrow and twisted stairs leading to a simple landing came an ominous *thump, thump, thump, bump da bump bump, thump, thump, thump.*

'Not exactly Miles Davis,' murmured Claire to Xavier.

'Sour face, sour milk,' he joked back to her, and put his arm around her encouragingly. 'We never found this place before. Give the woman some credit. You never know.'

Claire looked at him intently. 'I give her more credit than you could imagine. Oh, you bet, I reckon she's full of tricks.'

Two Chinese men had emerged at the landing to collect a cover charge, which Fabienne had already taken care of, from a fistful of cash in her pocket. For the first time, Claire saw Fabienne the Photographer in action on the battlefield, in the remote village, or under pressure of the studio lights.

Fabienne wasn't sexy simply because she wore cute clothes, although those didn't hurt. She was an '*allumeuse,*' a magnet of positive, unknown action. Claire felt more at home in one of her silk dressing gowns, tucked into a corner with her volumes of Chinese poetry, history and biography through which she escaped the claustrophobia of a dying colony through time and place.

The club stank of male sweat and cigarettes. A tall girl in a long red *cheongsam* and stilettos moved them toward a table near a small stage by pushing customers out of their way, leading with her strong thighs. One male customer laughed and squeezed her leg in appreciation and looking up for acknowledgement, laughed again. He ignored Claire and

Fabienne and looked questioningly at Xavier. The waitress dismissed the little harassment with a deep chuckle.

The next act started and without further ado, Claire's ginger ale was left melting in its ice as she stared at the strange apparition that emerged from behind a curtain. A Eurasian girl with an almost Korean flatness of feature, but gingery-streaked hair strode out on stage in a simple short black cardigan sweater, the sort that sold cheaply at the China Products Emporium a few blocks away, worn over a mini-kilt.

The Scottish motif was sustained by a comically small tam on her head and a real set of bagpipes which she made clear were far too heavy. The stripper laboriously blew at the pipes, but wiping real sweat off her brow, smiled at the audience knowingly and began to slowly unbutton her sweater.

'More hot in Hong Kong than in Edinburgh!' she yelled hoarsely over the general hubbub and thumping disco background to her act. The Scottish theme was a kind of insider's joke in Hong Kong, since many of the founding fathers of Hong Kong's powerful colonial trading houses, or *hongs,* had been Scots. Early intermarriages between Chinese and foreign devils, or *guay-los,* were commonly alliances of equally clannish Cantonese and Scots.

Claire surveyed the audience. Many were slight Chinese boys sitting with foreign men. She glanced more quickly around for women and realized—now that her eyes had adjusted better to the dim lighting— that Fabienne and she were the only two women in the club, unless you counted the stripper on stage.

Which clearly you couldn't, because the stripper, having revealed two natural-looking large, pale breasts, which made Claire surer of the girl's northern bloodlines, was now unwinding the kilt to reveal a small erection encased in white jockey underwear.

'*Ho yeh! Ho yeh!*' shouted some of the Cantonese drinkers with approval. The whole act was one big visual pun on mixed race, mixed sex, and mixed culture. The Chinese, whose monosyllabic tonal language lent itself generously to punning, started clapping with the beat of the disco bass in a kind of intent and hungry way.

'Well, I have to hand it to you, Fabienne,' Claire joked her uncomfortable way out of the first shock. 'It's my first Asian hermaphrodite, and you found it.'

The gingery brown pubic hair as well as the heavy, unsupported swing of the breasts made it clear that there was nothing artificial about this artiste.

'I could believe we were in Bangkok, not Hong Kong,' said Xavier. The music sped up a little as the erection grew larger under the stripper's guidance. Claire realized how far off the beaten track they were, by Hong Kong's standards, when the climax of the act lived up to its name. The audience yelled out some crude catchphrases as the 'Scotsman' exited with a lot less dignity than she'd arrived.

Claire had been dragged to sex shows years before during her first assignments in Bangkok, for the most part. It was a sort of initiation rite for women forcing their unwelcome way into the ranks of foreign correspondents in Asia. At least she hadn't had bosses coming in from overseas who made such excursions a job requirement, but she knew of many such instances imposed on her colleagues with the implicit understanding that being a 'good sport' included going along with the executive's off-the-record excursions and keeping quiet back at headquarters. Claire hoped that Fabienne's appetite for the kinkier side of the East was satiated.

'Exactly how long will you be staying in Hong Kong?' Claire asked her across the clinking of ice and insistent bass of the interval music.

Fabienne looked up in surprise at Claire's tactlessness. Such a full frontal assault was clearly not her style. She was more of the hide-and-seek type.

'You're afraid I might stay on forever?' Fabienne avoided Claire's direct gaze by lighting a cigarette.

'A lot of people do. In fact, you could say there are two kinds of people in Hong Kong at this point in time—the people who are staying on until they are due to leave, and the others who are just stuck.'

Claire's mind darted to Evans-Smith. He was actually leaving the colony, but lodged forever in its colonial history, the only context in which he belonged. But her friend Father Fresnay was staying on until his job was done, whenever he and the Church, and for that matter, the

Chinese government, decided enough was enough. It was more than a physical fact; it was the subtext of every relationship or encounter in Hong Kong. Are you staying until your tour, your time, your travel is finished? Or are you trapped by marriage or investment or time to a life in this uneasy future with the Communists?

'Oh,' Fabienne smiled understandingly, 'I'm only staying for a little bit, but what about yourself with the Communists taking over? Haven't you made China your whole career? Are you one of the people who is stuck?' The Genevan glanced minx-like in Xavier's direction, but he wasn't really listening. 'Or did the arrival of Caspar change that for you? Now you have a Swiss baby to consider and the father? Maybe you're not as stuck as you were before?'

Claire laughed off the offensive. 'I already had a perfectly good passport when I met him.'

She wants to know if Xavier and I are permanent, Claire thought. Is that why she suddenly has a photo assignment in 'nearby' Cambodia? She's really here to stake her claim. It's worse than I let myself imagine. That's why he hasn't told me much about their meeting the other night. He's afraid to let me know her real intentions. Does he think I'll panic? They both underestimate me, in their different ways, because Europeans so often confuse American transparency for stupidity. He thinks I might make a fool of him, or myself and she actually believes she can seduce him away from me and his child with an old suitcase of memories.

As if reading Claire's mind, Fabienne raised her voice to get Xavier's attention, 'Do you think I could take some photos?'

Xavier hated to draw attention to himself. It was a natural modesty and also arrogance born of knowing precisely who he was in the context of six hundred years of his family living in the same Swiss village.

'Oh, I don't think—'

But Fabienne was already squeezing between the tables toward the back of the room with her large shoulder bag in tow, extracting her camera, Claire realized with dismay.

'Xavier, I'm kind of tired!' Claire protested as soon as Fabienne had left their table.

'Do you want another juice?'

'No, um, frankly, I've had enough.'

Oh, God, she sounded like a martinet, a killjoy, a *mom*. She had become somebody's mother and there it was. All these people in the room had mothers who didn't know what they were doing right now. What a filter through which to watch the world's turpitudes. Now her figure was ruined and her mind was warped. She seemed to have left her sense of humor back in the maternity ward.

'You're right,' Xavier said unexpectedly. He kissed her lightly, 'The Swiss-Hong Kong Tourist Association does not approve.'

But Fabienne was already back, more victorious than ever in her quest for kink. 'The manager said I could take a photo when they finish the next act, and he promises it'll be great! What, is something the matter?'

'Well, if he said yes, we'll stay. Then maybe the jazz club, OK?' Xavier looked for compromise.

'It's my fault, Fabienne,' said Claire, 'There might not even be time for the jazz. I want to get back in time for Caspar's last feed.'

Fabienne was miffed at this show of solidarity between the two new parents. 'Okay,' she tossed her head, 'I might even stay without you.' Claire didn't quite believe her, but after more than fifteen years in Asia, she appreciated anyone trying to save face.

Over the sound system, a drum roll sounded abruptly and cheering started from some of the tables in front of the stage crowded with Hooray Harry's—British types who looked like they hadn't bothered to change clothes after a day trading stocks on the Hang Seng Index a few blocks away. Some incongruous, old-time honky-tonk music started up and without any introduction, a Chinese manager leaped on stage and led the audience in a familiar countdown, '*Yet, Yi, Sam*! One, Two Three, Who's There?'

'The Fairy Princess, who do ya think?' answered an astonishing vision sashaying across the boards to a wave of delighted applause in dripping pearls and sequins, feathers and platinum wig. It was a six-foot-plus 'Mae West' with shaven shoulders, hips and bosom heaving with padding, her enormous fan of feathers coquettishly wielded with all the subtlety of a jib sail on Hong Kong harbor.

'Mae' paused dramatically, and then came a bump of the hips and a drum roll and 'Mae' soaked up the guffaws from the flushed fans at her feet. 'Is that your real hair color, honey, or are ya burning up for someone?' Mae taunted a redheaded man sitting across the audience. Claire blushed out of solidarity for him. Thank God 'Mae' hadn't directed such a joke at her.

'Ley ho ma, and hello boys,' Mae swaggered and swept 'Although my mother says little *boys* should be in bed after nine o'clock at night.' More laughter. 'Little devils need their sleep for school, um-hmm, yeah.'

'Hello, hello, pleased to meet'cha,' Mae scanned the audience who had simmered down appreciatively. She focused on one guy sitting right in front, 'And you're not bad to meet either. Say, do you believe in love at first sight, anybody here? Oh, good, I see a lot of hands, c'mon get'em out of your pockets, there, save that for later. You do? You believe in love at first sight, do ya? Well, I don't know if I do, but it sure saves a lot of time, don't it!' Hoots and hollers.

Claire looked at Xavier and shook her head, chuckling resignedly. 'I have to admit, whoever he is, he's got the voice and delivery down perfectly.' Xavier was laughing, too.

'It's just Life to see you guys, c'mon, crawl to me baby, crawl to me.' Instead of a kiss, the audience got an extended pelvic grind, which drew yet more applause. Claire took in the unmistakable change in the audience. The few waiters on hand were delivering beers and gin and tonics to the Europeans, as all westerners were tagged in Hong Kong, at twice the pace, while the Cantonese in the audience sipped more gently at their fancy cocktails.

The show was like a smorgasbord of titillation, with something for everyone. And why shouldn't Hong Kong enjoy a transvestite evening when the whole city was becoming a metropolis in political cross-dress? Was it a capitalist enclave officially disguised under Communist sovereignty now? Or a Communist *entrepot* masquerading as capitalist? What did Deng Xiaoping's 'one-country-two-systems' slogan mean, anyway? A whole city in some kind of cosmic political drag, left in the care of some long-distance pimps who care nothing for the people here, but everything for how much money Hong Kong will rake in for the north. Claire surprised herself. She hadn't realized how cynical she'd become.

The soundtrack of some new music began, an authentic wind-up for a real vaudeville tune. It seemed like the performer had tried to do something with class and some genuine theatrical preparation. 'Mae' launched into a song tailor-made for Hong Kong's racetrack gamblers. With one hand on an ivory walking stick and the other on her padded hip, she purred to the lilting, suggestively syncopated backup:

Oh, I wonder where my easy rider's gone,'
I wonder where my easy rider's gone,
If he was here, he'd win the race,
If not first, he'd get a place,
I never saw that jockey trailing anyone before.

The impersonator never dropped from a pitch-perfect nasal impersonation of the Original Blonde. Claire thought it was such a good rendition, it gave her the impression she indeed watching someone she had met before, and the more she laughed at the song, the more she was got an eerie feeling that 'Mae' *was* someone she'd seen before—not the actress, although the likeness was beautifully executed, but someone she'd met before somewhere, *but where?*

The act took on a new fascination as she peered closely at 'Mae's' features for a glimpse of the man underneath. For Claire, this became by far the greatest tease of the show. She was drawn in completely, marveling at the evocative swaying of the hips, the delightful pursing of the lips.

'This guy is amazing,' she whispered to Xavier, 'What the hell is he doing in Hong Kong? Who is he?'

I'm losing all my money—that's why I'm blue,
If that boy was here, he'd sure know what to do,
I'd put all my junk in pawn,
To bet on any horse that jockey's on,
Oh, I wonder where my easy rider's gone.

The music built up for a slow final chorus, and the brokers and barristers slopping their drinks at the front, joined in for the last carousing phrase,

'Ohhhhhh, I wonder where my easy rider's gone,'

'*Merveilleux, incroyable*,' gushed Fabienne. I'm going to get a picture of this guy. I don't believe it! NO, better, you take a picture of us together!'

Despite the lift some genuine talent had brought to the evening, Claire was now truly exhausted. She glanced at Xavier who was oddly distant, as if he was watching the show with his eyes, but not his mind. She wondered where he was. Protectively, she closed the kimono closer over her chest.

Fabienne thrust the expensive camera into Claire's hands. 'It's my back-up camera while the other one is being repaired. Take care, just push here,' and without hesitation, she jumped onto the stage to embrace a startled 'Mae' in the middle of her bows. Claire hesitated for a moment, surprised that Fabienne had left her with a telephoto that needed delicate focusing. But she would take any photo if it meant she was then entitled to call it quits for the evening.

Putting her eye to the viewfinder, she brought their torsos into alignment. Rising smoothly to the occasion, 'Mae' put one hand on her gorgeous wig of marcelled curls and the other arm around Fabienne, obligingly striking a pose. Claire shot a couple of frames, then let the long-range lens linger for a moment on the performer's face.

The lens was like a telescope, bringing 'Mae' up close. Claire gasped as illusion fell away. The lips had been styled with pencil and gloss to look much fuller than they were. Underneath the powder, the evidence of a closely-shaven chin betrayed a dark-haired male.

The eyelashes, however, had needed little touching up. Naturally long, they framed eyes Claire had seen only the day before.

The brilliant impersonator—whose 'mother wanted little boys in bed by nine—was Inspector Antony Crowley.

chapter seven

'Aconi-what? Aconitum? What's that?' Claire frowned in surprise at Vicky over her steaming mug of coffee. She'd promised to drop over by nine, but that was already too late to catch Vicky's parents before they left for a day in Saikung, 'to get their minds off things.'

When she realized Miriam and Gordon Forsythe were gone from the apartment, Claire hid her relief from Vicky, but Vicky probably knew already that her parents required a fairly attentive audience at the best of times. On a normal morning, Miriam would have hooted her delight and approval over Caspar, even though she hardly knew Claire—such was her sense of loyalty to any new mother so far away from 'home.'

There would have been a lot of 'Do you know the whomever's' with unsolicited updates on people Claire had hardly met. Gordon would have grilled Claire for her impressions of the political situation, ending with his vague, 'Time will tell. Couldn't be avoided.'

Petey's death killed off inconsequential colonial chat.

Claire was also relieved that the elders were out of the house because she wanted to tell Vicky about the apparition of Crowley as 'Mae' at the nightclub. It was easier without Miriam around, her over-plucked eyebrows shooting to the ceiling in disbelief that Hong Kong had sunk to the level of the girlie bars in Bangkok's notorious Patpong district.

Anyway, Vicky had just divulged some startling news of her own. 'Yes, they found a herbal solution mixed with some chemical called aconite in Petey's stomach. Apparently it's a classic poison, but not very commonly used.'

'I never heard of it.'

'Neither had I. Neither had the Hong Kong police, apparently, but it turned up in Peter's autopsy. A very clever young man on their forensics team just back from Canada decided to go a bit beyond procedure because of some strange results, and that led to more tests, and anyway, it's the strangest thing and the forensics fellows don't know what to make of it. They asked me any number of questions about his diet, his medication, even the houseplants. Asked me about seeing Petey with any purple or purple-white flowers. I could never get Petey to stop chewing on rubbish from the ground—leaves and twigs. But I can't say I ever saw any such flowers around Tregunter Path. Well, at any rate, it proved me right and Ian wrong.'

Vicky's eyes were shaded from Claire's scrutiny by sunglasses, so it was hard to tell, even in the slanting morning light of the Sandfords' balcony, whether her expression matched a very slight note of triumph in her voice.

'Ian wrong? Why? He expected something else?'

'Oh, he didn't want an autopsy at all! I disagreed, I mean, what's the harm? There might be something, just something, we don't know. My parents backed me up, especially Daddy, and when Ian saw that Petey's own grandparents weren't sentimental about his remains, he couldn't very well object any longer. And you know what else the police told us? There were a lot of bruises on his body, more than they noticed on Sunday. John Slaughter said the lab man hadn't any theories, but insisted it just wasn't a simple case of fatal epilepsy.'

'Aconite and bruises,' Claire repeated carefully, 'as well as the normal signs of an epileptic attack?'

'Absolutely. But do you know they were also looking for signs of sexual molestation? Well, of course, there weren't any that seemed obvious, but I must say, they were remarkably thorough.'

Vicky expelled her satisfaction with a huge sigh of relief. The police procedures were obviously lending a supportive professionalism on which she could lean away from her grief.

'The saliva tests, the vomiting, not to put too fine a point on it, were completely consistent with Manny's story.'

'Thank God.'

'You can imagine her relief. The police questioned her all over again, and of course the other girls corroborate her story completely. Petey was already close to death when they reached him. The police wanted to know if they saw anybody else pass them, or talk or approach Petey while they were having their picnic. Manny insists she didn't notice anything unusual, but you never know. Maybe someone else was passing along the path or watching them without them knowing. '

'How is Manny?'

'She hasn't come out of her room, except to leave the meals and dust and vacuum while I'm in my room. As soon as we've finished dinner, she disappears into her room, of course, but she was like that before this all happened. She's a very sad woman. She lost her own son, you know, Ramon. Sunday was a nightmare for her as well. I think she also wanted to leave Ian and me some time alone. No, there's no doubt Petey had an epileptic attack, but,' her voice faltered, 'You see, the point, Claire? It shouldn't have been fatal.'

Vicky fell silent. Claire hesitated, not sure how to help. She had no idea of what suffering her friend was containing through sheer force of will, only four days after losing her beloved child. The funeral was tomorrow morning, rescheduled because of the autopsy. Maybe then Vicky would let herself go, release all her pain when it was over, her parents were gone and, Claire prayed, Leo was found.

A ferry horn sounded long and low in the harbor below. It was the natural music of Hong Kong, punctuating their days. After a while, Vicky poured herself some more coffee. Claire broke the quiet. 'Do you know the Franklins? Or Leo?'

Vicky screwed up her mouth in admission, 'Lily and I weren't as friendly as we could have been, considering our children swam together downstairs when they weren't out boating. But of course, you must know them better than we do, living on the same floor..'

'Not really, as we haven't lived here very long.'

'Well, once you've spent a full summer by the pool minding your child, you'll get to know people much better than you'd wish, not to put too fine a point on it. Leo was a very boisterous little boy, I've noticed—it seems a lot of Eurasian kids seem either terribly quiet or terribly noisy. Have you noticed that?'

'I can't say I have. Actually the parents seem noisier than the child. Lots of dinner parties. Leo is quite cute. He and I sort of have a running joke together, nicknames we call each other. But his parents are quite aloof, stick to their crowd. At least, there is certainly a lot of traffic on our landing on some evenings.'

'Lily entertains ferociously, mostly couples like themselves—you know, Chinese wife with *guay-lo* husband, very upwardly mobile, hothouse orchids on the table, custom-made Italian motorboats, charity dinners . . . They weren't much interested in us and our fuddy-duddy share in an old junk. Ian doesn't care for him—not because he's Australian, but because he's, well . . . ' Vicky stopped.

'You heard some rumors?' Claire hinted.

'The maids talk a bit.' Vicky's averted her eyes down and concentrated on her coffee. For a colonial wife, she'd said everything that needed to be said.

Just then, Manny slipped through the sliding glass doors of the balcony, but Claire knew the roar of the traffic down on the slope had muffled what they'd said so far.

Claire didn't observe the 'relief' that Vicky had seen. Manny's eyes seemed gorged with worry, but her manner was as gentle as usual. 'Shall I clear the coffee, ma'am?' Vicky shook her head and asked for more. Claire waited until Manny had passed through the heavy swinging kitchen door.

'She talked to me, I mean the Franklins' *amah*, Narcisa,' Claire was sure that for all of her preoccupying grief, Vicky was as quick-witted as ever.

Vicky's eyes widened with curiosity. 'Is it true?'

'Twice, at least. You'd think when she asked for a night off to date a Filipino boy Lily Franklin would have been more than happy to say yes. Narcisa admitted to me that she was expecting a clandestine visit from this new boyfriend, some gardener named 'Jun' who works up on Lugard Road, about the same hour that Leo was snatched.'

'Lily might not have noticed anything. The marriage wasn't in great shape. I could tell. It happens all the time. European marries Chinese, thinking he's getting a docile little poppet. It lasts about two years, and then he looks up one day and she's decked out in a fortune of designer clothes from the Landmark, expensive jewelry, a mobile phone in her crocodile bag, and she's off to the races—quite literally, off to Sha Tin—with her girlfriends for the whole of every Saturday afternoon.'

'They've already dismissed Narcisa. Given her the usual two weeks. That means she's got about ten more days to find another job or be deported back to the Philippines.'

Vicky had a sudden thought. 'Do you think this boyfriend took Leo, I mean, for money? There's no ransom note that I've heard of, unless John's keeping it a secret. They often do, I've heard, so as not to encourage more snatching, what with all these Asian-type kidnappings in Taiwan and all over now. It's all about money.'

'It also means that if Slaughter can't find enough evidence that Jun and Narcisa were involved in Leo's disappearance in little over a week, Narcisa will have to go home and that trail will go completely cold.'

Vicky sighed. 'Poor girl, I can't believe she deserves any of this. It's Giles Franklin's fault. It's not the first time somebody's husband went jungly with a local girl, but right in your own house, ugh,' Vicky's shook her head in disapproval, her tough, practical colonial streak showing itself again.

This moment of distraction for Vicky passed and she turned silent, again, obviously thinking of Petey. Claire reached over to hold her friend's hand for a moment of comfort. After all, that's why she was here, and she was grateful that she was on maternity leave and had all the time Vicky might need.

'You handled his illness so well. And now you're dealing with his death more bravely than anyone has a right to expect,' said Claire. She wondered momentarily if Vicky was taking tranquilizers, but she should have known better.

Vicky shook off her moodiness.

'Simply what one does, Mummy says. Manage through the next hour, then the next hour, then the next. She's very solid, Mummy, but you know I don't think that makes her cold, even though she seems a little unemotional at times. Did you know my mother was married before?'

'Miriam? As in Miriam and Gordon, your parents?'

Vicky laughed lightly. 'Oh, it wasn't always "Miriam and Gordon." She was quite a flirt in the "fishing fleet." In fact, the year she announced her engagement to my father, the old gang had a kind of catchphrase about my mother—"Miriam'll marry'em." Daddy's her second husband, you know. Her first husband, Ralph, was quite a bit older than she was, a real hero in the Malaya days.' Vicky pronounced the name, 'Rafe.'

'Daddy only came into The Emergency towards the tail end. Then one day, Ralph was gone. Dicky heart was the verdict. Broke her spirit for a while, you know, in a quiet sort of way.'

Manny had come in quietly with fresh coffee and smiled politely in acknowledgement of Claire.

'Thank you,' Vicky said properly, but she waited until Manny had left the room to continue her story. 'After the funeral, Mummy says she went on a long holiday to visit a rather racy aunt who kept her soaked in G-and-T's for at least a month. Then she came back and that was the end of it, or at least she would shrug it off. "Good or bad, it'll come in handy for conversation during the rainy season," my Great-Aunt Julia told her. "No experience is wasted, if not repeated, so don't waste your time over it." Course Great-Aunt Julia was a Wren in the war.'

Claire laughed despite herself. 'I'm sorry, I shouldn't laugh, but your family is really something. And, after all, what are we doing right now? Talking about it. '

Claire looked more seriously at Vicky. 'Is it possible to look forward to the new baby?'

Vicky thought the question over. 'Yes. And somehow this autopsy report makes me feel better. Leaves me something to latch on to, something more to find out. It doesn't bring Petey back, but it lets me gnaw away at it without feeling self-indulgent.'

Claire chuckled. 'Sort of legitimatized gnawing.'

'Precisely. You know, I'd like to hold Casper a bit,' Vicky said softly.

Claire reached across her chair to the small sofa of striped ticking and rattan. Casper didn't wake, but as Vicky took him gently, his little mouth started to twist over to one side in hope of a meal.

'Oh, I'd forgotten how they do that when they're so little,' Vicky managed a small smile, and then tears started to flow silently down her cheeks. She lifted her sunglasses away from her eyes. 'Got a tissue?' she laughed bravely, crying and smiling, and holding Casper all at once. 'We'll be all right in a bit, won't we, won't we?' she said, more to herself than to Claire.

Claire watched her friend and decided it was a poor time to talk about Antony Cowley and his jokes about little boys.

***

As Claire emerged from the Tavistock apartments, she saw it was too fine a morning to spend indoors. The police were still everywhere, their questions drifting along the hallways, their Chinese and British accents mingling with the sounds of the city below and the breakfast departures, front doors opening and closing, elevators rising and descending to the waiting shuttle bus. Claire didn't feel like going home after leaving Vicky's.

Instead, she decided to give Caspar his breakfast feed outdoors. Positioning him a little more comfortably in his harness, she crossed Tregunter Path and wandered past Ip's gardening hut, up the well-worn dirt footpath that left the paved road and rose in steep curves all the way through the thick, green trees to the top of Victoria Peak. The hammer of pile drivers from building sites across the city punctuated the crisp air, slamming against the Peak and reverberating off the wall of tightly-packed high rise buildings at the foot of the mountain.

Claire couldn't remember a time, political winds notwithstanding, when Hong Kong hadn't shaken with the deafening clanking and pounding of construction machinery. It was the symphonic industrial backdrop to all the new Asian capitals—Kuala Lumpur, Taipei, Shanghai, Jakarta, Saigon, and any day now, Hanoi.

Nothing was as comforting these days as the baby's warm weight lying on her body, almost as if he were still curled up inside her as he had been all those long uncertain months. She could bury all fears for him when he was this close. Like this, no harm could come to him. She hadn't minded letting Vicky hold him. But it had been strange to see

Vicky nuzzling her grief-stricken face against Casper's tiny breast without flinching at little at the stolen intimacy. Did every new mother resent sharing her newborn this intensely? Would she ever be able to protect him enough from the world? His vulnerable red-downed head collapsed against her breast with the lulling rhythm of her step.

Claire realized she was going to pass the picnic site where the amahs had eaten last Sunday. They were all back at work now, of course, and the little clearing looked forlornly trashy, littered with food wrappers discarded by the construction workers and barred by a police sign in English and Chinese. The rubbish can at one end of the clearing was stuffed with Tagalog tabloids, movie mags and hairstyling monthlies. The Filipinas' Sunday was a day of mutual praying, manicuring, politicizing, gossiping, giggling, eating, singing, dancing, and above all, shared loneliness.

Petey had died some fifty feet away near the dried up *nullah*. Claire guessed this when she saw the police ribbons still tagged around trees to mark off the site. She sat down gingerly, careful not to jolt or wake Caspar, on one of the impromptu plank benches resting on rocks. She glanced up the slope towards the *nullah* that ran from the Peak downhill towards Tregunter Path. Yes, she could make out the banks of the ditch. She swung Caspar and herself heavily back to her feet and wandered farther up the footpath, but nothing apart from the police markers distinguished the place where Petey died. If there had been any traces, Claire knew, the police had already examined them with Manny in tow to point out the way.

This part of the footpath was fairly wide, rising at a leisurely angle to the slope. Then it turned steeper and narrower as it navigated upwards to the Peak and the tram station at the top. Through the trees, Claire heard the rumble of the wooden tramcars as they ferried their passengers—mostly tourists at this hour—up and down rolling cables of wire through the overgrowth.

Claire started humming a little tune she had often played on the piano when she needed a lift in spirits, but was breathing hard when she reached a small bench covered by a wooden roof, another rest spot for joggers and lovers. This wasn't the kind of exercise that was going to trim her down to Fabienne's fawnlike figure, but it was a start.

A definite gloom was descending on her as she sat down to feed Caspar, the canopy of the semi-tropical forest shielding mother and infant from the sun. The tune died on her lips and she listened closely to the sounds all around here. There was the regular little sucking sound that was such a comfort to her. But still, she felt uneasy. Her breath slowed, as if the slightest movement would wake the stillness of the brush around her. She could not say why she felt the presence of something or someone around her. Some bird or animal? There were snakes in the undergrowth, she knew, and sometimes even wild dogs that roamed the Peak and ventured closer to the residential buildings in their hunt for scraps in the back of the parking lots where the rubbish was left for pickup.

She waited. She held Caspar closely to her heart. But there was no sound. None at all. She twisted her torso to the right, back down the path, and even directly behind her, where the forest floor slid sharply down some thirty feet to Tregunter Path. She saw nothing on the slope below her—no animal or bird. Perhaps it was something smaller, a gecko? She twisted to her left to peer through the trees to the back of the buildings lining Tregunter Path.

She waited, holding her breath. She couldn't shake the sense of being observed, and why not, she laughed to herself nervously? This footpath was a quick shortcut back to the residential buildings lining Tregunter Path for joggers returning from the two-mile run around the top of the Peak. In fact it was unusual not to see some spritely local health nut. But there was no *guay-lo* in a Hash House Harrier T-shirt and no leathery Chinese oldster in a flapping tank top and khaki Empire-builders.

A pall has come over the Peak because of the children, she thought. We all feel it. We want to find Leo alive and well, but it would be unnatural not to dread finding him any other way with each passing hour. We're all waiting for something more to happen. You can see it in people's faces in the elevator, and along the Path. It's nearly Christmas Day but it feels as ghoulish as Halloween.

Something unusual struck her eye. Directly across from the bench where she sat was a large rock, mossy and silent, piled high with dead leaves and dirt. But peeking out from the leaves was something odd, definitely furry and small, and bluish. In some places, it was smudged with mud. Had a small animal been stricken while she sat there? Perhaps that was the noise.

Caspar had fallen asleep without even tackling the other breast. Lifting herself with care so as not to wake him, Claire swung herself gently across the path and knelt slowly down against the rock. She glanced down the footpath in both directions and then started brushing the leaves away.

There lay Grover, his blue fur-splattered wet and muddy by the pre-dawn rain. He was still smiling his silly, lovable grin, waiting for Petey. Claire felt close to tears. At first she thought the toy had been dragged here by a live animal, but right next to Grover, also hidden under the leaves, lay a tape cassette labeled neatly, *Peter and the Wolf.* It was Vicky's handwriting; Claire knew from seeing her grocery lists, thank you notes and a short roster of phone numbers pasted up next to her kitchen door.

Most days, Claire had barely glanced at Petey, much less his ratty, threadbare Grover. In the days before she had Caspar, it was remarkable how little she distinguished between children and their individual worlds. Now she saw each as unique, and stifling her sobs for fear of waking her own baby, she wept deeply for minutes for Petey, picturing him alone there in the forest.

Her cleansing sobs subsided. Some of the tension was gone and it was not just to do with Petey, but the hormones flying around inside her, this silly Fabienne's visit, and questions that were coming as fast as blows. Did Petey hide his Grover this far up the hill? If it was Petey's Grover, was Manny lying when she said Petey was playing farther down the path, closer to Tavistock, just within sight? Or did someone move these things up the hill in a hurry? Why hide his toys if there was no way to hide his death?

She heard another sound, a twig crackling somewhere in the undergrowth down the path. She was not alone. She knew it. Someone was running quickly away, but not down the jogging path where they could be seen, but straight through the dense forest. The sunlight gleaming between the trees, glinting off the water below, made it impossible to distinguish anything moving down the slope.

'Hello?' she called hoarsely, trying not to disturb the baby. Was it Ip? A jogger? Crowley doing his rounds? She rose from the rock to start silently down the hill, but between the rock and the path, she immediately tripped on a long, hard root twisting over her foot. It yanked her and the harness. Caspar jerked awake and started crying. She rocked him too wildly, wiping her eyes of tears and staring down the footpath in a futile search for the unseen observer. She stuffed Grover underneath Caspar inside the harness, pocketed the tape, and headed home feeling defeated and confused.

***

Despite everything, Christmas was coming at them like a juggernaut of mindless manufactured cheer, Claire marveled, as she saw a truck arriving at Branksome with someone else's tree bouncing precariously off the end of the truck bed. Three toughened delivery men wearing baggy cotton shorts despite the brisk weather jumped out of the cabin, put out their cigarettes on the tarmac, and started to untie their cargo. Claire remembered she should drop off her presents for the office: a leather case for her much-appreciated secretary and researcher, Cecilia Chau, some Chanel body lotion for Cecilia's mother, and a cookbook of Asian grilling recipes for the guy filling in for her maternity leave, Hopkirk Wells. He had been seconded from the Tokyo bureau to cover for Claire, but his was a thankless job, so she'd decided she should demonstrate her gratitude.

She found Dovie and Connie finishing the vacuuming and laundry before taking their lunch.

'I'm going to leave him with you two,' Claire said, slowly released Caspar from his hot little nest in the harness. There was a wet spot left on her shirt where his sweaty cheek and drooling mouth had nestled for the last forty minutes.

Dovie looked at her with sympathetic efficiency in her voice. 'He'll be perfectly fine with the two of us. We're double-locking both the front and back and we don't answer the door to anyone, period.

Nobody. One of the Chinese policemen heard from one of the *amahs* in Century Tower that an *amah* in Tavistock said she had seen a strange young *guay-lo* hanging around Tregunter Path over the last few weeks.' Connie nodded from the corner of the kitchen.

Claire sighed, but made no comment. She should trust these women with something as simple as keeping the apartment doors locked. She forced herself to hand over Caspar to Dovie, noticing Connie's look of sheer jealousy at being left to fold underwear. Grabbing the Christmas presents, Claire forced herself out the front door and waited outside while she listened to Dovie draw the chain and shoot the bolt into the slot on the other side.

A few westerners and Chinese residents in business suits were waiting for the shuttle bus to depart for Central, while Narcisa and another *amah* waited slightly apart. Of course, the westerners all boarded first, and when Narcisa and her friend started to step into the bus, the Cantonese driver shouted, 'Ten o'clock only. Five more minutes! Not now! Not now! Not ten-o'clock yet!'

The residences along the Path had a rule that only tenants had priority to use the shuttle, while the servants had to wait for the rush hours to end. This was one of the conventions that was becoming more complicated each day, as Chinese became tenants, along with their Chinese servants, while many of the white tenants hired Filipinas, Thais or Indonesians. But Claire reflected, it was hardly necessary for the driver to slam the doors shut right in Narcisa's face when there were empty seats.

'No sense these girls trying to bend the rules or everything will come apart at the seams,' muttered the man standing in the queue on Claire's right. She recognized Fiona's husband, Deputy Secretary of the Public Works Department, Barrie Reynolds.

'It's falling apart anyway, isn't it?' Claire replied, 'if you mean the old caste system. In six months, it may be Party members first.'

Reynolds cocked a suspicious eyebrow. 'Trying to be amusing?'

Claire shrugged and then changed the subject, 'I'm sorry to hear your wife's car was stolen.'

'Nicked right out from under the car park attendant's nose. He must be in on it,' sniffed Reynolds, blowing his own nose noisily into a linen handkerchief. 'Frankly, Fiona's such a rotten driver, the city is safer without her behind the wheel. I should have personally arranged to have it stolen months ago. She borrowed my car and driver today to do a bit of Christmas shopping at the outlets in Hung Hom. That way there won't be any more accidents, but I don't fancy riding this bloody bus. I missed the 9:07 by a hair and I'm late for a meeting with HMG.'

He was the sort of man who wiped his whole face after sneezing. Claire tried to imagine him swabbing down his forehead during a long meeting with Her Majesty's Governor.

'An accident? Was she hurt?'

'Not just one. First, there was the whiplash two years ago down on Queen's Road East. Some taxi rear-ended her when she was tailgating a lorry. I don't really blame her for that one, although she could have signaled if she'd given herself more room in front. Then there was the run-in with—oh, well, why am I going on like this? Never drink and drive, myself.'

Their bus hurtled down Garden Road. The first stop would be the government offices near the Public Works Department and then the US Consulate. Along with a few others, Reynolds collected himself.

'Nasty business, this kidnapping the Franklin boy. Bright little chap. Got everybody jumpy. Well, got to jump off myself.'

Claire was left mulling over the unamusing image of an alcoholic Fiona Reynolds bashing into the ends of Hong Kong taxis. Cantonese taxi-drivers were for the most part volatile, rude, dishonest, and impatient. And they were monarchs of the roads. They didn't tolerate English ladies scratching their paint jobs.

It was a lucky thing Fiona hadn't hit anybody on Tregunter Path—like a playing child.

chapter eight

What a relief it gave Claire to gaze up at the old office building in Wan Chai, that half-shabby, half-glitzy district of silvery new office towers overhanging faded Vietnam era topless bars. Suzie Wong would not have recognized her old haunts, now replaced by 'Chuppie' restaurants, expensive gyms and four-star hotels overlooking the few quiet temples and sidewalk noodle shops that had survived the creep eastward of the high-rise cityscape of Central District.

Was it possible that in the six weeks that had passed since she hustled off to the delivery room, so little had changed here? On the ground floor of the building, the Choi family's flower shop was quiet at this time of morning with only a few funeral wreaths leaning around the lobby entrance waiting for delivery. This was the very spot a few years before where Jim had casually kissed her good-bye as if he'd be gone for only a few days. Without a word of explanation or warning, he'd never returned.

Now that same storefront reminded Claire instead of Petey's coming funeral. It would be a modest, dignified Anglican service at St. John's Cathedral, attended by Ian's fellow pilots and their families, a few of Vicky's English school friends who had married men working in Hong Kong and a few gray heads from Miriam and Gordon's days.

The doorman, Mr Shuk, was sitting on the same old perch behind his reception desk in the lobby, looking as lazy and nosy as ever.

'What? No baby? What happened?' he scowled in mock disappointment.

Claire laughed, waiting for the elevator to take her to the twenty-fourth floor. 'You want to babysit? Any time!'

He shook his head, laughing gruffly at the idea. 'No babysitting, never, never! I too old!'

'Claire!' Hopkirk and Cecilia jumped from their seats with a huge hug for her from each as soon as she had kicked open the bureau's wooden door, warped stuck in its frame by years of relentless humidity.

'This place looks great!' she cried, dropping into her cracked leather chair with its patches of adhesive tape, and gazing around her well-worn office, and then out the window, where a sliver of harbor could still be seen between the new towers thrown up on Queen's Road East.

She didn't care that what first struck her eye was how stained the carpet looked around Cecilia's little metal desk, how the corkboard above Hopkirk's desk was broken off on one corner, and how the tape on her chair was losing its battle against the foam stuffing. Since she'd rushed out of here midmorning, her waters broken, her step halted by painful contractions, she might have done the crawl across three oceans—she felt she'd traversed so many miles of experience in only a few weeks. Yet, the old chair fit her bottom just as well as before, even with the new pounds around her hips.

Claire had arrived at the office just as Cecilia was finishing the morning routine—photocopying and filing away news stories marked up by Hopkirk. Claire felt a pang, as she saw the *Bangkok Post*, *China Times*, *Wen Wei Po*, *Da Kung Pao*, *China Daily*, and her beloved transcripts of the Chinese mainland press airmailed by the BBC's listening service. Cecilia brought in the latest pile of mail and placed it next to two other bundles, 'Whenever you're ready, *Mom*.'

That pile jerked Claire back to reality and she begged off, 'Oh, thanks, but I'll wait until next week and my official return. I just came in to give you my holiday goodies.'

Hopkirk drooped his lanky frame around the sliding office partition. 'Tell us what's happening up there on Tregunter Path. MacDermott's back in New York from his tour of East European bureaus and I mentioned that the two boys' story is all over the front page here. He wanted to know if it ties in with any broader feature. He read a *Fortune* story about kidnappings of businessmen in Guangdong and Taiwan. They did it as a sort of travel advisory piece. You know he doesn't like playing catch-up.'

MacDermott was the testy editor of the international edition of *Business World*. He was loyal to his people in the field, but impatient and painfully honest when playing corporate middleman between the forty-seventh floor overlooking half of Manhattan and distant bureau chiefs.

'Frankly, it never occurred to me as a story for us,' Claire answered bluntly. 'When you're up there, it certainly doesn't feel like a business story from any angle. There's no ransom note or demand for money, so I don't see beating up speculation just yet.'

'Leo Franklin's father is an Australian businessman. He must be fairly successful. Did you see he's offering a million Hong Kong dollars for any information leading to the discovery of the boy?'

Hopkirk spread two Chinese papers down on the desk in front of Claire.

Claire paused, and searched mentally for her old reporter's point of view. But she still didn't see it as a story.

'If this were Taiwan, this story wouldn't even make the local papers, kidnapping is so common there. We've seen some horrific stories about kids permanently disfigured and turned into beggars on the streets of Taipei before the police could locate them in time. Really turned my stomach. I think the *New York Times* did something like it out of Delhi or Saudi Arabia.'

She shivered at recalling one account of a mother stumbling over her own missing child begging legless on the street in Taipei.

'Did you remind MacDermott of the piece we did back in '94 on the Cambodians seizing and killing western trekkers? We folded in a sidebar about the "kidnapping—a growth industry" in that,' she recalled.

Hopkirk nodded with thanks in Cecilia's direction. 'Luckily, Miss Elephant Memory slipped it under my nose while MacDermott was on the line.'

Cecilia smiled, 'It was my pleasure, sir.'

Hopkirk was a pro at covering the Tokyo forex market. He didn't have to hide his confusion. 'I don't get it. One kid died in a seizure, then another little kid just disappeared from his bedroom?'

'Like, on our floor?'

'You're kidding?'

'No. And I'm damn glad they didn't report that in the papers. We're already jumpy enough as it is.' Claire struggled to find the word, waving her hands in the air. 'Vanished. It's really strange. You can bet everybody is double-locking the front door. Just being down in Wan Chai makes me feel like I escaped the Bermuda Triangle for a few hours.'

Hopkirk had another thought. 'What about that story in '95 from Singapore about the Filipina who murdered another *amah* and the kid—?'

Claire nodded, 'The Contemplacion incident. She was innocent. At least that's what I think. I was convinced of it and so was everybody in the Philippines. But the Singaporean government got away with the cover-up, and hung her. The Philippines recalled their ambassador to Singapore over it. But nobody's blaming the Filipina *amahs* this time without some evidence. The Franklin *amah* working for the Franklins only got sacked with notice.'

'Sacked? You've been in Hong Kong too long,' Hopkirk laughed. 'You're starting to talk like a Brit.'

'Too right,' laughed Claire. 'At any rate, the police are keeping their cards close to their chests while they question the whole neighborhood. I wonder if they have any clues, really. And my head is full of questions about things that just seem a tad weird.'

'For example?'

'In the cold light of downtown Wan Chai, how do these things strike you two? The policeman near the picnic site the day Petey died, who was conveniently right on the spot, has a secret life as a transvestite diva at a little no-name club off Lan Kwai Fong. His act is full of double-entendres about little boys.'

Claire knew her tone was insinuating, but she gave full vent to her misgivings. Although she gave John Slaughter a lot of credit for his decades of service, there were inconsistencies she wanted to pull together, and to throw her questions into the face of the veteran policeman would be insulting someone who didn't deserve her disrespect.

'Second, just a minute after Petey Sandford is discovered dead, just before the policeman too conveniently rounds the corner, a car speeds away driven by the alcoholic wife of the PWD Deputy Secretary. According to her own husband, she boasts a history of "hit and runs." The deceased little boy's *amah* claims she tried to flag this woman's car down before the policeman turns up, but the wife behind the wheel totally denies to my face noticing any babysitter on the pavement.'

'Third, Petey's body is strangely bruised. Coincidence? Well, in case it's connected to Mrs Reynold's erratic driving, there's no chance of inspecting the car in question because that night it conveniently disappears from the Tavistock garage, right out under the nose of the gateman.'

'Finally, the autopsy confirms Petey suffered an epileptic attack. So why is some unexplained poisonous substance turning up in his little tummy?' For a minute, this point reminded her of something, something she'd seen—but what?

Cecilia and Hopkirk could only shrug.

'Fifth, only twenty-four hours later, Leo disappears.'

Hopkirk thought for a minute. 'Maybe there's a connection nobody knows about? Where was Leo during Petey's epileptic attack? Did he see something? Know something?'

Claire looked at Hopkirk. 'Good question. Very good question.'

Cecilia piped up. She was considering what Claire had said about Crowley. 'A lot of Chinese boys sell themselves to homosexual *guay-los* out in Repulse Bay. They wait on the rocks next to the beach, just in front of the hotel there, and the customers send boats to shore to pick them up for an hour or two. They might know something about your policeman, whether he is actively looking for boys or not. It's too cold to swim now, but my mother likes the buffet lunch at the hotel. I might be able to find out something this Saturday.'

'Your mother doesn't mind you scrambling over the rocks accosting Cantonese in G-strings?'

Cecilia wasn't Cantonese like most of Hong Kong's Chinese, but came as a toddler to Hong Kong in the sixties, fleeing the anti-Chinese rioting in Indonesia. Her mother had worked her whole life as a seamstress in textile factories and Cecilia had worked her way to a degree in librarian skills at the Hong Kong Polytechnic, earning her book and uniform money stuffing jeans and silk underwear into export packaging.

Cecilia shook her head that she didn't mind and laughed a little, a deceptively lighthearted chime for someone who had survived a nervous breakdown in 1989 over shock at the Tiananmen murders in Beijing, not to mention an unexpected incarceration in a Chinese prison in 1995 while on assignment in Guangdong for Claire.

'It's my pleasure,' she said simply.

Claire rose, refreshed by the respite from Caspar and the levelheaded atmosphere of the office.

'Well, I meet a different kind of deadline these days, so I better get going. You know, Hopkirk, a baby boy is exactly like an editor on the international desk. He makes you feel very important for a few seconds, he won't take no for an answer to any of his untimely demands, he wakes you up at all hours of the day and night, and like any editor, he never heard of such a thing as a weekend off.'

Hopkirk laughed, 'I'll find it very reassuring to know that I'm so well prepared the next time I get pregnant!'

Claire nodded, 'Well, enjoy your last week in our quiet corner of the empire. I liked the piece you did on Asiatech's new figures for Christmas sales. It's always hard to find a new angle on the Christmas manufacturing story. Thank God you managed.'

Hopkirk bowed ceremoniously, grateful Claire had bestowed her blessing on his tenure. Sometimes bureau chiefs resented any outsider sitting in for them.

'When's your flight back to Tokyo?'

'Right after New Year's Day. After trying to keep on top of events from Jakarta to Beijing, I really appreciate my simple life of yen forecasting.'

Claire felt light and happy, certainly more in the Christmas spirit than at any time since last Sunday morning. She missed Caspar, but it was a novel feeling she wanted to savor a little longer, so she figured that before heading home, she would enjoy her freedom for another half an hour. She would stop at Xavier's office for a kiss. He worked out of a high-rise needle-shaped building on Ice House Street in Central, right next door to the Foreign Correspondent's Club.

She checked her hair in the windows of a shop and was happy to see the way it caught the sun. She reminded herself that it had been days since she'd worn lipstick, and slicked on a glossy copper salvaged from the bottom of her bag. The taxi ride to Central took mere minutes and she hoped Xavier would be pleased to see her for once without Caspar clinging to her chest.

Opening the door to his outer office, her mood slumped. There was a woman's voice, querulous and emotional, coming from Xavier's private office. His Chinese secretary, Lornia, looked taken aback to see Claire striding in without warning.

'Claire, uh, Hi! How is the new baby?'

'Fine, just fine, thanks, Lornia. Um, Xavier in a meeting?' The door was closed. That was unusual for Xavier who prided himself on a relaxed and open atmosphere with Lornia.

Lornia hesitated, fingering the lacework holes in her hand-knit sweater. 'Yes. He was expecting you?'

'No,' Claire shrugged. Lornia looked nervous. What was wrong? Claire's hand flew nervously to an unruly red twist of kinky hair over her temple, the one that drove her crazy as a teenager by sticking out when all the other girls' hair was blonde or brunette and smooth. Lornia's anxiety was contagious.

'I'll let him know you're here,' Lornia nodded and kept her head down.

She went to Xavier's door and opened it. The sounds of a woman in tears slipped past her. Lornia said a few words about Claire waiting outside. In a second, Xavier was springing to the doorway to greet her.

'Claire, come in!' He gave her a warm kiss on the cheek and ushered her into the inner office, where Fabienne sat at the head of a small conference table, wiping her eyes with a Kleenex. She was wearing black suede pants and a black leather jacket with a baby blue *crepe de chine* shirt underneath. This was not an outfit anyone chose for a morning of weeping—quite the contrary. She looked up to see Claire in shock and surprise. Claire had obviously interrupted an intense moment between her lover and his ex.

Claire felt betrayed by her own flushing cheeks. She rarely dropped in on Xavier during the day because she was usually so busy in her own office. Occupied with her own life, she thought. She had already been counting on the delight of a loving reception when she arrived, a warm hug and the small relish of being alone with Xavier in fresh surroundings for a little time without the baby. These last days of maternity leave were so short, so precious, why did they have to be shared with this woman?

'Sorry, Claire, I was just catching Xavier up on some old gossip,' said Fabienne.

'A friend of ours suffered a terrible motorcycle accident recently.' Xavier looked solemn, and since Claire had never known him to lie, she felt her alarm subside as the pieces fell back into place.

'I'm sorry to hear that. Who was it?'

Fabienne was still collecting herself and didn't look Claire in the eye.

'A girl we were both close to, the girlfriend of a member of our old commune,' Xavier explained.

Claire waited for Fabienne to add something, to help Claire muster some commiseration over someone she'd never met. But the conversation seemed to have died with Claire's arrival. It seemed a fair explanation for the tension in the room, but Claire still felt uneasy.

'So!' Xavier rubbed his hands together, trying to set a more upbeat mood. 'I'll get some more coffee. Claire, show Fabienne the trail we'll be taking on our hike out to Father Fresnay's village!'

This hike had been the result of Xavier's 'planning session' over drinks with Fabienne the night Leo was kidnapped. They were going to stick to the plan, Claire insisted, because there was nothing else they could do. Privately the thought of getting Caspar away from Tregunter Path, even for a day, was a day of escape from heavy anxiety and dread.

The two women walked awkwardly to Xavier's wall map of Hong Kong, all 400 square miles of territory, showing the islands of Cheung Chau, Lamma and Lantau, and the sprawling New Territories reaching up to the border with China's southernmost province, Guangdong.

Still unnerved by the atmosphere of ill-explained tensions, Claire pointed to the eastern coast of the New Territories and the Sai Kung Peninsula. 'We'll be hiking from this part of the Sai Kung Country Park along a path to the bay of Tai Long and the village of Ham Tim. There's no road through these hills, which means the village is preserved as it was a hundred years ago. You see, it forms part of this trail that stretches for miles, the MacLehose Trail named after a former governor, Sir Murray MacLehose.'

Fabienne pretended to concentrate on the map, and Claire ran her finger along the coast until she found the village. They were both good actresses, but for how long?

'You must bring a camera. Did you get that broken one fixed yet?'

Fabienne bristled, 'A professional never goes anywhere without a camera. Like you with your notebook, I suppose.'

Claire nodded awkwardly, 'Yes, same thing. Well, good. You'll get great shots of traditional village architecture, and the old church where our friend Robert gives his little Christmas Mass is very charming. Be sure and bring lots of film.'

An excruciating silence followed as Claire settled herself in the chair opposite Xavier's desk, and Fabienne stood pretending to scrutinize Hong Kong's eastern coastline. Would Fabienne be excusing herself soon, or would she try to sit out Claire? Claire knew her rage was ridiculous, but she got so few chances to relax with Xavier, she was furious. At night she was too exhausted from childcare to stay up and chat to him about his day. No one who had not been a new mother could imagine that two people living together with a newborn had so little time to enjoy each other as two adults. Fabienne could never understand.

Suddenly, Claire pulled herself together. It was so ridiculous, she thought, she must forcibly remove herself from this scene. This was turning into a Henry James story, where you imagined everything was happening even though nothing was happening. Or was it? This did her no good and she wasn't vying during recess for a chance to play kickball, she was the mother of this man's child.

If there was a game going on behind her back, if there was an unspoken dialogue between Fabienne and Xavier—or worse—Claire hoped a strategic withdrawal might give her the upper hand, or at least some emotional buffer zone. If she had to share Christmas Eve with this woman, she still had Christmas morning with her man and child. She had almost thought *husband*, but caught herself.

She glanced at her watch, perhaps too theatrically. 'Oh, it's late!' she exclaimed. 'Time for another feeding. I'm sorry, I'm just not used to Caspar running our life yet!'

Xavier was returning with her coffee. 'I screwed up,' Claire laughed it off. 'Nature in the form of your son calls! Look, I just came for a kiss. See you tomorrow, Fabienne. Wear some comfortable shoes.' She could not resist this dig at Fabienne's expensive Italian boots. At five foot ten inches, Claire's own footwear tended toward flats, to her frequent regret. She gave Xavier a good, strong, hug, almost a football tackle, and sipped the hot coffee standing up. Xavier looked at her, clearly startled. Perhaps he wished to detain her a few minutes longer.

Once she had escaped them and safely bid her swift adieu to the still-embarrassed Lornia, Claire pushed the button for the elevator and leaned her forehead against the cool tile of the lobby. She wondered how she would get through Christmas Day.

The taxi ride home was difficult. Claire felt waves of childish hurt, the feeling she was shrinking into nothing, diminished by each encounter with Fabienne. The importance of Caspar, his centrality in her life was one shock to her system, but to consider the idea that Caspar was *not* central to Xavier, that his own life was less than turned on its head by paternity, wounded her deeply. There he was, in his private work domain, entertaining the latest news on his other life, his previous, carefree, single life. It was still there for him, as it would never be again for her.

She was lugging a stone of worry around in her stomach. She hoped she could sneak into the apartment without alerting Connie and Dovie and most of all, Caspar. She needed time to herself. But she had forgotten the barricade of bolts and chains Dovie had erected to keep out intruders. She waited for what seemed an interminable delay for someone to answer her own front door.

Dovie's face was a deep, frightening purple flush when she finally admitted Claire. She started to speak, 'ma'am,' and then stopped, shook her head, and walked toward the kitchen.

'Dovie, what is it?'

Dovie turned and spoke carefully. 'I have to speak to you alone, ma'am.'

'Well?' Claire tried to sound patient and warm, but in fact, she dreaded servant problems. She had seen many women lose their privacy and peace of mind over minor issues that blew up into domestic Cold Wars.

Dovie nearly whispered, 'Please, not here.'

Suddenly a burst of angry Tagalog exploded from the kitchen. Connie was standing near the sink, face turned towards the window, but she was sputtering in Tagalog, obviously furious over something. Fully aware that Claire was standing there dumbfounded by this unexpected confrontation, Dovie would only tersely shoot one simple Tagalog phrase back and then appeal to Claire, 'Please ma'am.'

But Connie was apparently determined that Dovie would not speak privately to Claire. She walked to the doorway, her face ablaze, and shouted in Tagalog to the older woman and then started crying and shaking. Claire took Connie gently by the shoulders and sat her down at a small table in the long, sunny kitchen, a room as big as Claire's living room.

'Calm down, where's Caspar?' she said, noticing a shake in her own voice at this unexpected explosion of emotion.'

'He's in his room, ma'am,' Dovie said. The older woman was standing behind Claire, breathing heavily, trying to hang onto her dignity and refusing to look back at Connie.

'Please come with me, ma'am. I want to show you something.'

Bewildered and alarmed, Claire raced Dovie to the nursery where Caspar was lying on a blanket in the corner, trying to pull the string on a squawking Big Bird toy but mostly wagging his fist in the air. Claire's breath rushed out of her in a rush of relief.

'Look ma'am.' Dovie reached up to a high shelf and pulled a half burnt-down candle from its perch next to some stuffed toys. 'I found Connie burning this over his crib during his morning nap. She was chanting the rosary.'

As a Catholic, Claire had nothing against the rosary, but the candle struck her as a bit theatrical. 'Why are you fighting with her now?'

'You see,' Dovie was anxious that Claire understand and she was getting excited, 'She put the candle up her on this shelf on a piece of tin foil, but the tin foil got folded here, and you see!'

Claire, indeed, was horrified now to see that the candle wax had dripped onto Caspar's mattress. 'Was he burned?' she turned immediately to inspect her offspring.

'No, ma'am, I found her kneeling here, like this, and the wax was dripping on this end and Caspar was sleeping over on this side, which is why she didn't see the wax, falling here, right behind his leg.' Now that she had got the story out, Dovie straightened her and stood more calmly in front of Claire.

Claire took a deep breath. They could both hear Connie protesting and sobbing to herself, all the while scrubbing the sink, pouring out the injustice of Dovie's betrayal over the Comet.

'I'm going to speak to Connie alone. But I think you can expect to be taking over a few days earlier than we discussed.'

Dovie's lips tightened with private satisfaction at Claire's decisiveness, but she was far too mature to feel triumphant. 'She has a lot of family who depend on her, ma'am.'

'Don't worry, she was always here temporarily, just until we found you. She has another job waiting for her after the Chinese New Year. We'll make sure she's fully paid until the new job starts. But I don't want her working here. She means well, but I've lost confidence in her judgment. I appreciate your explaining this right away.'

'I'm sorry, ma'am. She didn't tell me she was praying for him every day until I found her like this. She's very frightened that they won't catch the kidnapper. We all are.'

'Dovie, do the *amahs* around here know more than they're telling the police? About Leo's disappearance? Or about Petey's 'accident?'

'They don't talk to me, because they think I'm just an old lady and I'm new in this neighborhood. But still, I hear the gossip. Connie got scared yesterday because of some talk on the shuttle bus about a man hanging around Tregunter Path at night.'

'Do the police know?'

'Of course we told them. But they don't pay attention to Filipina gossip. And most of the time, I would agree with them,' Dovie shrugged.

Connie was waiting in her room when Claire knocked on her door. 'I'm sorry, Connie, but I hope you understand you put Caspar in danger, even though you didn't mean to.'

'He is already in danger, ma'am,' she whispered and gripped Claire's wrist tightly.

'What do you mean?'

'There are things going on that you don't understand.'

'Like what, Connie? You must tell the police if you know something. Are you talking about this rumor of a lurker around the neighborhood or do you know something else?'

'Did you talk to the policeman, ma'am? The one with the curly black hair?'

'What about him?'

'I can't tell, ma'am. But the Filipinas, we know when something is wrong. When someone is sick in the head, we can pray, but there is nothing we can do. We have to think of our jobs, and our families back home.'

'And there is nothing more you can tell me?'

'No, ma'am. But don't leave Caspar alone. I will continue to pray for him, ma'am. But he is in danger.'

chapter nine

The twenty-fourth of December started early for Claire with Caspar cradled in her arms before sunrise. Sitting tucked into the window seat in his nursery, she gazed down at the soothing stretch of harbor in the distance, still only a dark expanse of water undisturbed by ferry and speedboat crossings.

Visiting freighters dotted the waters far out to the west of the city's high-rises. It was traditional that during Christmas week, many of the fleets cruising the South China waters stopped for a rest in Hong Kong. It was only at such a crowded time of year that one could see their behemoth vessels were anchored in neat rows, not randomly, as if the whole harbor were a watery parking lot outside the world's biggest shopping mall.

Christmas calm had descended over the colony, despite all the greed, hustle, and racket Cantonese merchants and Johnnie-Come-Lately-Colonials could muster. Even the Nightclub from Hell must be dead quiet at this hour, Claire thought to herself.

She saw two police vans parked at the junction of Tregunter Path and May Road. The constables lounged inside, dozing, watching, recording, and waiting day and night, for someone, somewhere, somehow to slip up. Maybe Christmas was the time when people were weak, when sicknesses surfaced, sadnesses overwhelmed, and memories to painful to endure alone returned. Perhaps it was a time when evil claimed its little part of the day, unable to let the birthday of Christ be an unchallenged balm to the world.

Something or someone might break.

'Let's bloody hope so,' thought Claire, morbidly. The possibility that there would be no resolution to Leo's disappearance was incompatible with her sense of the world.

Casper was now deep, deep asleep, a milky lump. He'd sucked so hard that a little blister puckered the center of his upper lip. Claire rose carefully and transferred him to his crib and breathed easier. It was an echo of those first moments when the midwives at Adventist Hospital had helped her off the delivery table and she felt, momentarily so light she was sure she could have defied gravity and floated away.

She moved stealthily to her books, stuffed less than methodically into shelves during their hurried move, and found her *Concise Oxford Dictionary*. Aconite was easy to find; 'acme, acne, acolyte, aconite: poisonous plant of genus aconitum esp. monkshood or wolfsbane; drug obtained from this.'

Claire was startled by the sound of Xavier already in the bathroom, clearing his throat and humming some Christmassy tune to himself. He had a deep baritone, a wonderful voice. Claire thought this is the first time I have ever heard him sing. She felt bathed in the fullness of the moment, her first Christmas present from him ever.

His family had always celebrated the birth of Christ on the eve of Christmas. Claire's parents had made the morning of Christmas a wonderland of present opening, music and singing, and then Mass. Well, she thought, this way I'll get two Christmases every year from now on instead of one. And just in case Fabienne ruins today's hike, I'll get a second chance tomorrow at our first Christmas morning together without her. All in all, the spirit of the holiday seemed to be nudging Claire's enveloping melancholy to some more peaceful corner.

The rising sun now reflected off the silvery waters of the harbor. Where was that other book? She ran her index finger along so many beloved titles: *The History of Private Life, Volumes 1-4*, three volumes of *The Cambridge History of China*—two bootlegged editions from the old Taipei rip-off bookstore Caves and one genuine edition from London, all her Iris Murdoch, P.D. James, Ngaio Marsh, Robertson Davies, Robert Van Gulik, John Le Carré, that biography of Truman that had been a doorstopper in her old apartment, popular American political bestsellers, a fistful of Asian cookbooks, Chinese language dictionaries, textbooks, here we were, getting warm, her assorted guidebooks for all the capital cities she'd worked in across Asia, the dog-eared maps, art auction brochures for ceramic sales by bankrupted Chinese ship owners in the bank crash of 1983, her Carrian Trial files, warmer, warmer . . .

Casper stirred a little, but merely pursed his lips and went on dreaming. She started along the next shelf . . . There it was, buried under a scrapbook of old clips, a thin little medical dictionary she'd found in one of the mainland-owned bookstores ten years before. She'd needed it for a ten-day job translating in Henan for an obnoxious BBC camera crew shooting footage of Chinese esophageal cancer patients. It included an appendix of chemical terms. 'Aconite in Chinese: *chuan wu tou* . . . Sichuan crow's head.'

'That tells me precisely nothing,' she mused to herself. 'But it sure sounds like strange stuff to end up in Petey.' She resolved to run it past the smartest guy she knew, and that was certainly not the well-meaning Chief Inspector Slaughter busy investigating baby food and houseplants. And luckily they would be meeting him in less than an hour.

***

In fact, Fresnay was late by almost half an hour, but then, they were all running behind schedule. Claire and Xavier had packed up for the overnight trip as usual—frozen home-made spaghetti sauce, some bottles of good wine, bread, cheeses, salad and hardboiled eggs—and having filled all the available space in Claire's backpack, realized they still had some six diapers to accommodate, wipers for the baby's bottom, and a change of spare clothing for Caspar in case of accidents.

When they were packed and just about to head out the door, they realized they had forgotten to account for one more new burden— Caspar himself, sitting innocently blowing little saliva bubbles in a carrier seat in the kitchen with Dovie.

Fabienne was waiting punctually outside her hotel, dressed in a dapper photographer's vest, jeans and well-worn shoes. Claire was almost grateful to see how slack the Frenchwoman's backpack looked; for once, this person's presence made sense. It was agreed already that Fresnay, who had the strongest pair of legs, would handle the two-hour hike with Caspar on his back. But Fabienne would carry the diapers and baby-wipes.

Claire had secretly packed her Christmas present for Xavier in the bottom of a sock. It was a travel clock she'd ordered from New York, compact and expensive, a gold-rimmed face encased in a handsome lizard case and guaranteed for many years. It was the sort of thing she always wanted for herself during her many abrupt mornings in strange hotels on assignment, but she never bought expensive status goods for herself. She never bought less than top-quality for presents. She was happy with her choice, and knew he would think of her whenever he was visiting one of his projects in Beijing, North Korea, Mongolia, wherever, in the coming new year.

She was disappointed to see Fresnay wasn't waiting for them as arranged. So they had parked Claire's 'rust bucket' on the side of a two-lane road winding through the brushy hills of Sai Kung Country Park, and made idle, polite conversation about the history of the New Territories, distribution of Business World in Asia, and Fabienne's assignment in Cambodia. She was proposing to retrace the steps of foreigners who had been seized and murdered by straggler Khmer Rouge troops at one of the ancient Angkor tourist sites. It sounded like a fairly dangerous project for a first-time visitor to Cambodia.

'You have experience avoiding land-mines,' said Xavier, so I won't worry about that, but you don't have the language. I hope you have an excellent guide.'

'You know I'm a survivor,' said Fabienne, brushing back her dark hair and lighting a cigarette with panache. 'I'm in-des-tructi-ble,' she said. Her tone implied something more—or was it Claire's imagination?

Just then Fresnay's motorcycle engine sounded reassuringly beyond the hills behind them and in a moment, he was unscrambling his long legs and discarding the helmet from his unruly hair.

'Salut, salut, c'est un plaisir to faire votre connaissance. Je suis Robert.'

'Damn!' Claire thought. On top of everything else, she'd forgotten that her Jesuit friend was half-Scottish, half-French, which combined with Xavier's multilingual skills and Fabienne's atrocious English meant that Claire would be spending two days as odd-woman-out in the language department. The only other person in their party who didn't speak fluent French was Caspar.

She'd forgotten how beautiful the Hong Kong countryside could be. Not heavily forested, but low-brushed and lush at this time of year with ferns and heavily fronded trees lining the water. Banana plants had to be brushed out aside as they moved along the inlets of the South China Sea forming tiny coves around which villagers and fishermen had planted a few two-story villas or fishing shacks. At each rise, they could cast their eyes toward the eastern horizon, knowing the sea lay just beyond these hills, while below them stretched one valley after another. Sometimes they passed a herd of cows peacefully chewing on the plastic debris left by city backpackers or overheard the happy Cantonese racket of campers inside a neon nylon tent, their radios and CDs preventing too much panic from urban withdrawal.

Still, they were out of the city and its shadows, personal and political. The fierce old battles of Sai Kung villages during the war—some pro-Communist, some pro-Kuomintang—had faded now, while the new forces still loomed, like an invisible army poised on the border to the north of them.

If the villagers who watched the hikers passing by now cared about politics, the simple fact was that there were fewer of them left for the political parties to bother about. Their sons and daughters had fled to the factories and government-designed new towns, to the urban crowds of Hong Kong and Kowloon, and along with a thousand other Hong-Kongers each week for the past five years, to new lives in Canada, Australia and the US, gone for good.

The incline started slowly and Claire paced herself carefully, knowing the steepest challenge came only at the end of the morning. Their rhythm, Fresnay leading with Caspar's small head bouncing slightly up and down to his enthusiastic step, followed by Fabienne, then Claire and then Xavier. No one had said as much, but Claire knew that Xavier's slightly arthritic knees would be troubled, thanks to decades of merciless skiing and motorcycling.

She also knew that Fabienne would know that, and would understand if Claire hung back, giving Xavier 'face' for lagging slightly behind. At a turn near the crest of the first hill, they paused and saw the entire peninsula stretched out before them, preserved for the teeming city as a recreation area, but also protecting, as much by accident as design, the area's few remaining authentic villages of traditional Chinese peasants.

'*Merveilleuse*,' Fabienne exclaimed. 'I would never have imagined such peace so close to the city.'

'It's my refuge,' Fresnay said. 'At least once a week I have to get away from that pile of Chinese newspapers, radio transcripts and the political database, just get away from the deadlines of the newsletter to remind myself of what I am doing here. Oh and now, we use the Internet, and instead of less work, that just means access to more information than before. Anyway, it's my job, and not a bad way for a farmer's sixth child to end up.'

'You mean spying for the Pope,' Claire shouted ahead, which only brought an annoyed glance backward from Robert. Certainly, Fresnay showed no interest in making converts, and apart from his Sunday obligations to the Filipinas, along with all the other priests in Hong Kong, he carried none of the duties of a parish priest. He and his team of Chinese analysts burrowed away under reading lamps—sifting, collating, and dissecting the news from the mainland.

Claire knew he was also secretly in touch with the Chinese religious underground on the mainland, keeping close tabs on the welfare of imprisoned priests and clandestine cells of Catholics loyal to Rome rather than to the Party. This was a subject they never touched on, and Claire had never discussed it with anyone else, even Xavier.

As for the two men, their relationship was warming slowly, even though it carried the undertones of competition between two healthy, virile men. She had introduced them more than a year ago, well before she had discovered her pregnancy. Fresnay had been cordial to Xavier, but in that challenging tone he always had. To understand him, you had to remember that without a wife or children, he invested all his identity in his priestly scholarship.

'Xavier is a very Jesuit name. Maybe you should have been a priest,' Fresnay had joked.

'Eight years of monastery school with the Benedictines in Switzerland cured me of any such vocation,' was Xavier's riposte.

'Benedictines! Well, of course you went astray!' Fresnay had laughed.

'We kept the Jesuits out of Switzerland for a very long time, presumably for a reason!' Xavier joked back.

'Are you so sure we weren't there anyway?' the priest insinuated.

Remembering this banter warmly as the fresh sea breezes struck her nose for the first time today, Claire smiled to herself with a shock of wellbeing. Part of the trick to surviving life overseas as more than a laboring drone was to create some sense of family, some belonging precisely where you didn't belong. Fresnay had accepted Xavier and in time, Xavier would find a way of fitting in with her other friends, she felt surer every day. Was she giving Xavier the benefit of the same effort when it came to Fabienne?

They swung down the first serious slope to one of the bay-lets used as a dock and fishing port by a few locals. The narrow concrete path was only a short section of the MacLehose Trail. At some points, it skirted the inlet waters by only a foot or two, and Claire would have loved to have stopped there and cooled off her feet, but they had settled into their pace now, and had not even reached the halfway mark.

Fresnay burst into poetry, partly to show off his prodigious memory to Fabienne. He was a priest, but liked admiration from both sexes, and performing extemporaneously was the closest Claire ever saw him come to flirting with new acquaintances:

La langoureuse Asie et la brûlante Afrique,
Tout un monde lointain, absent, presque défunt.
Vit dans tes profondeurs, forêt aromatique—

Fabienne joined in,—*Comme d'autres esprits voguent sur la musique,*
Le mien, ô mon amour! Nage sur ton parfum.

Together they nearly sang,

J'irai là-bas où l'arbre et l'homme, pleins de sève,
Se pâment longuement sous l'ardeur des climats;
Fortes tresses, soyez la houle qui m'enlève!
Tu contiens, mer d'ébène, un éblouissant rêve
De voiles, de rameurs, de flammes et de mâts.

The unexpected camaraderie Fresnay and Fabienne had discovered in Baudelaire promised to dispel some of the tension, Claire hoped. Oddly, Xavier couldn't muster a smile at the sight of Fresnay pounding up the hill, Casper's tiny legs bouncing forward and back against his torso, with Fabienne close behind, swinging her arms in time to the poetry.

'There's a possibility these two are going to get on my nerves,' mumbled Xavier.

Was he jealous? Claire examined his expression. It struck her that Xavier *was* jealous, not of Fabienne's flirtation with the priest, but of Robert's proprietary ferrying of Xavier's first-born son. She realized Xavier was moving more slowly as they got into the second half hour of climbing. His face was flushed and even in the cool breeze, his forehead had broken into sweat. He was in pain, but too stubborn to admit it, and the second more serious ascent was just ahead.

'You want to stop?'

'I'd better just keep going.'

'Xavier, what is it?' Fabienne had turned and was loping back toward them cheerfully.

'My knees are giving up. I'll be all right . . . just have to take it slowly. Go on, go on, don't stop because of me.'

Caspar was starting to wake for his 'brunch munch,' as Claire called the late morning feed. She suggested they cross a small valley used by campers and grazing cows before stopping on the last and meanest hill of all. There was a cool stream where it would be good to eat some of their fruit and cheese while Caspar had his snack. They leaned against some large rocks and surveyed the neon dots of high-tech tents favored by Hong Kong teenagers on overnight adventures. Here and there a cassette player broke the rural stillness with some 'Canto-pop' crooning by Anita Lui or Andy Lau.

'Does that remind you of Sicily, hmmmm?' Fabienne was talking quietly to Xavier as he stretched his legs in the stream to cool down his muscles and knees. Claire overheard her, but didn't turn her head. She already felt self-conscious about breast-feeding in front of Fabienne, while Fresnay's presence didn't trouble her at all. Fresnay came from a very full house of siblings, nieces and nephews tumbling around rambling houses in Caen and the countryside outside Edinburgh. No, she felt unfairly exposed to her attractive rival.

Fabienne's trilling voice carried along the soft breeze. 'The tent fell down one night! Oh, it was so funny, trying to put it up again in the dark with the wind blowing and we were so drunk. *Tu te rappelles?*'

'Of course,' Xavier said, putting his arm around the vivacious Fabienne for a moment for a comforting squeeze.

Claire heaved a deep sigh . . . She's not giving up, this chick, she's just not going to give up . . . and looked up from Caspar's intent little labors to find Robert's eyes firmly watching her expression from where he sat discreetly to one side. She smiled wanly. Her clerical friend was a quick study of more than poetry and Chinese politics.

'So! Mademoiselle! We take the lead and I will show you the best view in the entire territory within twenty minutes!' Fresnay was actually lifting Fabienne from the stream's side and thrusting, as much as helping, her back into her backpack.

Claire tucked herself back up as Caspar was loaded gingerly back onto Fresnay's sturdy back. She took Xavier's hand and they returned silently to the path together. He stopped for a moment and looked quietly and tenderly at her troubled face. Words didn't come. His expression was somber, and he stroked her face as if she were a small, injured animal. Was this a sort of pity? Claire's uneasiness deepened.

Fresnay and Fabienne had already gone around a curve in the hill, and Xavier was clearly making an effort to get up to speed and maintain some dignity in the face of the priest's obvious fitness.

'I would never have suggested this if I had known you'd be so uncomfortable. Last year you didn't have so much trouble with your joints.' Claire said.

'I'm fine, I'm fine!' he protested. 'It's just all those years of banging my knees around, a couple of accidents, and now I just have to live with it. You should have seen me a few years ago on my bike!'

Claire's patience and sympathy were running thin. 'Well, she knew you then, as she's making clear every five minutes! I don't really need this, and it's hard to enjoy something I had really looked forward to with her around.'

'Well, your pal Fresnay is here, so we're not exactly alone!'

'I thought he was becoming your friend, as well. And he's a priest, not an ex-lover! That's completely different.'

'And she was always mostly a friend. Can you understand that? And now she's really only a friend, so let her be.'

'Me let her be.' Claire paused to collect her temper. She re-pinned some of her flying hair back away from her damp forehead. '*Me* let *her* be. Okaaaay.'

Xavier had already started up the slope and sheer willpower seemed to have temporarily cured his arthritic knees.

Fresnay and Fabienne must have been waiting for some minutes when Xavier and Claire caught up with them. Fabienne looked cheerful in a forced way but there was a wariness in her eyes.

Still, the view was breathtaking, looking beyond the little two-alley village of Ham Tin's tall, skinny Chinese houses, beyond the dilapidated village wall of toppling stones, beyond the stretch of thick low brush and paddy fields to one of the broadest, whitest and most untouched beaches in Hong Kong. One backpacker's lonely orange tent sat defying the Pacific winds on a bluff at the southern end of the beach, but otherwise, the scene was unbroken and natural.

'*Incroyable, n'est -ce pas?*' Fresnay helped Fabienne unload a camera to take some pictures, while Xavier favored the weaker knee with a massage for a minute or two.

'Don't forget, going down can be rougher on your legs than going up,' the priest warned them, but Claire felt like a colt returning to the stable, or in this case, one of Ah Fok's cooling beers on the cement veranda of his little three-burner café. There were familiar faces greeting them from the benches and tables Ah Fok had added for the Christmas Eve festivities. A Chinese professor and hiking aficionado

had brought a new girlfriend, and an Irish gym teacher from Kowloon
had gamely dragged his seventy-year-old mother along the same path
the day before.

On the side of the veranda, a local crone in a broad circular straw
hat edged with bobbing black cotton balls laughed a toothless greeting
and waved one hand in recognition, then grabbed Caspar without
anybody's permission and stroked his hair and shrieked, 'Ho leung jai,
ah,' sturdy little fellow, at the top of her lungs.

Fresnay lost no time in settling them in rooms along the row of
empty houses, long abandoned now by the children of farmers for a
life in the crowded industrial neighborhoods of Kowloon. Claire could
hear the priest showering under a hose behind his house as he prepared
to offer his tiny congregation their Christmas Mass, so she fed Caspar
in a corner of their large cement-floored house, and washed herself off
in a sunken stone basin that had once served as the cooking wok for
the former tenants.

The little chapel behind Ah Fok's café was her favorite place of
worship in the world, and as she and Xavier took the host from their
friend's hand, Claire prayed fervently that the contentment she felt
within these cool plaster walls would last. She prayed for Vicky and
Ian, she prayed for Leo and his parents, and she dared to pray that her
doubts about her future with Xavier would be dispelled somehow,
sometime very soon.

As she prayed, the day's small and large fears subsided, draining out
of her as she knelt by Xavier's side. She took his hand. She loved him
and she could not afford to lose him and this new happiness for the
sake of her pride. As soon as he asked her to marry him again, *if* he
asked again, she was going to say yes without hesitation.

As soon as Fresnay clapped his hands together and said, 'The Mass
is ended, go in peace,' Caspar woke up and started crying.

Laughing, they all retired to Ah Fok's veranda. Fresnay slapped
some French accordion music into Ah Fok's battered cassette player
and started dancing with the wailing bundle. To Claire's astonishment,
Fabienne grabbed *her* and started a sort of jitterbug, dancing the way
French girls do, without any of the self-consciousness engulfing Claire.

Claire's awkward torment ended within a minute or two, and they settled down to their well-earned beers, while Xavier returned from Fresnay's weekend house only a few feet from the café in a pair of knee-length shorts. One knee looked frighteningly swollen.

'Let's open our presents now!' proclaimed Fabienne.

'Fine,' said Claire. After five minutes' hustle and bustle in different directions, they reassembled at the small table and began Christmas formalities. For Caspar, Fresnay produced a tiny pair of overalls with the words, 'Future Foreign Devil,' embroidered on the back in Chinese and on the front in English. 'Might as well be prepared for the worst,' they laughed together.

'This is for you,' Claire said to Xavier shyly producing the tiny box. Xavier looked very touched when he opened it and tried to set the alarm. It gave off a clear, musical chime. 'Very elegant, and I can't wait to wake up in some comfortable hotel to this, instead of that little 'hiccup, hiccup' at four in the morning when that guy wants his breakfast!'

Fabienne couldn't let this rest unchallenged. 'Only an American would buy a Swiss an American-made clock!' she said, trying to pass this off as a joke, and hoping the others would see how obvious Claire's miscalculation would be. Xavier chuckled, because frankly he too, thought it was a funny thing to receive a timepiece not made in Switzerland.

'Here are my presents,' Fabienne smiled, and as they were opened, Claire realized that the gloves she had coughed up at the last minute for Fabienne were too large for the woman's delicate hands. Fabienne had bought a small bottle of perfume for Claire and for Xavier, an elegant sleek Swiss Army knife.

'But I have one already!' he said, producing his battered Victorinox.

'But the corkscrew is still broken, isn't it?' There was no mistaking the love and familiarity in her voice—some damn shared memory again, thought Claire with angry frustration!

Fresnay was staring fixedly at Xavier's left knee. 'That needs some kind of poultice overnight, if you ever want to see Hong Kong again,' urged Fresnay. 'Since the eleventh century, monks have used rosemary to ease swelling. There're still lots of it in my kitchen garden. Let's give it a try.' The industrious scholar was also a superb chef, growing standard herbs on a stretch of field alongside Ah Fok's kitchen. Claire followed him carefully along the rows of basil, oregano, thyme, lovage and finally . . . 'Ahhh, here it is . . . *ros marinus* . . . fond of the sea . . . that's why it's doing so well in this sea air.'

He spent some minutes in the kitchen, where Claire watched him grind up a huge pan of the spiky branches and then mix the fresh needles into a paste of isopropyl alcohol with some of Ah Fok's rice starch for thickening. He wadded it all into gauze, which he wrapped tightly around Xavier's mean-looking knee.

Maybe it was just the support of the bandage, but Xavier managed one slow dance with Claire before they all sat down to heaping plates of pasta covered with freshly-grated parmesan cheese and salad, with a desert of fruit and a tart heated up in Fresnay's little oven inside his humble but comfortable 'getaway.'

The sun had long disappeared behind them, retracing with its fading rays the footpath to the west of them that they had struggled to conquer. Ah Fok brought out old-fashioned green mosquito coils, placing one at each corner of the little cement terrace. A brash bare bulb illuminated the terrace, but a string of colored Christmas lights along Fresnay's windows facing them told Claire that the priest, who seemed so cerebral and independent of emotional ties, had lovingly prepared for his guests with a wonderful sentiment he was shy of expressing in more obvious ways.

The wine and beer were flowing and they chatted with the other visitors sitting at nearby tables, while Ah Fok's mother, the crone who wouldn't relinquish Caspar any more than she intended to relinquish life, rocked him vigorously. But even she began to flag with the late hour and the boisterous music from Fresnay's cassette player.

To Claire's surprise, Fabienne took Caspar on her lap and began to cuddle and amuse him, giving Xavier and Claire a chance for an impromptu and guarded two-step. And she even seemed to enjoy lifting the tiny boy into her arms for a short waltz of their own along the edges of the terrace. Caspar was delighted, his laughter rippling through the adults like a stream of champagne.

She'd misjudged Fabienne. Perhaps this interloper just needed time in Hong Kong with Claire, Xavier and their newborn to find her way of digesting Xavier's new situation. Fabienne was an adventurous professional—like Claire herself—and was still so young and beautiful. Was it too much to imagine that in a few years' time, Claire would dance with a newborn belonging to Fabienne and another partner, a man who loved her for her *chic* and courage?

Everything was going to be all right, after all.

'Robert, I think this medicine pad may be working on my knee. Can you make another for my other knee?' Xavier ventured over this third glass of wine.

'Certainly one for every bone in your old body!' Fresnay teased him, 'But don't think for a moment, man, you can ingest my magic potion. Excessive doses taken internally are fatal!'

'You're kidding,' said Claire. 'We eat rosemary all the time and it doesn't do me any hard.'

'But not in the doses they tried in the Middle Ages. People believed that drinking infusions of rosemary water would do away with all the evils of the body, but found that too much of a good thing killed them as surely as a poison,' Fresnay said, clearly in all seriousness.

Claire started, remembering her intention to tap Fresnay's encyclopedic brain. 'What about monkshood? Do you know anything about that? Ever heard of it?'

Fresnay looked at her with surprise. 'Of course!' He looked off into the distance, 'Aconitum . . . '

'That right! Aconite!'

'Derived from *akno*, or dark in Greek,' interrupted Xavier who never lost an opportunity to remind everyone he'd studied Greek in a Swiss monastery school for eight years.

Fresnay nodded. 'The shape of its flower resembles the cowl of the Benedictines, your friends, Xavier, which is why we Jesuits all know how sinister this stuff is,' he chuckled.

'According to Greek mythology, the poison of the monkshood was the foam that dripped from the mouth of the mythical three-headed dog Cerberus, when Hercules performed his twelfth labor and dragged it from Hell. Whenever the dog spit, these plants sprouted. Many educated Europeans would know it, because we learn in history that in ancient times monkshood was used to poison wells and springs in the face of the invading enemy. And it was used among common people as a sort of working class alternative to hemlock. It was a sort of classical form of euthanasia, forced on the infirm and old when people wanted to get rid of them.'

There was an appreciative silence filled only by the cheerful fingering of the accordionist on the cassette player at the back of the veranda.

'It was found in Petey Sandford during the autopsy,' Claire announced at last. 'The forensic men told the police it might be some kind of flower Petey ate randomly while playing around the *nullah*.'

Fresnay looked meaningfully straight back at her. 'We must explain this to Inspector Slaughter right away, so that he doesn't spend another day wandering the hills in vain.'

'What do you mean, Robert?'

'There is little likelihood that Petey just stumbled across a plant like that in the wild. Someone must have fed it to him intentionally.'

Claire looked at Xavier. 'But everybody agreed that Petey had an epileptic fit. The police, his doctor, and his *amah*. Even his mother, who's a close friend of mine, accepts that.'

Xavier wasn't so sure. 'You're thinking that possibly someone fed him the poison and the results were mistaken for one of his seizures, Robert?'

'If I had to guess tonight, I would said that the presence of this substance in Petey is hardly likely to be an accident.'

Claire looked at the priest straight in the eyes. 'What you're saying is that—'

'That this has a bearing on Leo's disappearance beyond what the police already suspect. That you may be living, not with some random snatcher who spied on Leo and grabbed him for his charming looks when the opportunity arose, but with a very well-educated, very determined and very, very sick murderer hiding in your midst.'

chapter ten

It was impossible to reach John Slaughter on Christmas Day, even though they left messages for him everywhere they could think of, and Father Fresnay spent half his morning speaking Cantonese to various Chinese constables left on duty. Tomorrow was Saturday, so Claire swallowed the frustration of returning to Tregunter Path with her fears doubled, and no more answers than during those last few days of horror since Petey's death and Leo's disappearance.

Fresnay had left before nine for his solo hike back to Central. Claire was amused to see that, having warmly offered his private Mass to friends in Ham Tin, he treated the next day's schedule of standing-room-only Masses and confessions with all the professional aplomb of a corporate CEO giving shareholders a quarterly report.

Hong Kong's harbor was jammed full of junks, ferries, small sampans and tugs—and most dramatic to see from the hills above—military ships. Destroyers, cruisers and ships of all sizes and nationalities were still arriving for Christmas leave. Would this wonderful tradition, which always culminated with these hundreds of ships blaring their horns on midnight, New Year's Eve, end soon with the takeover by Beijing? Claire wondered sadly.

Central District was full of beautifully-dressed and made-up Filipinas attending Christmas Masses, while the English-style pubs were full of sailors of all nationalities; some of them were spilling out into the streets of Wan Chai, beers in one hand, girlfriends in the other, singing Christmas carols in an unseasonal midday blaze.

All of this was punctuated by the never-ending construction racket; the resounding boom of pile drivers a reminder that this was an Asian Christmas, and with the handover to Beijing imminent, only nominally a Western outpost and for not much longer. While a few hundred thousand Westerners and Filipinos celebrated Christ's birthday, it was just an ordinary Friday working morning for millions of others in soon-to-be Communist China where speculation and profit would always reign unchallenged by mere concerns of the soul.

They dropped Fabienne off at her hotel. She said she would spend the rest of her day taking a jetfoil to Macao to photograph a children's choir of Vietnamese refugees singing on the steps of the ruins of St. Paul's Cathedral and a Portuguese Christmas parade.

Meanwhile, here in Hong Kong thousands of Filipinas in their festive flounces, laces, and red and gold high heels streamed into and around St. Joseph's Church on Garden Road in Central. The largest corporate landlord in the city, Hong Kong Land, had installed a towering tree flown down from China's Manchurian north to the atrium of Central's cathedral to consumerism—the Landmark Shopping Center. In the middle of this incongruous setting, splat in the middle between the Dior and Versace boutiques, a bagpipe band was playing Handel.

Middle-class Chinese who had the day off would be at sporting events or shopping malls—eyeballing goods that were sure to be marked down for a mammoth shopping spree before Hong Kong's true annual holiday, the Lunar New Year break.

To her secret surprise, Claire genuinely wished Fabienne well. As soon as she'd waved the woman off as sincerely as she could without actually going, 'Whoopee,' she forgot her. She hoped Dovie had remembered to turn on the Christmas tree lights for their homecoming. Connie had packed up her things and moved out by now. Dovie wouldn't return to work until Monday, although Claire knew that after she spent Christmas Day with her daughter she would move into the servant's room at the back. Now that Connie had decamped, Dovie could shove the partition aside and occupy the entire space.

So Claire would be with her man and child in their own home for the very first Christmas of her new life. Xavier drove in silence and she sat quietly, almost contently now, but as the festive atmosphere of the city faded from earshot below, Claire couldn't help noticing the grim aspect of Tregunter Path all over again.

Leo Franklin's smiling face stared out at them from reward posters attached to all the lamplights and fences along Cotton Tree Drive, along May Road and flapping in the sunny bluster of the late winter morning along Tregunter Path. Giles Franklin's reward for information a million Hong Kong dollars. Obviously no one had come forward.

Claire knew it would be a very difficult day for the Sandford family. She'd put off showing them the Grover toy for fear of upsetting Vicky. Nevertheless, she intended to pay her holiday respects at a quiet drinks gathering they'd organized for the 26th in lieu of a funeral reception. The day after Christmas was known to the English, and therefore most of Hong Kong, as 'Boxing Day,' when it was customary to throw open the doors for relatives and friends. This year Miriam Forsythe had called to say that it was meant as a sort of memorial get-together for friends who hadn't been able to make the funeral. Claire thought she would find the moment with Vicky then to return Petey's things.

So today would be unnaturally quiet for Xavier and Claire. As they collapsed, knapsacks dumped onto the sofa, and shoes shrugged off sore feet, into their under-decorated living room, the tree stood near the large picture window, its backdrop the bare balcony and beyond, the glittering harbor. The string of colored lights twinkled, just as Claire had hoped, but there seemed to be so many of them! The ornaments she'd feared were too few shone from every angle of the branches. She left Xavier standing there, drinking in this all–American spectacle with a look of amusement and affection on his face, while she laid the sleeping Caspar in his crib, and came back and entwined one arm in his.

'So if you celebrate Christmas with the whole family on Christmas Eve, what's left over for the 25th?' she asked Xavier shyly.

'That's when the very private celebrations begin,' he said, taking her in his arms.

***

The Sandford gathering was bound to be a subdued affair. On arriving, Claire's first duty was to say hello at last to Miriam and Gordon and introduce Xavier, and then to deposit Caspar in the nursery. Claire paused in the tiny too-neat little room, and gazed at all the toys sorted away by Manny: the Thomas the Tank Engine slippers, the plastic dinosaurs in a row on the shelf, the foam alphabet blocks, surrounded by striped wallpaper with its trim of clowns dancing under the edge of the ceiling. It was deathly tidy.

She stashed the diapers, bottle and Petey's Grover and cassette tape under the crib for later, if the moment came. Caspar settled comfortably into the crib for his post-brunch nap and Claire sighed, returning to the living room with an even heavier sense of their loss, if that was possible, than before.

She saw a group of older people catching the fresh air on the balcony, but decided against joining them, and for the moment, seized on Gordon's offer of a gin-and-tonic and braced herself for a solacing chat with the bereaved grandfather.

'Quite a loss, our little chap,' said Gordon. He added his thanks for Claire's support for Vicky. Claire demurred and so the formalities continued for a few minutes. But Gordon was bearing up well, and soon she found herself in the middle of a political conversation between Gordon and Ian.

—'I'm not entirely convinced the results had so much to do with democracy or any understanding of political parties,' Ian was saying about the last round of colonial elections before the 1997 takeover. 'A couple of independents—one of them was that columnist, Margaret Ng, got a tremendous vote just on the basis of her personality, I think.'

Gordon nodded. 'Well, it was their last chance to show the Communists they want these elections to continue after the handover. In England the reporting made it seem like a clear-cut victory for the democrats, something to really stick in the craw of the Party.'

Ian sipped his drink. 'What stuck in their craw was that the Communist elements ran their own candidates in elections they condemned outright, and then were utterly trounced. Beijing claimed it had to do with their lack of election experience, *of course* nothing to do with their pro-China, anti-democracy positions. So they turn around and appoint a rubber-stamp Provisional Legislature on the basis of nothing but their own whims. Which just shows how much good faith they put into their guarantee of elections in the first place.'

'Oh, surely back in 1984 they intended to keep their promises. Thatcher wouldn't sign a document of that historical weight in bad faith. Not like the old girl,' Gordon argued.

Claire joined in: 'It's not about elections anyway. It's the content, not the form I worry about. The Communists are going to have their finger in every pie, whomever is elected to Legco. My friends in the local press tell me that there is already a *bo suk*, a Communist party 'uncle,' sitting in on every single editorial meeting in town, watching everyone who goes in and out of the office of the editor-in-chief from his new desk directly across the corridor—'

'—Even at the *Post* and the *Standard*?' Gordon interrupted.

'Of course,' Claire shrugged. 'It was a decision taken right over the head of the editor-in-chief. The owner Robert Kwok isn't about to offend Beijing. He intends to keep doing property deals with them for a long, long time. And up in Beijing, they're having meetings in the Hong Kong and Macao Affairs Office every week about how to turn Hong Kong into another ruffle-free Singapore—no free press, docile judiciary, controlled elections. Lee Kuan Yew has been personally advising them for years.'

'Another Singapore? God help Hong Kong,' muttered Gordon, who had seen the rancorous split between the Malays and Lee Kuan Yew in the early sixties. 'What else do your friends in Beijing tell you?'

'Well, it's not just the press. A friend of mine who works in the Beijing press corps overhead an official saying with great satisfaction that since around '91 or '92, the Communist Party has had a live body sitting in all the main corporate offices of every foreign company represented in the city, if not actually on the board—'

Ian nodded, 'Gordon, you must have read how they strong-armed our board into giving them a big chunk of our airlines shares at a discount to a company under direct State Council control.'

Claire added, 'And you heard that they're lining up their ducks to get control of Hong Kong Telecom? Another case of "greenmail."

Threaten the local monopoly with mainland Communist competition and the local has no choice but to hand a piece of the action over to Beijing.'

Gordon drank his gin. 'Wouldn't have believed your bosses would have caved in if you told me ten years ago.'

'Everybody talks about something dramatic happening on July first,' Claire said, 'but the Chinese will make sure that if anything changes, it happens once all the foreign journalists and CNN go home. After that, they have all the time in the world. They're already making it clear to each of us journalists that we have to show our loyalty one way or another or we won't get visas into the mainland. The sinister part is that their grasp will slowly tighten without ever looking ham-fisted. I heard out of New York that Beijing had hired Burston and Marsteller to handle C.H. Tung's public relations six months ago, but he was only officially elected two weeks ago.'

Gordon turned to Claire, 'But it's all good grist for you overseas reporters, eh? Won't you be sitting in the press box at the handover ceremony?'

'Of course I'll be there, but as the years have rolled closer to the date, it doesn't strike me as the Big Bang we envisioned when they signed the deal in '84,' she said thoughtfully. 'More of the proverbial whimper. Well, maybe it's just the change in my personal perspective. Before the baby, I thought about it non-stop, but lately, I've been off work, of course, and frankly, I've been so upset about Petey and Leo—'

It was the kind of feminine response that practically ensured the two men would turn away slightly and drift back to business. Claire felt a tug at her elbow and turned to see the white quiff of Alistair Evans-Smith on her right.

'How's Dovie working out?' he asked. 'Everything all right?'

'Oh, hello! Of course, you worked with Gordon years ago, didn't you?' How the old colonial Asia hands stuck together.

'Actually, we're going to be seeing a lot more of them in England once I join Althea. We have a cottage not far from their village. We've been family friends for years. I think it was Gordon who nicknamed the Evans family on the low ground below the village, the 'Evans-Below—'

Claire laughed, 'Making you the 'Evans-Above?''

'Precisely. Anyway, Dovie making out all right?'

'Well, she had a little set-to with our temporary *amah* over saying prayers of protection over Caspar's crib, dripping candle-wax on his mattress in the process.'

'Oh, Good Lord, Dovie wouldn't stand for that kind of Popery, I'm sure.'

'My confidence in her doubled because she told me right away. One thing hitting me all week is how these Filipinas stick together, even to the point that they won't tell us the most terrifying things going on in those back corridors. Actually, there's something else I'd like to talk to you about. Something that troubles me, but I can't really raise it with Inspector Slaughter, because it might do the person in question a lot of unnecessary harm.'

Evans-Smith and she slipped out of the living room and found a quieter corner in the study around the corner. It was clearly Ian's sanctuary, filled with photos of him playing rugby with the airline's team and a collection of antique toy planes lined along the shelf above the television.

There Claire unburdened her tale of the nightclub visit with Xavier and Fabienne. Evans-Smith didn't hide his astonishment.

'You're sure it was this same Inspector Crowley?'

'Well, I think the photos must be with Fabienne, if there's any doubt. But yes, I'm sure it was Crowley. It just left a terrible shadow in my mind over his being there right on the scene of Petey's death. But you know, I'm afraid it's some kind of unacknowledged homophobia buried inside me just leaping out and raising questions about his relationship with Petey that are just inappropriate.'

Evans-Smith seemed distracted by something else. Finally, he spoke up. 'I never go to Lan Kwai Fong myself, since my bailiwick tends to land me at clan festivals drenched in incense and gongs, not feather boas and beer,' he chuckled. 'But you're old enough to remember when buggery was a capital offense in the colony. Didn't take it off the books until the early '80's.'

'Of course I remember.'

'For years Chinese up in Beijing gave us pretty strong signals they wouldn't let us decriminalize it—kind of a convoluted argument that it was alien to the nature of the new Chinese Socialist Man and an English vice.'

'Well, it's not as if the police and legal circles didn't have their scandals,' Claire recalled. 'Remember that policeman's murder or suicide. He was found dead in the room and shot over and over? Remember he was about to name homosexuals in the police force?'

'Yes. Those were rough days for all of us. Goodness, times have changed if coppers are prancing around in public in drag!' Evans-Smith said emphatically, slapping his thigh in surprise.

'Well, I'm not so sure it was in public, so to speak. His act is unbelievably convincing, he does it anonymously, and I only identified him through a telephoto lens. I think everybody else was too inebriated to care who he was,' Claire reflected. 'I wouldn't have mentioned it but for the salacious reference to little boys. Anyway, would it matter if the very senior ranks knew?'

Ian suddenly popped his head in, 'Refresh your drinks?' But Claire knew it was really to make sure she wasn't trying to work on family time—grilling an invited guest. Ian was the sort of corporate personality who suspected reporters of taking advantage of every waking minute to invade the privacy of others. He only respected Vicky's friendship with Claire from a slightly wary perspective.

Evans-Smith waved Ian away reassuringly and turned back to Claire. 'Of course the police force wouldn't be able to officially drum Crowley out of town. But it would look very closely at him from now on, you know, check his record for any signs of putting a foot wrong. You say he's on Tregunter Path every day? I don't like the sound of those jokes about little boys, either, I must say—'

Claire leaned forward and felt she had to whisper, 'Exactly. But if I raise anything with John Slaughter, I might be doing real harm to an innocent man's career. He's entitled to his hobbies, I guess, and in fact, he's talented in a way. Nobody's ever accused me of being judgmental about homosexuality before, but recently I saw a report in the Herald Tribune about child pornography and pimping little boys to respectable men and it made me sick. Of course, now that I have a little boy of my own, I'm getting a little paranoid about the entire outside world. I feel like raising him in a social bubble just to keep him safe.'

Evans-Smith patted her shoulder and rose to return to the party. 'If Caspar turns out to be anything like his mother, he wouldn't sit still for life in a bubble very long. One thing I learned with Viola and Freddy, you can't save them from their own destiny.' His face clouded and he said abruptly, 'Leave this Crowley matter to me, my dear,' and returned to the party.

Vicky found Claire sitting alone in the study a few minutes later.

'Everything all right?' Vicky asked.

'Shouldn't I be asking you that?' Claire replied.

'I'm putting one foot in front of the other. Really. I'll tell you an awful confession. It's almost better that Daddy and Mummy are going home tomorrow. I want to be alone with Ian or just sit in the nursery and be with Petey and take care of myself without having to put up with Mummy's constantly asking me if I'm all right.'

'Sorry.'

'Really.'

'Vicky, may I show you something? Or rather, return something to you, not to upset you, but because it's something that belonged to Petey.'

Vicky looked understandably startled and stiffened a little. 'Of course.'

Claire moved across the hallway quickly into the little nursery and brought back the baby bag. 'I found this in the most unlikely spot. 'Way up the footpath above the road here, and looking as if it were hidden very deliberately. She tugged Grover out of the bag, but Vicky had gasped even before Claire had managed to deposit the well-worn toy in her lap.

'This too. I recognized your handwriting.'

'My God, this tape! I chucked it into the rubbish bin almost a year ago, on Doctor Trythall's orders.'

'Why?'

'Claire, I can't tell you how strange this is!'

'I don't understand.'

Vicky looked up at Claire. 'Well, I wondered about Grover last Monday or Tuesday—I can't remember when it hit me he was missing—because Petey never went anywhere without him. It was all Manny could do to get Grover out of his arms long enough to wash him every few weeks. But that's not what I can't understand. It's this tape. It makes no sense.'

Claire waited and waited, feeling the edges of her patience fray as Vicky fell into a cryptic silence, lost in her own frantic search for an explanation.

'Vicky? Vicky!'

'There has to be an explanation of this. Do you remember when Inspector Crowley was here? I told him there were certain triggers, like little electrical connections, that might fire off in Petey's mind, things like noise, or stress or certain things, specific things that could set Petey off. It's one of the strangest things about his sort of epilepsy.'

'Yes. So?'

'Well, the songs on this tape disturbed Petey. It wasn't anything we could make out, I mean, we didn't know why or how. It triggered his episodes of babbling nonsense. But Dr Trythall had monitored Petey closely and said if there was any reason to suspect the tape, just bung it down the rubbish chute at the back. And we did.'

'When?'

'Well, that's it. I mean, let's see, it would have been last spring sometime.'

'Did anybody else know about this tape?'

'I told Manny not to save it. Sometimes she found Petey putting things in the wastebasket that shouldn't have been there, so she tended to be careful. But I specifically told her this tape had to go.'

'She didn't understand. Maybe she saved it, worried she might be doing the wrong thing.'

'She's always been devoted to him, especially because her own son died, you know.' Vicky looked at the Grover toy. 'I'll put this up with his other things. Petey loved him so.'

Claire took the Grover from Vicky, who was starting to cry, and placed him firmly on the highest shelf.

'Don't you want the tape, too?' Claire said offering it up.

'I hope I never see it again,' Vicky said, brushing it away with her hand. Claire put it back into her baby bag and they left the study together, arms linked and returned to the living room.

***

Claire wanted to spend Sunday evening at the piano. It was, she had explained to Xavier, her Christmas present to herself. For someone who had studied the piano to an almost professional level, it was amazing she'd left the keyboard untouched for so many weeks. It was a measure, she reflected, of her intense love affair with Caspar, an attachment so filled with joy and doubts from the very first hours of labor, all other pleasures became secondary. The distractions had only compounded since then and she sat down on the piano bench and rested her hands on the keyboard lovingly as if it was a reunion with a neglected old friend.

Xavier had promised that while she played, he would take Caspar for a long walk along Queen's Pier in Central to show him the neon Christmas lights flooding both sides of the harbor and shimmering back off the waters. Claire wondered if Xavier needed some time alone. She said nothing as her two men had set off on the shuttle bus bundled in warm clothes against the wet breezes coming off the water.

She pulled out her piles of music and furiously tackled the *Hanon* exercises first. She had done these scales and finger puzzles in machine-gun time for thirty years now and her fingers scarcely needed coaching from the pages as she spent nearly twenty minutes on her warm-up. 'Pumping ivory,' her teacher had called it. Her mind relaxed into the routine, worries receded by the rhythmic rise and fall of her hands. Then she stopped and flexed her fingers. The apartment was so quiet. She realized she was completely alone.

Xavier, Caspar, Dovie—they were all gone. She didn't feel as comfortable as she had hoped.

She returned to her music, working through a favorite Grieg piece and then tackled 'Fast zu ernst' from Schumann's *Kinderszenen*, a syncopated piece with five sharps that eluded her. She had to stop repeatedly as her fingers seemed to be determined to tangle themselves among the black keys. With each pause in the music, the silence of the darkening living room closed in on her. She tackled the music more intently each time. She started again but it really wasn't the pleasure she'd anticipated so happily when Xavier had asked what gift he could give her.

She put her hands into her lap. A chill seemed to hang over her shoulders from the wall behind her bench. She felt so very, very unprotected and alone. Of course, it was the external wall of the building. Being solid concrete, it was likely to be colder than the rest of the building.

She played ruthlessly now, forcing her fingers along, even though their stiffness disturbed her. The old adage about practice—the first day of missed practice, you notice, the second day your teacher notices and the third day your audience notices—certainly rang true. She would get it back, she thought, but it wasn't the trade-off of Caspar for dexterity that was troubling her. Something in the silence of the room mocked her good intentions.

She stopped playing again. She heard no sound, even the pile drivers and hum of construction had stopped early today.

She turned on the small lamp on one side of the piano. She started again. But Schumann's phrases wouldn't come smoothly. She shoved him aside and tried something to keep her interest. She was so rarely alone these days, why waste the time on the gloomy thoughts that kept intruding? She tried something grand, some Paganini variations. She'd just started when a knock on the front door startled her so much she half-jumped off the piano bench and knocked the sheet music on the floor.

Standing frozen, staring at the front door, Claire was strongly tempted not to open it. There was no denying she was afraid. She wasn't expecting anyone. But what was she afraid of? Thank God Caspar was with his father, safely far away in the harbor-side crowd. And it came to her without any warning that she felt guilty. She'd meddled in the whole affair of the little boys and she had no business approaching Ip, turning Crowley's innocent music hall routine into something sinister or half-interrogating Vicky about a harmless tape.

The ringing continued and then someone started pounding on the door, again and again. She waited, bewildered at her own state of indecision. She was actually backing out of the living room when she heard a voice.

'Claire! I know you're in there, Madame! Open the door and tell Xavier to pour a man of Christ some wine!'

Fresnay! She ran to the door and let the priest in, with a wave of relief. What had she been thinking of? 'Xavier isn't here. He's taken Caspar out for a walk. Please come in.'

Fresnay hesitated, and Claire remembered that for all of his motorcycling, hiking and dining-out habits, he was always mindful of his priestly profile in a Godless city. He was wary of gossips and didn't like to visit a woman alone.

'I'll just stay for a moment then, but I thought it couldn't wait. I still haven't been able to reach Inspector Slaughter by telephone, but I expect I'll talk to him tomorrow about this whole affair.'

Fresnay leaned in the doorway and fingered the strap of his bike helmet carefully, clearly pondering his words before her spoke. 'You see, something else has come up, and I think you can help, as you live in the building. I want to talk to your *amah*.'

'Well, Connie has left for another job, and Dovie went to visit her daughter for the evening. Why?'

'Well, I heard confessions through Christmas Masses all yesterday—most of them Filipinas of course. It was the usual, you know, hours and hours of impure thoughts, gossiping unnecessarily, and fiddling the grocery money. Then without breaking the seal of the confessional, I can tell you this much. A woman came into the box, her voice was shaking with fear. She confessed she wanted forgiveness for conversing with "the Devil." The "Devil that is killing children on Tregunter Path".'

'No! So they know who it is! The *amahs*, I mean!'

'At least one does, indeed. I don't know the identity of this woman, and even if I did, I'm bound to keep it secret. And I don't know how reliable she is. She rabbited on and on, "The Devil knows my sins, and the Devil will get me too".'

'Those were her exact words?'

'Oh, I won't forget her words, lass. Exactly as follows: "Everyone always thinks the Devil looks like a man, but he can look like a woman, too." Then she started sobbing, and before I could even blurt out some kind of penance for her to say, she raced out the door.'

Fresnay looked sheepishly at Claire. 'I must confess something myself. I shouldn't have done it, but I stuck my head out in time to see the back of a Filipina in a heavy coat rushing away. I've heard a lot of things in my time, but I don't mind telling you this gave me chills. Because, well, simply because it had the ring of truth.'

chapter eleven

Claire couldn't sleep Saturday night. She tossed back and forth, painfully aware that Caspar would wake for feeding at five a.m.

The meaning of the *amah*'s confession was crystal clear to her, if not to Fresnay. Had Fresnay been to the nightclub with the three of them on Tuesday night, he would have accused her of jumping to premature conclusions. For pretty much the same reason, she didn't mention her thoughts that morning to Xavier. But Claire was sure this was no theological discussion Fresnay had heard. 'Everyone always thinks the Devil looks like a man, but he can look like a woman, too,' was obviously a simple Filipina's description of Crowley's antics in drag.

The *amahs* must know more, but would they risk telling the police? Naturally, they'd be wary of Crowley. She'd seen that fear on Manny's nervous expression from the very first, when the poor woman asked Claire to stay and witness her interview with the officer in her private quarters. If Manny's story of seeking help from Crowley wasn't true, no one knew better than Crowley how she had lied.

Now, could she prevail on Manny to tell the truth? Manny knew Crowley could have her or any of the *amahs* deported back to the Philippines in a matter of days on some trumped-up immigration charge. Would the Labor Tribunal take up a case against a Hong Kong policeman? Not likely.

Claire finally rose, hollow-eyed to Xavier's offer of coffee. She wondered if Fresnay had told Chief Inspector Slaughter about the significance of the traces of aconite in Petey's stomach. However Petey had ingested the poison, aconite might be a complete red herring, perhaps even an inaccurate identification from the lab.

Maybe the police should be thinking in a completely different direction. Following the lead of an exotic poison was unlikely to connect with Leo Franklin's whereabouts. Claire wondered if she should talk to Fresnay again, but realized that it was Sunday, a busy working day for Hong Kong's priests down at the Catholic Centre with shift after shift of crowded Tagalog Masses, those great distaff assemblies of prematurely ageing virgins, lonely wives and absentee mothers. But that thought led to another; today was a day off for most of the *amahs*. Manny and her friends might return to the picnic site for their usual mix of prayer and partying.

Around eleven she left Caspar sleeping in Xavier's lap in the study to set off for the picnic site. She wasn't sure how to approach the group, how many there would be, or even whether Manny would be willing to talk to her in private. Her hunch was right; women's voices singing to guitar strumming came from the clearing on the hill above her. She quickened her pace along the Path, crossed the bridge just wide enough for a single car that spanned the drainage *nullah*, and reached the entrance of the familiar footpath ascending to the Peak.

She paused. The music stopped. She heard a low chant of prayers, very light, like Tagalog ripples along the recital of rosary beads. She didn't intend to interrupt their prayers, so she started up the footpath and aimed to settle a little bit above them to wait for their lunch to begin.

From above, she saw four women kneeling on garish beach towels in the dirt of the construction site reciting Hail Mary's. The gaudy plastic pink and blue beads of their rosaries caught the sun. It was a startling tableau to see these women removed from their hours of servitude. They looked entirely different females.

With their hair dressed, their faces made-up, their plain blue and white uniforms discarded for the day in favor of tight denim jeans, bright shirts, hair ornaments and incongruous high heels, they seemed to have morphed into fully-fledged female citizens. Having painted their faces, they'd reclaimed their personalities from the anonymity of domestic service.

Manny, being the oldest, was the least flashy; she wore a black dress with a white collar and black flats. Claire saw Regina, one of the girls who had prayed with Narcisa in the parking lot, but Narcisa wasn't there. The other two girls looked vaguely familiar.

Claire resigned herself to a long wait. In fact, she was losing interest, her idle thoughts drifting dangerously back to Xavier and Fabienne and wondering if they'd arranged any other meetings in his office, when suddenly, Manny started strumming on the guitar. The other three women took up the song, and for a few seconds, it sounded like nothing more than a 'modern' religious tune—trite, and certainly an insult to the ears of any god who'd once enjoyed the services of Handel and Mozart.

The strumming grew more insistent. Without warning Regina switched from singing to a kind of moaning babble. Claire strained her ears for clues of Tagalog dialect, but nothing she could make out from where she sat sounded like language. The utterances turned animal in nature. Taking her cue from Regina, the third woman, whom Claire now recognized as an employee at the Tavistock building and the fourth woman joined in with their own uncoordinated mumblings and groans, their bodies shaking and hands waving rhythmically up and down according to some otherworldly dictate.

Claire felt she'd intruded on something too private; it smacked of sexual hysteria. Only Manny remained cogent, strumming the guitar undisturbed by the wildness emerging around her, with an unemotional expression Claire found more frightening than the antics of the three younger women, as if Manny incited them into these fits intentionally. The longer it went on, the more Claire realized that this was a ritual of some sort. She'd heard of the 'Charismatic' movement, an evangelical offshoot of the Catholic Church that priests like Fresnay frowned upon, but could do little to stem in a relatively uneducated community of Filipinas. It was so unrelated to the cerebral theology Claire had learned; it hardly seemed the same religion.

Claire found it unbearably embarrassing to watch. Just when she started to think of abandoning her mission, the creepy performance wound down. Slowly the three twitching, howling women drew themselves together, and at Manny's behest, joined hands and began another simpering song, this time in English, about being all one together. Claire remembered home Masses of the sixties back in

Berkeley with her parents working hard to seize on the results of
Vatican II.

When the song ended, the festivities began. Claire felt free to show
herself by walking back down the Path and waving hello to Manny.
Manny nodded and smiled, apparently assuming Claire was striding
down the footpath like just another jogger. She looked startled when
Claire turned toward them and entered the circle of construction piles.

'Manny, could I talk to you for a few minutes?'

'I'm busy now, ma'am, could it wait until tomorrow?'

Manny clearly knew her rights to ignore all employers other than her
own during her sacrosanct hours off.

'I would appreciate very much if we could talk privately,' Claire
pleaded, leaving Manny the privilege of showing her companion how
generous she could be with her time.

Manny joined her near a flat rock wide enough for them to sit on
side by side, but the Filipina pointedly refused the place Claire offered.
She wanted this to be a short interview.

'Manny, I can't help but notice that a lot of the Filipinas look up to
you as their big sister, and I thought perhaps you could help me, or
rather Father Fresnay.'

Manny's eyes widened at the mention of the priest. Perhaps it was
an honor to be singled out by a priest, such an important man to the
Filipinas all over Hong Kong.

'Yes, ma'am.'

'Father Fresnay heard a confession that, well, alarmed him and
although he doesn't know the identity of the woman who confessed
and would never divulge her identify even if he did know, he was
worried about something she said, something to the effect that there is
a Devil killing the children of Tregunter Path.'

'Really, ma'am? A Devil?' Manny's eyes widened with curiosity.

'Yes, a Devil who can be "like a man or a woman." Claire stressed
the exact words. 'Can you imagine what it means for a Filipina when
she says that? I mean, do you think this woman was trying to tell us
something useful in helping answer questions about Petey and Leo?'

'I don't know anything, ma'am.' Manny looked confused. She was starting to redden and look as if she would burst into tears. 'This upsets me, very much, to talk about Petey. I miss him very much, every day.'

'I know, I know. It just occurred to me, just between ourselves, that the person confessing might have been Narcisa.'

'Narcisa? Why Narcisa?'

'Because on the night Leo disappeared, she was screaming something about the Devil taking Leo, as if she really knew who it was. When I asked her about it, she said she really believed in the Devil.'

'I don't know, ma'am. Why don't you ask her?'

'Where is she today? Doesn't she usually come her with you?'

'She spends the whole day crying in her room, ma'am.' Manny's face had hardened, Claire thought, and it became clear why with Manny's next words. 'Mrs Franklin went to her mother's house—'

'Yes, I know,'

'And her mother has a lawyer asking for Narcisa to be charged with neglecting Leo. She wants to break the contract with Narcisa and send her home right away. Mr Franklin doesn't want the lawyers. He is fighting all the time with Mrs Franklin on the telephone. Mr Franklin told Narcisa to stop working and just stay in her room in case the police want to talk to her. Anyway, Narcisa won't see anybody now. She is ashamed. You should leave her alone.'

Claire saw no reason to give in that easily when Narcisa might know something.

'Don't you know her well? Couldn't you help us out a little?'

Manny considered for a moment and turned unexpectedly talkative.

'I feel very sorry for Narcisa and also for Mrs Sandford. I cannot tell you how sorry. You know I lost my own little boy because he got pneumonia in the Philippines. I asked Mr Sandford for airplane money to go home and take care of him, but he said it wasn't necessary, that all we had to do was send the money for antibiotics back to my village and that pneumonia was an easy sickness to cure.'

'So he gave me a lot of money to make sure we could buy the best, the kind that come from a famous company and not one of the phony imitation medicines the poor people in Bontoc use to save money, and fortunately, another *amah* was going home on her vacation to a village near my village, so I gave the money to her.' Manny paused for breath.

Claire waited, unwilling to stop Manny from talking, even if it had nothing to do with Petey and Leo. Manny had tried to tell her once before about Ramon's death, during the interview with Crowley. It was obviously a story that Manny needed to retell. Somehow the death of Petey and Ramon were tied up emotionally inside her. Why not? She had lost two little boys she loved, not one.

'How much money?' Claire asked.

'Two hundred US dollars for the medicine, plus another fifty dollars for her to travel to my village and buy food for Ramon and my family. I was very grateful to him then.'

'He could have let you go home,' Claire said against her better judgment.

But Manny was graceful enough to overlook this disloyalty on Claire's part to her friend's husband.

'This *amah* was so stupid, ma'am. She spent the money on makeup and clothes to make a good impression on one of her boyfriends, thinking Ramon could be cured by traditional herbal medicine instead. When my mother got a letter from me telling her the money was on its way, they caught her and she told the truth, and then this Filipina tried to raise more money from her own family and I did everything I could to get more cash too. I didn't dare ask Mr Sandford for any more, so I worked Sundays cleaning other apartments.'

'And did you get the money together?'

'We almost got it from friends and everybody, but not fast enough and Ramon died.' Manny's expression of composure threatened to disintegrate as her grief surfaced with the telling of the tragedy. Claire took her hand.

'I'm very sorry, Manny,'

Manny nodded needlessly, 'I know, 'ma'am.' She withdrew her hand.

'What happened to the other Filipina?'

'The priests said I should forgive her foolishness, that God wanted Ramon in heaven, and that my boy was happy at God's side. They told me that forgiveness and friendship would bring grace to my soul for eternity.' At that Manny collapsed into sobs and there seemed to be nothing for Claire to do as the woman shook off Claire's gestures of sympathy.

Claire waited for what must have been two or three minutes before she spoke again. She thought it might help to change the subject back to Tregunter Path.

'Manny, excuse me, but let me ask you the most direct question I can, because I know you want to get back to your friends. Do you know something about Inspector Crowley that we need to know in connection with Petey and Leo?'

Manny wiped her eyes with the back of her hand and looked up surprised at Claire.

'No, ma'am. Did anybody say anything about him to you?'

'No, nobody. But Connie, who worked for us between regular jobs, was scared by talk of a man hanging around the Path. Nobody said he was a policeman, but I wondered if without the uniform, maybe someone would mistake Inspector Crowley for a loiterer, you know, someone with no business hanging around watching the kids. That's really what I wanted to talk to you about. And just one more thought. Petey's body had strange bruises on his chest and it occurred to me that perhaps he was hit by a car and you didn't want to say so for fear of getting into trouble, or getting someone else into trouble, because he shouldn't have wandered down to the road.'

Manny wasn't stupid. Her eyes flashed with recognition of Claire's drift. 'You mean Mrs Reynolds, the Crazy Lady.'

'Is that what you call her, the Crazy Lady?' Claire had to suppress a smile.

'She drinks a lot of wine all day from a bottle in her dressing table. Her previous *amah*, Concepcion, told me.'

'Yes, she's very lonely, Manny.'

'She misses her boy a lot, but she could bring him back to Hong Kong any time she wants. Nobody wants to work for her, ma'am, she is always changing her mood and firing and hiring the Filipinas who are sent to her by the agency. Nobody wants to recommend her to their friends anymore.'

'Did she hit Petey with her car that day? Is that what really happened?'

Manny seemed shocked at the suggestion. 'No, ma'am, although everybody is very careful walking around the curve to the vegetable truck because maybe she is driving out of Tavistock at the same time.'

'Really.'

Manny saw no humor in Mrs Reynold's driving skills.

'She is a drunk driver, ma'am.' Manny drew herself up, apparently impatient to rejoin her friends.

'Thank you, Manny. I appreciate it. Oh! I nearly forgot to ask you something.'

Manny was turning away to return to her friends, who were unsuccessfully trying to hide their curiosity, casting glances from lowered faces.

Claire reached into her backpack and pulled out the tape cassette of *Peter and the Wolf.*

Manny gasped.

'You recognize this?'

'Yes, of course, ma'am. It is an old tape of Petey's.'

'You seem surprised to see it. So was Mrs Sandford. She said she threw it out or rather, that you threw it out, but I found it up in the forest, way up there by the gazebo with Petey's Grover.'

'Where, ma'am?'

Claire pointed up the path.

'Petey was never higher than the place over by the *nullah* where I could see him.'

'So you said. But what I can't figure out is why something tossed into the garbage would turn up again.'

'I don't know, really, ma'am. I threw it out a long time ago.' Manny did look bewildered. Claire detected something behind Manny's eyes— were new questions occurring to her, some realizations that hadn't hit the woman before?

'Please try and help us figure all this out, and think over what we talked about, I mean about the Devil stuff.'

'I will, ma'am,' Manny nodded slowly and walked away.

***

Claire wanted to talk all this over with Xavier when she got back to the apartment, but the phone interrupted her return. Fabienne was back from Macau. Claire knew this because Xavier took the phone call in his study and closed the door before continuing the conversation in a voice well below his usual Swiss mountain-man volume. Claire was too proud to ask what her rival's plans for the day were or whether she had booked herself a flight out of Hong Kong soon.

She felt as if she were literally choking on her own pride. It was hard to admit to herself even that on that lovely return to their bed on Christmas afternoon, the first time they had made love since Caspar's birth, she had hoped he would propose again.

He hadn't.

His silence had grown very heavy since she had decided to seize this chance at happiness without any of the guarantees she had foolishly thought were necessary. Just watching Fabienne swinging back and forth on an emotional tightrope without a net was enough to embolden Claire. Life didn't come in fairy tales with happy endings. Fabienne had arrived armed and ready to battle charmingly to stay in Xavier's life *on any terms*. The gloves were off—and suddenly Claire's ring finger looked awfully bare.

About midday, the phone rang again. Claire raised her eyebrows meaningfully at Xavier, unable to hide her annoyance at the possibility that Fabienne was pushing for yet another adventure. Instead it was Alistair Evans-Smith.

'Whether your curiosity was fed by homophobia or not, some quiet inquiries with some retired friends at the London end have turned up something quite distressing about our young Inspector Crowley,' he said.

'Did you ask Slaughter?'

'No, no, no. Not at first. I was afraid John might see it as unwarranted meddling and it might have just created ill will. However, as it turns out, he is now very aware of Crowley's history.'

'He has a record? As a criminal?' Claire sank down slowly into her well-worn rattan desk chair.

'Not quite. But there was a troubling reason he left England and joined the Hong Kong police.'

Claire felt the journalist's selfish satisfaction of her instincts being on target.

Evans-Smith was obviously being careful in his choice of words. 'Crowley was once questioned, then totally exonerated, totally, on suspicion of child molestation. There was a case involving a young boy in his district in south London. Crowley had taken a friendly interest in the boy, to the annoyance of the boy's mother. Then the boy reported some hanky-panky with a friend of Crowley's—not a police officer, as it turns out. But Crowley was questioned, and another police colleague reported seeing some, well,' Evans-Smith cleared his throat as he reached for an appropriate phrase, 'some so-called 'man-boy' love magazines in Crowley's locker.'

'My God!' Claire exclaimed. 'How did he manage to get into the Hong Kong forces?'

'Times are hard for recruitment here as far as Europeans are concerned. There's absolutely no opportunity for promotion to the upper ranks, as you know, but we still need Europeans on the beat. And to be fair, I warn you, Claire, before you speak to anyone about this, it turned out there was no connection between the case and Crowley's private life. None whatsoever.'

'He wasn't involved at all with the little boy?'

'Beyond friendship, apparently not at all. The little boy's mother was away at work a lot, and she'd given the father the boot long before. But Crowley's career in England was over. The other men in the ranks leaned on him to get out.'

'So, what happens now?'

'In the end I rang Slaughter because he should be aware of it, which he wasn't. But I think that should be the end of it, my dear. It doesn't answer the question of where that poor little chap, Leo Franklin, has spent his Christmas. By the way, the investigation had turned up one strange new fact—Leo's passport is missing.'

Claire started at the implication, 'Isn't that good news? That means he's been taken somewhere else? Maybe across the border or to Macao?'

'That's what we hoped, but there's no record of him of departing the territory at any of the border controls,' said Evans-Smith

'Anyway, it leaves some hope that whoever took him had a plan to keep him alive. Each day I pick up the paper expecting to see they've found his body somewhere in the harbor or up on the Peak.' It was the first time Claire had admitted out loud that she feared Leo was dead.

'I promise you that at least out here in the New Territories, the Field Patrol Detachment teams are on alert for anything like a dead body, and believe me, what with the sharks and the gangs coming across the border every day in vegetable trucks, it wouldn't be their first, by any means.'

***

That evening, after a long bath, she fully faced herself naked in the mirror for the first time. She had someone else's body, frightening and strange. The breasts had slipped at least an inch lower and their shape was even more conical, less wide and high. Her stomach was pulling in nicely and there were no stretch marks, thank God, but around her navel was a halo of little, tiny puckers. It wasn't exactly as bad as a painting by Lucien Freud, and it wasn't Rubenesque any more. Well, it was, at any rate, Claire's body. They would just have to go on together.

She reached into the back of her closet where she had stuffed all her kimonos of yore, a proud collection of antique silks and newly-tailored satins she had routinely worn after meeting a big deadline to New York and returned from a particularly grueling assignment outside Hong Kong.

Her kimonos were a sort of secret costume party for the soul, a departure for a few hours from the stress of sustaining long distance working relationships and making cold calls to people who generally didn't want to talk to the press. Retreating to a world of Chinese poetry, tea, her books and music had often helped her through a lonely week. They were the wardrobe of the girl who'd seduced Jim, her silken robes gliding over her naked body, easily sliding apart for his embrace years before.

All that was before she met Xavier and moved with him to Tregunter Path. Where had her sybaritic side gone? In the diaper wash? Why was she being such a ninny over this Fabienne? Claire brushed her red hair high up onto her head and clasped a long tortoiseshell comb into the depths of the wave at the back. She found her *L'Air du Temps* bottle still behind the hair conditioners and nursing pads, exactly where she'd put it when they first moved, for God's sake. What had she been wearing each morning? Baby oil mousse? It was time to rise like a phoenix from the ashes of self-pity, self-examination, and self-mourning. She wanted this man. For Caspar's sake, she had to have this man. He would never have another father and her child deserved more than a halfway, half-uttered, or half-defined family life.

Claire had just pushed her arms through the long sleeves of a favorite dark green damask robe and tied the cider-colored sash when she heard the doorbell ring. Xavier was working in the study, and she called, 'I'll get it.' She pulled the robe more tightly across her bust for modesty's sake and opened the front door without hesitation.

She instantly regretted it. Antony Crowley stood within a few inches of her, and lurched halfway through the doorway, yelling, 'For my own good? For my own good, he said! A voluntary request for temporary transfer, oh yeah, right! Bloody right! Voluntary! You bloody, meddling, cunt! You think I've got a chance with me asking for temporary transfer voluntarily?' Crowley crowed bitterly at the top of his lungs, 'and everybody asking why? You're going to regret this. I'm innocent of anything. I was trying to help, you stupid, stupid, cow.'

Claire stood back, but as she gave ground, he moved right into the living room, trying to grab her arm with his right hand and hold her rigid in front of him. He missed once, and grabbed at her gown instead, catching hold of the belt.

'You'll regret this you bitch! You can't do this to me without paying for it.' He leaned into her ear, 'Just a little word in the ear of some ponsy colonial twit, just a little harmless inquiry, eh? I finally figured it out. You were in the club that night, weren't you? You were with that "nice gel" with the camera?' He wheedled in a frighteningly good imitation of an upper-crust English accent.

Inches away, Claire saw his eyes flicker strangely. She felt the blood draining from her face and her feet rooted to the floor. She saw him pulling back from her and knew in the next minute he was going to slap her or worse. She knew it and yet she couldn't move. She heard a roar from Xavier coming down the hallway, but even before she could turn, Dovie was pushing Claire aside, wielding a huge Chinese cleaver threateningly in Crowley's face, and forcing him back into the corridor.

As Claire pulled back, she saw the two men struggle, the violence coming out of nowhere to fill the room, while Dovie stood like a rock. There was a split second when the men parted slightly. Dovie seized the moment and slammed the front door on Crowley's startled, raging face. As the three of them stood there, stunned into silence, they heard Caspar whimpering in the nursery.

chapter twelve

"I am afraid, I am afraid,' that's all she cries all day,' Dovie sighed. She was leaning her matronly torso over the railing of Caspar's crib to whip the little bed sheets under the mattress corners with an efficiency that belied her age. Her strong brown hands worked expertly, fixing one corner of the sheet tautly over the other. The thin pad sprang to attention.

Caspar was replaced firmly but gently in the center of the bed where he stared obediently up at a mobile of dangling ducks. Claire admitted to herself that Dovie's confidence translated itself through touch to her baby who seemed more settled than before. He was squalling less and less and practically gurgled with happiness as Dovie swung him unceremoniously from nursery to kitchen. He was just as composed when she bounced him up and down in the balcony doorway in a kind of swing on a mini-bungee cord suspended from an old ceiling hook installed years before by someone keen on hanging plants.

Claire was jealous of Dovie's experience, but wasn't ungrateful. There would be a time any day now, she knew, when it would make all the difference between giving her job full concentration or feeling nagging doubts. And if she had harbored any doubts about Dovie's physical agility or quick-wittedness, she had seen ample proof in the way Dovie had wielded her cleaver in Crowley's face until Xavier had managed to grapple one arm and then the other to twist the younger man around and out the doorway.

The two women had fallen into a conversation about Crowley and Narcisa as Dovie started her morning rounds of the bedrooms. 'Having seen that police officer throw a wobbly last night, I don't wonder the *amahs* around here are scared witless. What a display! That's not the kind of young man they sent over in the old days.' Dovie threw her shoulders back and surveyed the crib. 'I'll change over to the Paddington Bear sheets on Wednesday.'

'What made you visit her?'

'Narcisa? I was worried about her, ma'am. She missed Mass. That's a mortal sin. She's been hiding in her room the entire week. You would think she'd want a day away. She told me there were a lot of things I didn't understand. ' Dovie paused, as if to wonder what kind of things she, another, older *amah*, couldn't understand, then shrugged. 'Of course, we all know what Mr Franklin had done to her and why he can't just dismiss her. She might tell on him, how he abused her body. And then his wife would know and Narcisa says she would never get another job.'

'It seems so incredibly unfair. All the *amahs* know?'

'Of course, ma'am. They all try to avoid Mr Franklin. They say they cannot look that kind of master in the eye.'

'And Narcisa? Is she hiding information? Not just about Giles Franklin or Jun? About Leo's disappearance? She's got to go to the police. She can't go on forever if Leo's in danger.'

'She knows about the passport missing—she told Inspector Slaughter it was gone from Leo's baby book where his birth certificate and medical records were kept.'

'Isn't it odd she was looking for his papers in the first place? Did you ask her why?'

'Yes, I did. But when I asked her why she would have thought to check such a thing, she said she was dusting and said I didn't trust her, because I am from Manila and not from the north, and then she shut up and just cried and cried.'

'What about the boyfriend, Jun? Does she talk about him?'

'Probably up to no good, that one, ma'am. She hasn't seen him since the police questioned him the very morning after Leo disappeared. Narcisa says he's gone away because the Chinese police beat him up, but I think that's a Filipina exaggeration. I don't think the Hong Kong police would ever do such a thing.'

Claire wasn't so sure, since the number of complaints about police brutality had risen sharply in the last year, but she had to smile to herself to hear Dovie talking as if she were an English village dowager rather than a Filipina herself.

Dovie's conversation was a welcome distraction, but Claire felt uncomfortable getting too chummy with the older woman. Already Dovie had the edge of simple age, not to mention experience with children, over Claire. Claire had heard of women losing their authority over domestic servants who did everything from selling their shoes secondhand out the back door to borrowing cosmetics and perfumes on the sly.

Yet she liked Dovie more and more.

As if the wet winds of the South China Sea had lurked stealthily off Lamma Island to carry off what little Christmas cheer the colony had mustered, Monday had given birth to an ugly watery haze. Claire faced her last hour of maternity leave in her study ruefully reliving Crowley's attack. Only someone driven by impulsive fury would have caused a scene that could only backfire by drawing more negative attention to himself. She'd considered reporting him to the police last night, but thought better of it. Why not give him more leash and keep an eye on him? Let his frustration grow. Let him betray himself once and for all, if he had any real reason to be fearful. If not, let it go.

Her hair at this time of year seemed to suck up half the humidity in the harbor, ballooning into a coppery cloud. She brushed it back into a long, unyielding plait for work. She was due in the office at 9:30. Everything was supposed to be back in place now—child, *amah*, career, sanity. Instead, she was terrified of stepping outside her own door because even though Crowley was suspended, he was free to make trouble for her wherever and whenever he liked. Moreover, he was a police officer and in Hong Kong, police officers were the only people allowed to carry guns.

She stared out at the windswept roads sweeping the slope below Branksome and shivered, 'Well, who you gonna call?'

She felt little cheered by her feeble joke. Everyone knew the police force was in a shambles. People like Slaughter had already booked the moving men for next June. In a matter of months, Major General Liu Zhenwu and his People's Liberation Army troops, some 8,000 strong, would be taking over the military garrison of Hong Kong. The nervous breakdown of a Johnny-Come-Lately Brit cop would be of no interest to the new regime. Her eye travelled along May Road as a green pick-up turned down Garden Road and headed towards Central. The back of the truck held a delivery of carefully wedged-in potted trees, swaying side to side. Ip was off to see a customer, she mused.

Claire jumped up, knowing that staying hidden in her study was the silliest possible response to Crowley's threat. She dressed quickly for work, squeezing into a khaki pantsuit. She threw on an ankle-length rain slicker and rain hat and tucked her well-worn leather carryall that doubled as purse and briefcase under her arm. Reminding Dovie once again to double lock the door behind her, she headed out to the parking lot.

Crowley was nowhere to be seen. Her nerves settled a bit and she knew what she had to do. A dense fog closed in behind her, obscuring Branksome's lower stories as she moved across the one-lane bridge and branched off the jogging path over to the lowest of Ip's green terraces cut evenly into the slope.

Now was as good a time as any to get Ip off her list of niggling doubts and to answer a question that had lingered in her mind since that dinner with Fresnay in Tailong Bay. Crowley was their man, she was sure of that, but Ip could well have played a role. Somehow . . . She had half an hour before she had to head to the office. And Ip needed at least half an hour to do any kind of business in town.

The undecided drizzle drenched the beds of low brush plants, ferns and bougainvillea pots set in neat rows, crosshatching the gardener's property. Ip's finely dug irrigation gutters were overflowed with last night's rainfall. Claire noticed for the first time that behind the ramshackle hut that doubled as Ip's residence there was an herb garden. She saw at least fifty bunches of sweet basil in the distance, but closer to the hut lay dozens of little plants, some with tiny flowers, some with spiky branches of no aesthetic appeal whatsoever. She wondered who the customers for those could be.

The door wasn't locked since Ip wouldn't be the kind to keep valuables in a structure that could be carried off by tomorrow's typhoon. Nonetheless, the hut's interior was a shock.

The tiny building was completely whitewashed inside from top to bottom. Claire would have expected a dirt or wooden floor, but instead she was treading muddy footprints on spotless white-painted cement smoothed and varnished right to the edge of the wall. A chart of a naked young man was pinned on the wall. Claire saw that its main feature was a grid of meridians running from the head to the feet and hands. The rest of the hut's little wall space was jammed with bookshelves, some loaded with reference volumes, and others lined with jars of roots, seeds and unidentifiable compounds of earthy colors and unworldly textures. She stepped back for a moment as the glistening eyes of snakes met hers from their resting place in large glass vats next to animal penises and horns.

The desk's wood surface was freshly polished. There was a cheap large radio and a small cellular phone recharging next to a simple lamp. Apart from the desk and a simple chair, there was a narrow wooden cot doubled up and propped against the wall for the day. An antique dehumidifier sucked and rattled noisily next to the cot, laboring to filter the mist into a plastic bucket of water slotted into its back. Smoky wisps coming off a musk incense stick penetrated the moist air. Ip had put an orange and apple with the still-smoking joss sticks in a small red shrine to the Chinese kitchen god. The kitchen itself consisted only of a wok sitting next to a teakettle on a two-burner gas stove in the remaining corner.

'He's not just a gardener,' Claire said to herself with finality, feeling the bone-heavy chill of the cement penetrate her leather soles. Pungent chemical smells coming from the fleshy jars around the room mixed with the incense. Fresnay had feared a murderer who was 'very well-educated, very determined and very, very sick.' Ip did not strike Claire as very sick at all, and she saw the room as belonging to someone with an orderly mind, albeit an orderly mind in an ornery, stubborn old body. But then, Crowley had not struck Claire as a very well educated man, certainly not one to make an obscure poison his criminal signature. It was all coming together in her mind—but at the same time, something about the picture felt wrong.

She heard an engine along the road close to the hut and quickly dodged to the door to see if Ip was returning, but it was only the diesel grinding of a taxi moving slowly in the fog along Tregunter Path like a heavy bottom fisher cruising along the seabed for wayward passengers to gobble down. Claire realized she'd been holding her breath and moved back into the hut. This expedition was rash. She resolved to spend only five more minutes in Ip's home.

So *who was Ip?* Claire took a tiny tour of the room but couldn't risk the leisure of scrutinizing the heavy volumes lining the shelves. She ran her eyes along the jar labels, feeling each minute tick off as she struggled to translate the traditional characters of complicated botanicals she had never studied.

Many, even most of them, were beyond her training in standard newspaper-level Mandarin, and taxi-driver Cantonese. She took a small notebook out of her bag and worked her way along the shelves, noting what she could.

'*Ban Xia*,' she wrote, 'Middle Summer.' It was clearly a root, and Ip's faint handwriting in scratchy fountain pen underneath had recorded, *Pinellia ternata*. The next jar carried an identical label, but appeared to contain processed powder and smelled of sulphur. She continued down the row, searching for any others she could make out. She found a jar of dried white flowers that looked to her untrained eye like common clematis, but Ip had labeled them with the characters, *Wei Ling Xian*, meaning the 'holy root of the temple,' and underneath, *Morus alba, spatholobus suberectus*.

She lost more valuable minutes before she found an easy one, skipping the Chinese and translating, 'Ox gall stones,' from Ip's Latin, *Bos Taurus Domesticus*. The gallstones sat next to *Cou teng*, 'hooky branches,' called *Uncaria Rhynchopylla*, according to Ip's precise labeling. Claire moved the jar of creepy-looking twigs to see another glass jar of strange tubers, and read *Chuan Wu Tou*.

'Crow's head.' she murmured to herself. *Aconitum Carmichaeoli Bex, Radix Aconiti*. It was the herb from Petey's stomach, found during the autopsy. She had known she would find it. She had feared she would find it, and at the same time, hoped she wouldn't find it.

She stood still for what must have been more minutes she shouldn't have spared, wondering what to do. The dehumidifier churned away accusingly next to her. She should alert Slaughter, let him go through the right procedures, get a search warrant. She wasn't supposed to be here. Ip might come home at any minute. But he would know what to hide, and where, in an instant's notification of a search. She put the jar in her bag and glancing around the hut to make sure her exit hadn't been observed, darted towards the road. She was negotiating the final, expectedly dangerous leap across the *nullah* that had filled with water when she heard another engine coming towards her.   Standing   still on the hillock at the foot of his terraces, Claire and Ip's eyes locked. His truck veered away from her path, but she had registered the shock of surprise on his face at seeing her descending from his slope. There was no old man's confusion in his glance. Could he guess from her guilty expression where she had been and what she had discovered? She would call Slaughter as soon as she got to her office.

***

Reaching the Inspector wasn't as easy as she had expected. Cecilia put in a call right away, while Claire called Father Fresnay with the news.

'Tread very carefully now,' Robert said. 'I will pull out some of my reference books here on Chinese pharmacology.'

Slaughter was on the telephone immediately, just as livid as he was impressed that Claire had discovered the source of the aconite in Petey's stomach. 'Illegally obtained evidence is useless in court,' he shouted at her. 'I appreciate your interest in solving our problems, but with Crowley suspended and Ip's poison in your pocket, you've made my life bloody complicated, Claire. Bring the stuff round to the lab by lunchtime.'

Claire put the phone down, shaken by Slaughter's entirely justified tirade. She was going to be glad to unload the evidence into official hands. She was sure that Slaughter would find a way to handle Ip. Cecilia would personally take a taxi with the herb to Police Headquarters. Before she could reach for her raincoat, however, the phone rang and Cecilia passed it to Claire, 'It's your *amah*.'

'Ma'am, the Immigration Department has telephoned this morning. They say that the transfer of my papers to your name is ready and I have to go to Kowloon Immigration to collect them.'

Claire sighed. 'Don't they usually give us more notice?'

'Yes, ma'am, but as a favor to you, Mr Evans-Smith asked them to waive the usual six weeks' delay because he is leaving for England before that, so they are urging me to come right now.'

Claire hadn't ever imagined there could be a downside to Evans-Smith's old boy network. Now Connie had been dismissed and she had too much work piled up on her desk to return straight home the first day. She knew there would be conflicts in the life of a working mother—but not in the first ten minutes. She called Xavier.

'I'm sorry, but Dovie can't take the baby with her today when she goes to collect her immigration papers. Could you work from home today? I can't be seen my very first day back at work spending five minutes in the office and then going right back to Caspar.'

There was a long pause. Xavier would try to do his best, she felt sure.

'I'm sorry, but it's impossible. I'm sitting in a planning session right now with Chinese provincial officials from Hunan. After this, we're supposed to straight into another session with the financial people and the engineers.'

I don't believe this is happening to me, thought Claire. She tried to focus. She looked at Cecilia, but Cecilia had to leave now for Slaughter's office. It saved Claire from herself, in a way. She knew within an instant that asking her secretary to babysit was a major breach of Cecilia's employment terms.

'Xavier, I have a job too, and this is my first day back! Maybe you don't realize what Immigration is like—second only to the Transportation Department's Vehicles Licensing Bureau, they can be the Great Sucking Hole of Hong Kong. There'll be a black mark on her file if she isn't there. Filipinas don't win trying to negotiate with this bureaucracy. She has to go today.'

Xavier's tone made it clear he was drawing the line. He had offered a lot, but never had he been willing to play the househusband or second fiddle to Claire's career. She had run up against a brick wall of Swiss chauvinism.

'I know who would be happy to babysit!' he crowed with male pleasure at solving a domestic problem. 'Fabienne! She has nothing to do! It'll give her a sense of belonging and being useful. She'll be happy to do it.'

Claire felt her face flush. Hating the other woman already made her feel guilty, but now on top of her jealousy and suspicion, she had to be grateful to her for small favors. Every fiber in her body wanted to say no.

Then she looked at the mountain of newspapers, BBC broadcast transcriptions, correspondence and E-mail messages, all printed out and neatly readied on her desk by Cecilia. If only she had cleared this off last week during her little Christmas visit. How blithely she'd assumed there would be time and tranquility on her first day back!

'It's unnatural,' she said to Xavier in a sullen voice, 'Anybody but her.'

'Why, Claire? Don't be like that. She'll probably be thrilled. Remember how good she was with Caspar in Tailong? How happy it made her to be included like that? Call her right now. She's probably at the hotel just counting the hours until her departure.'

That's right. Fabienne was actually leaving, having filled the last day or so with sightseeing and camera maintenance. Why begrudge her this final gesture of acceptance? Why be so mean-spirited? The woman was leaving. Claire had survived her. Sheer time, the extraordinary exercise of keeping her lips pressed together one day at a time had won her an important psychological victory.

'All right. You call her. She can't say no to you. And I don't have a spirit generous enough to beg. Caspar is your child, too.'

Xavier's male ego was pleased with his solution—two of his women tending his tribe. Ancient Man's polygamous prerogatives were actually proving useful. 'I'd be happy to. Any instructions?'

The emotional crisis seemed to have passed. Really, the only problem had been in her head. Xavier was right. Fabienne had been good with Caspar. Claire tried to sound practical, even matter of fact. 'I'll call Dovie back and tell her to give Fabienne all the instructions she needs, the back-up bottles of my milk are there in the fridge. It won't be complicated.'

'Fine,' Xavier's tone sounded loving and managerial at the same time. 'Everything will be fine. So don't worry. When shall I tell Fabienne that Dovie will get back?'

'Probably not later than five. It'll take an hour for Dovie to get there, pull a number and wait for her file to be delivered to the right officer. As I recall, they stop calling new cases to the window around four or four-thirty every afternoon.'

The only way to cope with this development was to file it in the back of her mind as fast as possible. She called Dovie and told her that their friend would be babysitting, to relax about the Immigration appointment, and to give Fabienne all the instructions on care and feeding she needed and then to attend to her affairs as completely as possible so that there would be no call-backs. Dovie sounded as competent as any mother could have wished.

Meanwhile Cecilia was eager to brief Claire quickly on what she had found out in Repulse Bay the previous Saturday.

'It wasn't so hard. It was so cold that instead of sitting on the rocks to be picked up by the *guay-lo* launches, they were all sitting in a *daipaidong* eating noodles. My mother went to the hotel for her buffet lunch with a friend, and the friend's daughter came with me. We said we were looking for my little brother who might have gone with a policeman with dark hair, good-looking. It was a family emergency. The boys I asked know Crowley very well, but they said the policeman hadn't been around lately. They had a dirty nickname for him.' Cecilia blushed before she uttered the Cantonese equivalent of "Big Badge."

'Any details on him?'

Cecilia nodded. 'He likes young Chinese boys, that's certain. But so do a lot of them, Claire, that's why they go there. Some of these boys were maybe thirteen, fourteen, hard to say. There was an older one there who didn't like my questions.'

'Did they know anything else about him?'

'They knew he sang at a Lan Kwai Fong club. They said he liked them to teach him naughty songs in English and they would teach him some in Cantonese. He told them he was trying to get together a new act and maybe one of them could be in the show with him. He seemed to be very popular, but none of them had seen his performance. Said it was too expensive unless you got a *guay-lo* to pay.'

'Then they knew it was Crowley for sure.'

'Oh, yes. They even knew he organized day trips across the border into Shenzhen. Looking for virgin boys like a lot of the foreigners who are afraid of AIDS. Sometimes they said he took one of them along as translator.'

'More like purveyor,' Claire mused. She'd heard about the hunt for HIV-free conquests—and not just in Hong Kong. Burmese virgins, peasant girls from the mainland interior, and Vietnamese orphans were all valuable commodities on the international sex market.

Cecilia looked intently at Claire. 'You Europeans are so inscrutable,' she joked. 'Do you think now that Inspector Crowley intentionally hurt Petey and Leo behind the *amahs'* backs?'

'No, I'm not sure at all. Considering the way he lunged at me last night, he certainly seems to be acting guilty. But since I found the poison on Ip's shelves, I've been confused. But I'm not sorry now that I reported him to Evans-Smith. He shouldn't be a police officer. He should leave the buggery to its traditional home, the Legal Department.'

They both laughed, knowing well that Hong Kong's most famous queen was not pictured on the colonial currency, but had enjoyed two decades as a Queen's Counsel in the territory's courtrooms.

To keep her mind off Fabienne's invasion of her private domain, (turnabout and fair play from the gods for her own trespassing on Ip's property?) Claire buckled down to work. It was going to be a nightmare of cramming to catch up with six weeks of past news. But Hopkirk had done a magnificent job of not letting too much of the drudgery pile up on her desk.

For today, the most important thing was to edit down a stringer's file from Bangkok and to work through the story ideas tentatively suggested by Hopkirk and propped next to a welcome bouquet of flowers on the rickety metal typing table that had outlived its usefulness, but never got thrown out.

The day passed in a trance of concentration achieved only by blocking out all thoughts of Tregunter Path. The fog burned off and the sky across the harbor cleared. By four she was exhausted. Her eyes were red-rimmed from staring at the computer screen and her wrists throbbed with strain. She had known she could skip one feeding, but now she'd pushed her luck. It seemed like a very, very long time since she had held Caspar, as if he was a stranger from another life, a brief dream between yesterday's working agenda, and this morning's labors. This desk and this chair were more familiar to her than her own child.

She leaned into the cracked plastic backseat of a spacious old taxi with appreciation for its surviving the newer fleets of low-slung Japanese interlopers. The driver happily chatted to himself in broken English about his own children, his family in Guangdong, and God knew what else. Claire felt she'd been away from Branksome for a week, and she wondered if Caspar would greet her with recognition after a whole day away.

She was paying the taxi driver the fare and heaving herself out of the car when she heard herself hailed, 'Claire, back so soon! How was your first day?'

Claire stared at Fabienne in bewilderment. She was dressed in jeans and a cotton knit cardigan that clung to her petite figure, leaving a sliver of tiny, flat belly visible above the waistline. She was, inexplicably, carrying one of Xavier's squash rackets. It was all too obvious that babysitting had soon palled and that Fabienne had run downstairs to practice her forehand.

Claire felt sick to her stomach and then remembered that she hadn't eaten lunch in an effort to get her work down and get home early. She should have something to drink and eat before she wakened the baby for his feed.

'Is Dovie back already?'

'No, no, she called and said she'd be back by five. So, how was your day? I can guess, 'Fabienne cocked an eye confidentially at Claire like an indulgent older sister, 'Maybe it was a relief to be back on the horse?'

'Back in the saddle,' Claire muttered. She mustn't lose her temper, not yet. But she wanted to buck and run up the eleven flights to her apartment, the elevator seemed so slow.

'Oh, Oh, don't worry about the little one. He is taking a deep nap. He was actually snoring just like his father! We played and played and played. He kept trying to flip over and he learned to clap his hands!' Fabienne made a reassuring face and said firmly, 'He is really a very intelligent little man.'

Claire unlocked the front door, slightly consoled, and Fabienne followed, tossing the racket on the rattan sofa and heading to the kitchen. In a second Claire heard her run water from the tap into a glass.

She slung her leather case off her shoulder and her immediate thought was to open the nursery door to check on Caspar. But first she wanted to get cleaned up into something fresher than the sticky shirt she'd been wearing all day. There was crusted mud on her trouser hems from Ip's gardens that morning—an adventure belonging to another life.

She struggled out of her jacket and shirt and checked the mail left by Dovie on her dressing table that morning. She saw with pleasure that even though Dovie had left midway through the day for her appointment, the bathroom was spotlessly clean, the bedroom dusted and swept and the dry-cleaning ready for the pickup the next morning.

She ran a quick shower and stepped under it for a moment. She chose a clean cotton kimono instead of one of her silk one, laying it out on the bed. She brushed out her hair and retied it in a more forgiving knot at the back of her head, jamming a couple of geisha needles through it.

In a couple of minutes she felt transformed and capable of continuing with what had already been an extremely full day. Her thoughts glanced back to Ip's hut. The story was coming to an end, and approaching an explanation, she thought to herself. There will be someone held responsible, at least for Petey. It would lead somehow to Leo, or at least to some truth about Leo. There had to be more. Branksome Building and its unhappy tenants could not live in a limbo of fear forever.

She returned to the living room to perform the minimum of courtesies.

'Can I get you a drink or something? Some wine or something more interesting than water? I have to feed Caspar now, so you'll have to excuse me just for a few minutes.' Claire was determined to be alone for this important reunion.

Fabienne's uncertainty flickered in her light glance. She seemed unwilling to impose herself any further on Claire's privacy, but Claire had tried hard to sound sincere and conciliatory. Her gratitude towards Fabienne was more genuine than it had been this morning. With Dovie on the job within a few hours, the poison found and delivered to the police, Crowley suspended, and Fabienne leaving Hong Kong for good in little more than a day or two, all the tectonic plates of Claire's life seemed to be shifting slowly, if still unclearly, into normal position once again.

'No, thanks, but I'll stay a bit, if I may. I'll be fine with my water here. You go ahead. I understand.'

Claire was actually humming to herself a snatch of music learned as a child, 'In the Evening,' by Frederick Low, a duet she had played with her Viennese teacher in the low, orangey dusks of a Berkeley autumn. She looked forward to the day she and Caspar would play at the piano side by side, his little pale face intent on the simple melody and his small white hands playing the parallel octaves as her freckled fingers supported him with the interweaving harmonies on the lower octaves. Oh, the pleasures they had in store!

She returned to the corridor, and gingerly entered Caspar's little nursery. And there, in an instant of immeasurable scorching hurt, she felt herself hit like a soldier on a battlefield pushed off the ground by a shell and hurtled emotionally through the air like a legless doll.

Caspar's crib was empty. She screamed.

chapter thirteen

—Monday evening—

Claire's eyes were swollen shut, but even with them closed, her reclining body felt settled in a pool of cold fear. What had happened? She reached through the clammy fog, wondering why she felt so dull. No, not even dull, she felt nothing but a humid blanket of sleep. Nothing at all.

She turned and was falling back into sleep when a thought pierced her sedated mind. Caspar was missing.

This was a terrible thing, but her medicated emotions didn't protest. Her mind crawled back in time. She saw herself walking into the nursery, screaming with shock, then controlling herself with all her might and rushing to ask Fabienne where Caspar was. She'd insisted to herself, the way rational adults do, 'There's an explanation, there's an explanation.'

Lying quietly, she heard a lot of pacing and conversation outside her bedroom door, short exchanges between Cantonese men. She breathed out, waiting for the feeling of horror to flood back over her. She turned over. Pulling the curtain aside, she glanced out the window and saw the lights of the territory spread out below her, broken by the dark stretch of harbor. Night had fallen.

Claire tried to rouse herself, but her body tried to pull her back under. *So heavy, so very tired, I've been so drained lately, literally by breast-feeding, of course, and then this woman showed up. This woman who left my child alone. This woman who lost my child.*

Xavier must be home by now. He had to find Caspar. He had to call the police.

Oh, yes. Fabienne had called the police while Claire had been trying to hold back her tears of panic. That's right, Xavier had come home just as Fabienne had been asking for Dovie to help her find Dr Sui's telephone number. Xavier had called Inspector Slaughter. Dovie had started screaming, but then she had stopped and controlled herself, and Xavier had taken Claire off to the bedroom. So the Cantonese voices outside were the police.

There was a lump underneath her damp midriff, Caspar's white knitted blankie, fresh from the morning laundry. Her emotions rallied from somewhere deep below the sedatives holding her under the danger zone. She knew there was a hole inside of her. The drugs filled the hole with numbness, but for how long?

She must talk to Xavier. Where was he? Where was Fabienne? He would talk to Fabienne. He would know what to do. He would find out what she had done with Caspar. What had happened?

Her foot knocked over something off the end of the bed; an electronic toy hitting the floor started playing a nursery ditty. She let it play, as a call for help. The last lines were just ending when Dr Sui leaned her head into the room.

She sat down on the edge of the bed and took Claire's hand. 'How are you feeling?' Her doctor was a Chinese woman of northern stock and over six feet tall, with a hint of a moustache and a penchant for spotted or lacy blouses and heavy shoes. She would have made a perfect senior officer in the women's ranks of the People's Liberation Army. Trained at McGill University, Dr Sui had delivered Caspar decked out in a yellow slicker and matching shower cap that made her look like a mad Chinese pirate in a sou'wester steering through a storm between Claire's knees. Her only concession to Claire's discomfort was handing her a facemask connected to a tank of laughing gas— childbirth colonial Hong Kong-style.

'Where's Caspar? Do they know anything yet?

'Xavier is doing everything he can. The police need to come in pretty soon; they're doing the fingerprinting and examining the whole house for fibers and hairs.'

'What did you give me?'

'I knocked you out. And I'm going to give you another sedative to see you through the night.'

'I thought you didn't believe in painkillers. At least not when I needed them.' Claire feebly joked. Why did she always feel obliged to perform for doctors?

'You didn't need them then. You need them now. And these aren't painkillers, they're tranquilizers.'

'I want to see Xavier.'

'He'll be back in a few minutes. He went outside with the chief inspector. Your friend Fabienne is outside. Do you want her to come in and keep you company?'

'No, thanks.'

'I didn't think so, but she offered.'

Claire glanced up. It was dark outside where Xavier and Fabienne had gone. It would be hard to find Caspar on such a black night. Claire realized her thoughts weren't making much sense. She heard new voices.

'Can you get Xavier for me?' she asked Dr Sui.

'That's the police crew finishing outside. Try to be patient. It's a critical time right now, when any clues are fresh. They have to talk to everyone on the street: the jitney drivers, the *amahs*, and the vegetable truck salesman—anybody who was around the building. They radioed all the bus and taxi drivers on shift asking if anyone had carried a redheaded baby away. I heard them.'

Claire started to cry, slow waves of fear for Caspar engulfing her in terror. Wasn't he hungry? How many feeds had he missed? Dr Sui's tablets started to work, and she fell into a dreamless sleep, cold and sour.

***

Angry voices outside her door woke her; Xavier's low, threatening rumble and Fabienne's familiar chirp. Only now, the light Gallic tone sounded more like a broken flute, the air caught in wrenching sobs.

'They haven't found him yet,' thought Claire, her breath shortening as the fear returned and clawed her breast. Determined to get up before anyone had the chance to sedate her again, Claire swung her feet to the floor and bracing herself against the wall, started down the corridor.

They were speaking French and English, back and forth, as if English was the language in which Xavier could think clearly and Fabienne could only bare her heart in her own tongue. Claire fought down the drugs to stay upright. She was almost halfway toward the living room, moving hand by hand, sliding and heaving against the corridor wall. She realized the conversation wasn't about Caspar at all.

'*T'as dit, non, non, je ne veux pas des enfants.* No children, that's what you said. *Il n'y avait pas de discussion avec toi, pas de question!*'

'It was a different relationship, a different time in my life!' Xavier argued in a voice somewhere between a shout and a hiss of fury. 'When I said I didn't want to have children, I was speaking as a man of thirty-five, not forty-five, or forty-eight!'

'I know the little boy is everything to you, but she, this American woman, can't mean that much. She's not your type, Xavier. Whatever happened, *tu es revenu a moi, j'étais sur, il ne m'inquiétait pas, mais maintenant . . .*'

'Well, I'm not coming back this time. It is totally different now. You have to see that.' Xavier pounded a piece of furniture with his fist.

'It's more complicated, that's all,' Fabienne sniffed. There was a long pause and Claire struggled to control her panting. The Frenchwoman seemed to be finding her composure, her voice was sweeter now, more cajoling: '*On peut parler, faire des arrangements. Je peux accepter le petit—*'

'You can accept him? I don't recall putting him on offer to you or anybody. Thank you, thank you. You know, you're talking as if you were accepting the discovery of a mistress, being generous and accommodating, as if you were my wife of twenty years—which you are not. Try to remember that. It was never like that between us.'

'*C'était possible, c'était simplement que tu ne voulais pas, mais pour moi, c'est toujours possible.*'

There was a long pause. Claire held her breath. She leaned, sodden and sleepy, against the corridor wall. They couldn't see her, but she could hear every movement between the two, only meters away.

'How many times?'

'What?'

'How many abortions did you have?'

'Two. And they disgusted me, but so finally I made it final. *C'est fait.*'
Fabienne's voice assumed a taunting air.

'Oh, but you could change your mind, after all, you didn't really
know, did you, what you wanted and what you didn't want? You just
said something for convenience at the time. I realize that now! And
when I heard you had this baby, when I realized, it was too late for me.
The operation was done.'

Xavier didn't reply. An entire minute ticked past in the pained
silence in the next room. Then Fabienne refueled her bitterness and
burst out again, this time from a different part of the room.

'Whatever happened, *tu es revenu a moi, après le projet en Malawi, et après
l'autre fille a Beirut*—"

'That was diff—'

'Let me ask you something,' Fabienne spit at him. She'd moved
across the room, closing in on Xavier in a fury so intent on punishing
him with her resentment that she didn't notice Claire, now visible to
her from the living room. Claire pressed herself back against the wall.
She felt unable to enter the room and unwilling to retreat, stuck to the
corridor wall by her frayed nerve endings

'Will you still want to marry her, would you want to marry her at all
if there were no child? You told me you didn't want children! And I
agreed because I loved you! What did she ever do to earn your love?
Would you have wanted her without that child?'

'Of course, I would. That is why there *is* a child. Because I wanted
to be with her in the first place. And I will stand by her, because I want
to be with her. Do you have to hear every single word of it, word by
word by word?'

There was another long pause. Claire heard Xavier collapse heavily
into one of her old rattan chairs.

He sighed, 'I can't stand this kind of fighting. You love it. You
always loved it. Sniping, bickering, snide allusions, carping, sarcasm, I
don't know any more words for it. You lived for it–fighting and
making up. I think it makes you feel more real somehow. Maybe you

can't feel much without this level of animosity to get you going. And anyway, why didn't you tell me all this before? When you were pregnant? You should have told me.'

'I didn't think you needed to know.'

'But now you do.' He laughed derisively.

'It just came out.'

'No, it didn't just come out. You picked the worst day of my life to get back at me. I can imagine what you thought when you saw Caspar.'

'*Non, j'avais peur jusqu'au moment quand je l'ai vu. Il n'était pas comme toi, pas du tout.*'

He roared, 'Don't you dare say that he wasn't like me, he *wasn't*, as if he's gone. He's alive!'

'Xavier, Xavier, where're you going?'

'I'm going back out there with the police to find my son before Claire wakes up. I swear it. You can stay here or go to hell. If you'd stayed in the apartment, this wouldn't have happened.'

'It wasn't my fault. Someone must have been watching all the time, just waiting for the chance. I've upset you, I'm sorry. It's the wrong time.'

'What a bitch! What do I care about your sterilization? Your self-mutilation is none of my business! How could I trust you with my son? Because you made nice noises and danced with him in Tailong? Because I felt sorry for you? Was I crazy? All that bullshit in my office about how you could accept my new family, how you liked Claire, how you needed my help to get used to the idea, the tears, yes! I felt sorry for you! I even felt guilty! Why? I never made any promises to you. *Jamais, jamais!*'

Claire had noiselessly slumped to the floor, as she sat and listened to what Fabienne had been feeling all this week. Her arms clenched around her own midriff, she could only imagine the emptiness, the defiance, and the finality of Fabienne's decision to have her tubes cut. Not only had Fabienne not given birth to Xavier's children, she hadn't even *kept* Xavier's children while she carried them.

All week she must have looked at the child of the man she had loved for so long, knowing that she would never have anyone's children. Though Claire had never given the matter much thought before, there was a horror in the timbre of Fabienne's voice, the outrage of someone who had seen herself making a practical birth control decision only to realize she'd undergone a virtual amputation of her deeply repressed hopes. What if things had been different between Claire and Xavier? What if he'd been cooler at the news of Caspar's conception, what if she'd panicked and taken the 'easy' way out? Suddenly Claire felt too close to Fabienne, pretending over and over she didn't want what she might have *allowed* herself to want by challenging the course of events.

'Get out of here before Claire wakes up. I have to think of my family now,' Xavier said in the other room.

'What family? You have no family, you are no husband, you have no rights over anyone, nor they over you.'

'That's enough!' Xavier roared at her.

'It is a truth of life, a fact, and no child gives her permission to own someone!'

'I want you out!' Xavier yelled, as if all the force in his body were behind it.

'Let me stay and see Claire. I want to say I'm sorry. I should stay until Caspar is found,' Fabienne said weakly.

'Get out and wait at the hotel. No, go to Cambodia. Better yet, go to hell.'

Fabienne was moving around the room and gathering up her bag, jacket and cigarettes. 'I'll be in my room if there's any news,' she said in a small voice.

But for a few moments, Fabienne didn't move. Claire knew, as any woman would know, that Fabienne was waiting for more, for some good-by that would reassure her of a place in Xavier's life. That was what she had waited for all week, and Claire realized with a wave of relief, it was what she had not received. Finally the front door slammed shut.

She had had enough. The only thing that mattered was their son.

'Claire!'

He held her so tightly it was as though he was pushing the fear right out of her pores, fear of losing him and not finding Caspar. The fuzziness in her mind was expelled like a foul cloud. She felt even weaker than before his embrace and he led her over to the sofa. They sat down as she fought back more tears, and asked him, 'Where's John Slaughter?'

'He's with his officers right now running checks on the taxi and bus drivers by radio. They're interrogating the watchmen of all the buildings along Tregunter Path, doing all the routine things they have to do as quickly as possible.'

'Routine, routine! Routine hasn't found Leo Franklin, now presumed dead. Xavier, there must be something we can do besides sit here.'

He wrapped her in his arms, 'Give them a chance, Claire, give them a chance.'

'Where's Robert? Does he know?'

'I called him. He's on his way, and should get here any minute. He's going to stay with you while I work with the police.'

'Where's Dovie?' Claire mumbled.

'She's in her room, or maybe in the kitchen, I think. I excused her to get a rest. She's deeply upset, too. No one had any time to spend with her when she got back from the Immigration Office. John talked to her for a few minutes. I asked her to make you some soup.'

'I'm not hungry.'

Xavier sat quietly with Claire stroking her hair back from her damp forehead. Claire spoke quietly. 'The front door was locked. I unlocked it myself. Did they check whether the back door was locked?'

'Yes. It was locked and there was no sign of breaking in.'

'Xavier, that means that whoever took Caspar had a key. But Dovie was in Kowloon. I have my key and you have yours.' Claire couldn't think beyond that.

'No, no, Claire, you're still a bit confused by the drugs,' Xavier said. 'Fabienne had Dovie's key. We had to let Dovie in.'

She thought of Crowley. 'Do the police have keys? Like skeleton keys?'

'No. If they need access to an apartment, the gatehouse man uses his and comes with them. We've gone over that already with John Slaughter. He was asking me how many keys we had.'

Fresnay arrived just then and the sight of him was so comforting that for a moment, Claire could almost believe he might have stashed Caspar in his backpack and the whole nightmare was over. After comforting Xavier with bracing hug, the priest said down and gently took Claire's hand.

'I can't just sit here like a drugged zombie, Robert. What can I do? I will not just sit here!' Claire pounded her free fist on her knee. 'You've seen what the Franklins have done for over a week now, and how much good it did!' she glared at Xavier. 'We can't just let the police put up their posters, play their stupid announcements on that weekly police show and even if we had a million dollars to offer as an award, you see how much good it did Giles Franklin?'

'Calm down, Claire,' Robert said, but he looked at Xavier and nodded. 'She's right. What's happening downstairs?'

'Exactly what we've seen twice already,' Xavier told him. 'They're interviewing everybody in the building, door by door. They're stopping cars leaving the buildings and coming into Tregunter Path at the junction of May Road. They're radioing all the taxi drivers and bus drivers.'

The drugs were wearing off Claire. She started crying, despite all her intentions to stay composed.

'Crying is not going to help Caspar,' Robert said to her, abruptly withdrawing his hand. 'Think, Claire. Stop crying.'

She took a deep breath and wiped the back of her hand across her exhausted face.

'I have one idea,' the priest said, finally putting his motorcycle helmet at the foot of the sofa and leaning back to catch his breath. 'I was already trying to work on it when Xavier called me. As soon as I heard that Petey Sandford had aconite in his stomach, I had one of my friends in the doctoral program over at Hong Kong University fax me some research on it. You remember when we were treating Xavier's knee with rosemary, I said something can be both good or bad depending on the dose?'

Claire nodded. 'Ip has aconite on his shelves. We handed it over to Slaughter this morning—Cecilia did. I though it proved Ip was Petey's murderer. Ip knows I found it. He saw me coming down his slope this morning.'

Xavier interrupted. 'They released Ip after questioning. The police told me this afternoon. Ip was in police custody the whole afternoon, literally with them when Caspar was kidnapped. He has a perfect alibi. Ip told them someone must have taken the aconite without him knowing it and replaced it. He doesn't lock the hut. He's been completely cleared and he's back home. They're running fingerprint tests on the container.'

Fresnay shook his head. 'He may be telling the truth, or he may be lying, but why? We have to confront Ip ourselves. I think he gave Petey the dose and I think I know why. Read this.' Fresnay shoved into her hands a couple pages of fax paper.

Claire read out loud. '*Sconitum Chinense Paxton* and *Aconitum Carmichaeoli Bex*, or *Radix Aconiti*, is a tuberous root, pungent flavor, toxic in crude form, used to relieve spasms of arms and legs, paralysis of limbs, twitching and numbness, to remove "wind".' She looked up at Fresnay. 'Wind?'

Fresnay nodded. 'When people with certain kinds of epilepsy suffer a seizure, they sometimes give a shrill cry and fall unconscious. The Chinese ancients called this the "goat wind" referring to an imbalance in the system of "winds" and because in traditional lore, Chinese herbalists reported that the cry of an epileptic in seizure was similar to the bleating of a goat.'

'Robert, are you saying that they used aconite as a medicine?'

Fresnay nodded. 'In combination with other natural herbs. Read on, Claire. '

Claire's eyes skipped across the lines, as she scanned. 'Used in combination with dried bodies of centipede, *scolopendra subspinipes multilans*, for tetanus and convulsions, decoct with un*caria rhynchopylla,* in Chinese *gouteng*—'

'Hook-like branches' Fresnay translated.

'—Common name *gambir*, from the *rubiaceae* family, the branches, have a sweet flavor, their energy is slightly "cold,"' um, let's see, to reduce anxiety, stop involuntary movements, calm down convulsions, stop dizziness, stop convulsions in children and twitching, counteract epilepsy and convulsions, *gouteng* is an ideal herb for light cases of convulsions at the beginning stage.'

Fresnay spoke rapidly, almost as if talking fast would help them find Caspar all the faster. 'Aconite is a powerful poison, and it wouldn't be very hard to obtain. But it has such a classical history in both East and West, the presence of aconite in Peter's stomach implies a murderer with training—a doctor or a botanist. It didn't fit with the profile of an ordinary gardener, but I couldn't discount it. My guess is that Ip—'

'Was trying to treat an epileptic attack but it went wrong and Petey died?' Claire said.

Xavier shook his head. 'But why would he just happen to have a dose of epileptic tonic around the house, even if he was an herbal hobbyist? It's too much of a coincidence.'

'We have to ask him, now—tonight. Are you ready, Xavier?' Robert turned as if he expected Xavier to follow him immediately right out the door.

'No, you're not leaving me here.' Claire pleaded.

'You want us to leave it to the police?' Xavier moved towards her, his arm reaching for her understandingly.

'God damn it! Xavier, don't you know me at all? Leave it to the police? I have no intention of leaving this to the police and sitting in a heap of secluded sedation like Lily Franklin, hiding in her mother's apartment all week.'

'Well, someone has to stay here to coordinate with the police force.' Xavier was trying hard to be practical. He was looking at Fresnay and Claire as if they'd lost their minds. But Claire was already headed back to their bedroom. She reached for a T-shirt and sweater and realized that her breasts were overflowing with milk. She would have to release the milk and it would take valuable time. She ran to the kitchen to get the breast pump and a small spare bottle. They were kept cold in the refrigerator after Dovie sterilized them. But now she discovered another mystery.

'Xavier?'

'Yes, Claire?'

'Where are all my bottles of milk?'

The two men rushed to join her in the kitchen. Dovie joined them from her room. The two women stared into the refrigerator at the shelf along the inside of the door where bottles of her own milk ready for Caspar were stored. There wasn't a single bottle left.

'I don't understand.' Claire looked at the two men.

'Someone has taken the milk to feed the boy,' Xavier muttered in explanation to the priest.

Fresnay murmured, 'Maybe we can allow ourselves a little hope, Claire. Whoever took Caspar isn't going to kill him.'

'Why? What could anybody gain from taking him, especially if they are taking care of him? That means they intend to hand him back safely? Do you think he's being held for a ransom?'

Fresnay took his pipe out of his pocket and rubbed it thoughtfully. 'Finish changing, Claire.'

She ran back to the bedroom and grabbed a fresh shirt, her shoes and a bush jacket.

The two men were staring at her with expressions of near accusation. Xavier was the first to speak, as if by right.

'Claire, do you have anything, anything of value, that someone would want in exchange for Caspar?'

She glanced at Fresnay. Xavier knew about her discovery of the tape recording of *Peter and the Wolf*. She hadn't fully explained to Xavier yet everything about her discovery in Ip's hut. But she had telephoned Fresnay within hours. She felt that the accusation was prompted by the priest, who dared not directly imply she was responsible for the danger Caspar was in now.

The priest didn't wait for her answer. 'We're going now.'

Fresnay grabbed her arm and said to Xavier. 'You know where we are, just up the slope. If the police have anything to tell us, come right up and get us. Otherwise, this won't take long. We're going to make Ip talk.'

chapter fourteen

—Tuesday morning—

Claire first went through the back of the kitchen and knocked on Dovie's door. She heard the faint rattle of a rosary as Dovie rose and answered, still clutching the chain of beads in one hand. Her expression was calm and grave but her hair bun was awry, as if she had been fiddling with it in her distress, or holding her head between her fists.

'I'm going with Father Fresnay to ask the gardener some questions about Caspar. My husband is staying here with you in case the police come with anything new to report.'

Dovie nodded gravely and went into the kitchen, leaving her bedroom door open. On Dovie's nightstand, Claire saw a brand-new photo of Caspar next to the one of Freddy Evans-Smith standing on the English lawn and another of a Filipina bride, presumably Dovie's daughter on her wedding day.

Seeing Caspar's happy toothless smile in her mind caught her by surprise. She felt like vomiting up her cold, nauseous fear. She spent the few minutes retching in Dovie's small bathroom off the back door, her empty stomach wrenching up Dr. Sui's drugs colored by bright yellowish-orange bile. Robert waited patiently in the corridor.

Finally, she took a deep breath and feeling the surge of fresh anger fill her lungs, followed Fresnay out to the servant's elevator. It was much larger than the residents' posh elevators, since it was designed to accommodate furniture and machinery as well as people. Fresnay seemed very far away as he leaned against the opposite wall.

'You looked almost guilty when we asked you what evidence you have that might frighten someone into taking Caspar.'

Claire nodded. 'The aconite came to mind but I immediately I thought of Crowley and how angry he is—angry enough to attack me the other night. I wondered if he realized Fabienne still has that photo of him in full drag at the nightclub. He figured out it was us that took the photo, but of course he would think that because I took the photo, the camera and film were mine. I don't know. It just seemed to me that if he's denying anything to his superiors, then he might want to get the photo out of our hands. Do you think he could be holding Caspar ransom for that photo or something crazy like that? He was insane enough when he attacked me.'

Fresnay held his tongue. They exited into the night air cooled by the heavy stucco of the building on one side and a few feet away, a cemented wall about ten feet high damming up the fertile, lush hillside. The cicadas' relentless chant filled the air now that most of the traffic had died down for the night. What remained was a muffled, undifferentiated urban rumbling from the tightly-packed, overflowing city spread out below, hundreds of feet down the slope and stretching away into a blanket of garish Chinese neon lights broken by the dark blue stretch of harbor and the strange hulking shadows of the distant Kowloon mountains.

In this darkness thick with bamboo trees and brush, anyone could sneak down the slope and enter the building, climb the back stairwell slowly and quietly to avoid servants and handymen using the elevator, and then, very gently descend the steps again, carrying Caspar away. But not by car; since Leo had disappeared, every vehicle on Tregunter Path was checked out—discreetly but effectively—as it went through the gatehouse by policemen now standing duty with Mr Lui. The shuttle-bus drivers were also on alert. The taxi drivers were reminded each day on their radios to scrutinize all passengers travelling with small children.

How many redheaded babies were in Hong Kong? Who could enter her apartment without a key? How would they escape without being seen?

They rounded the back corner of Branksome and exited the parking lot gate. On the other side of the road two policemen in a police van quietly passed the time making notes and talked into walkie-talkies to colleagues taking stock somewhere nearby.

Her lanky companion led the way to the left. They drew no comment from the police who had identified him on the way in. They made their way swiftly along the twenty or so feet to the bend in Tregunter Path where the *nullah* came closest to the Peak side of the road. They leapt it easily. It was the same spot Claire had chosen to return to the Path when Ip's lorry had nearly collided with her.

Ip's single desk light was lit. In the glow of his desk lamp shining out the window, Claire could make out the silhouettes of potted plants readied for delivery near his door, moist and glistening in the bulb's glare. Everything else around the hut lay in darkness. It was hard to find her footing and she leaned on her friend's arm.

A young Chinese police officer stepped out of the shadow to block their path to Ip's door. 'Would you mind to inform me what you are doing here?'

'This is Ms Raymond, the mother of the child who was snatched this afternoon.'

'Excuse me. I'm very sorry, ma'am.'

'I'm Father Fresnay, attached as a pastor to the Catholic Cathedral on Caine Road. Ip Sin Saang. Hai 'm hai do-ah? We'd like a word with him.'

The officer wasn't budging out of their path. He regarded Claire cautiously and then turned back to Fresnay. 'Inspector Slaughter was talking with you today, I think.'

'Yes, I'm the same priest. I'm a family friend of Ms Raymond, and also spiritual advisor to many of the amahs who work along Tregunter Path and attend Mass at the Catholic Centre.'

The officer's silver identification numbers pinned to his epaulets reflected the light streaming from Ip's window. It was hard to see his features beneath his cap and it was easy to see why Claire and Fresnay hadn't spotted him in his blue-black uniform, standing on surveillance duty on a dark night.

The officer was a careful man. 'You want to speak to Ip? We've already interrogated him. He was just released from questioning this afternoon. I'm not sure—'

'We won't be long, officer.' Fresnay. said.

Claire turned to the priest. 'Robert, I need a minute to think about what we're doing. I only want to save Caspar. We know Casper isn't inside here. I want to avoid doing anything that might harm my baby. Are you sure we're doing the right thing?'

'Think clearly, even though I know you've been medicated. The doctor was trying to keep you numb, so you wouldn't feel the shock. But think! This man was in custody when someone took Caspar. That someone has a key to your flat. We've never been able to completely trust the stories we heard from Narcisa about Leo—the timing, her attentiveness, or the door left open for the boyfriend. But this time we know for certain—the back door was locked. Someone took Caspar, took his milk supply, and maybe will ask for something back in exchange. The thing you must remember, you must cling to, is the assumption that your baby is alive. He's alive. Maybe this man can help.'

'I'm confused, Robert.' She was leaning on his shoulder, dizzied by the quick sprint up the slope.

'Claire, more and more, I'm convinced that nobody poisoned Petey intentionally. But as of today, I suspect this story is much more complicated. Ip has an alibi but he had the aconite that was found in Petey's stomach. Whatever his story is, he hasn't told it to anyone so far. But maybe he'll tell it to us. Think of him as your only link to your son. Stay calm.'

The officer had turned away from them to report to headquarters. Claire heard the rumble of the Peak Tram wagons rolling down past them through the trees covering the steep slope, their brakes creaking to stop at the May Road station, and then descending on towards Robinson Road.

A thought suddenly struck Claire—more an image of the tram in her mind, but it was instantly interrupted by an unfamiliar voice. '*Chin lai,*' said the wraith-like silhouette standing in the light of the hut's doorway. It was Ip, inviting them to enter. He gestured to the officer to move aside. The officer hesitated, wondering whose authority came first. Claire guessed he was supposed to watch the old gardener, but had no orders to hinder him.

The priest led Claire past the officer with a nod of thanks. They followed the bent old man inside. Claire felt Fresnay's hand still holding her upper arm steady. She was shaking now with cold fear, hunger and fatigue. She sat on the edge of the cot next to Fresnay, as Ip slowly lowered himself back into his chair behind his desk.

There was a long pause. Claire realized there was a tiny radio on the desk, barely audible, broadcasting in Mandarin. Ip had been listening to the mainland news broadcast, distancing himself from the day's events in the grief-stricken neighborhood.

As she glanced at the radio, Ip's slender hand reached out and gracefully turned down plastic dial. They endured a long and complete silence. Finally Ip extended a pack of cigarettes, but both Fresnay and Claire declined. Ip put the cigarettes back into a drawer.

Fresnay took the cue, and removed his pipe from his pocket, tamping it down as he began to speak to Ip in Mandarin, his Scottish burr unable to completely obscure the northern Chinese 'rrrrring' accent that betrayed his long secret years spent disguised as a mere foreign student—a lay wanderer—in Beijing. 'We've come in the hope you will help us, not frustrate us. Three women in that building have lost their sons. This mother and the father of one of those boys are my friends. I am a priest.'

'From the Catholic faith?'

'Yes.'

Ip sniffed with visible disdain. 'I've seen your worshippers every Sunday down there,' he pointed to the *amahs'* picnic site. 'Throwing themselves around on the ground, screaming and singing like crazy women. I thought the Catholics were very good people. We knew Catholic missionaries in my families for many generations in Jiangsu province. But I don't understand that way of worship.'

'It's a movement called the Charismatics. I am not a follower of the Charismatic movement myself, but it is a powerful community in the Philippines.'

'I see,' Ip answered quietly. His long fingers riffled the pages of a thick volume opened in front of him. Otherwise his entire posture, expression, and especially his silence, frightened Claire. She realized she was still not breathing very evenly.

Ip spoke suddenly. 'But I didn't know until this afternoon that two more little boys were dead.'

'Not dead. So far just missing,' Fresnay corrected him.

Claire examined Ip's face for any clues to his emotions. There were none she could fathom. She needed this man's help. She had to rely on Fresnay.

Ip continued suddenly, 'I didn't know anything about these two little missing boys. The police told me this, today.' He pointed with a slender finger at the desk to mark his point. 'Just today. I thought I understood before. I understood the questioning. I know you came into my home without my permission.' He glared at Claire, 'and I saw today what you gave the police. I have been thinking about this all evening.'

There was a seemingly endless pause. They could see Ip was considering something carefully. *This man knew something.* Claire and Fresnay waited long seconds while the elderly man gathered his thoughts. Claire started to speak, but a slight pressure on her arm from Fresnay silenced her back into patience.

Ip drew himself up. He had made a decision. He walked to the door and opened it. He returned quietly, and Claire realized he wanted to make sure the officer outside was beyond earshot.

He switched into English. 'You will have to understand why I have said nothing. When you came to me demanding help before,' he turned to Claire, 'you probably thought I was protecting myself—a poisoner and a killer. Now you're confused, because you must be wrong! I was detained by the police when someone took your son. But you still think I had something to do with poisoning the little Pei-tei.'

Ip cleared his throat and looked up at the rows of books and medicinals along the narrow homemade shelves.

He shook his head with resignation: 'You will be wrong. I *was* protecting myself. No, no, I am not the killer of that little boy. But I have killed, *accidentally* killed. I was protecting myself, yes, and someone I felt very sorry for; well perhaps not really sorry but I want to say, someone I understood. Someone who has killed without understanding.'

Ip's face was drawn. His tones, his diction, were clear and slow, enunciated carefully for Claire, whose comprehension would have been dulled by drugs and panic, to focus on as a drowning woman clings to a floating shard of wreckage.

Ip turned to her directly, his face shadowed sharply by his harsh, single lamplight. 'What you said on Sunday was right. I could see what the *amahs* were doing, as I could on every Sunday. They would pray like crazy people, crying out, wailing in strange sounds like animals, waiting for signs from their God. Waving their bodies and hands. Curling up on the floor like dogs in pain.' Ip shook his head in disgust.

'Pei-tei made fun of them when he was with them. He was the only one who wasn't scared of his *amah*. The foolish little boy loved her. But the other women, they are afraid of her. They called her the Witch of Tregunter Path.'

'Why?' Claire burst out. Again, Fresnay restrained her, but too late this time.

'Because she charged them money for prayers to their dead, for casting spells to keep their husbands faraway in the Philippines faithful to them, or to get better jobs, a new dress or even to put a curse on an employer who was too harsh.'

'How do you know this?' Fresnay asked. After all the Filipinas were his business, not Ip's.

'Oh, they don't confess everything to you, Father. I saw them take the money out of their pockets and their coin purses. I saw this *amah* take their money every Sunday. I saw a lot. I said nothing, but I saw a lot. I saw the money given and taken. I heard the silly women give their thanks to this *amah*.'

'What happened that Sunday?' Fresnay demanded.

'I will tell you. You must understand everything first or you will understand nothing at all. It is very simple. One Sunday last September, I think, I saw Pei-tei in the middle of their group. I thought he was playing, but I didn't understand more.'

'A few weeks later, they were holding one of their meetings, and Pei-tei was with them, right there again in the middle of their group. This time, I could see from here, he was having an attack of the sickness. I shouted down to them. They came running to me for help, probably because I was right there, they saw me watching them, but also because they were afraid of their *guay-lo* bosses. They were afraid, and I saw, they felt very frightened, very guilty. I told them I could give Pei-tei a concoction for this type of sickness. The wind in his system was very bad. I ran back here right away, and took some ginseng tea I was drinking and mixed crowshead and—'

'We know, we've already guessed.' Fresnay nodded.

'You are a knowledgeable man, then. You have my respect.' Ip cleared his throat and sighed. 'This is what you don't know. The medicine worked. When Petey's attack had subsided, he was very quiet and needed to rest. I asked this *amah*, her name was Manuela, how the attack began. She went wild with anger and told me to go back to my hut. But later, many days later, another one of the *amahs* came to me.'

'Which one?'

'I don't know their names. They all look alike to me. One of the younger ones.'

'Would you, or could you, identify her if we asked you to?'

Again, Ip had to silently acknowledge to himself what he had given in to. Finally, he conceded, 'Yes. Yes, of course. She came to me and explained what had really happened,' said the old man.

'Was it something to do with the policeman Crowley?' Claire could not wait for this old man to tell his story. She wanted her son back now.

'No, no. He is a troubled man. I see him walking up and down the Path, up and down, sometimes in his car, but often walking, just walking. But he was not part of this other *amah's* explanation.'

'What was her name?'

'Her name was Narcisa. She told me that Manuela had used a tape recording to trigger Petey talking nonsense, '*hu shuo ba dao,*' bullshit talk, blind talk. She believed that through these babbling trances, she was communicating with her dead son. She believed this dead son talked to her through Petey.'

'Ramon!' Claire exclaimed in English, turning to Fresnay in astonishment. 'Why then, Manny told us the truth herself, *from the very beginning.* I was there when Crowley first questioned her. She asked me to stay and listen. She seemed to be afraid of him. She started crying, saying, 'if only I could talk to him once again, but now I will never talk to him again.' Crowley made her shut up, cut her off. Neither one of us saw the connection. With Petey's death—'

'She lost her medium.' Fresnay said.

'She must have thought Petey's seizures were some link to the afterlife.'

Ip nodded sadly. 'She used the little tape cassette to make him shake and babble. I warned this girl Narcisa that she must stop this woman from playing witch.'

'Manny did it again?'

Ip nodded to Fresnay's question. '*Duey-le*. Of course, she was sad and sick. She was happy to be powerful over the other women.'

Claire turned to Fresnay. 'So that was why Manny looked so startled and defensive when I asked her about the *Peter and the Wolf* cassette. Vicky had thrown it away months ago because she knew it aggravated Petey's attacks.'

Claire thought back to her conversation at Vicky's small drinks party when she had returned Grover and the cassette to her saddened friend.

'But we never guessed at the importance of it. The idea that someone would use it to make Petey have episodes never crossed our minds.'

Fresnay added, 'That's also why that Englishwoman, Mrs Reynolds, didn't see Manny on the road trying to flag down help for Petey. Mrs Reynolds wasn't so drunk as you suspected—'

'Because Manny never went down to the road when she said she did. It never occurred to me that Manny was lying and the soused old Mrs Reynolds was telling the truth.'

As the implication sunk into, anger flooded Claire in waves. 'Why didn't you tell anyone? You could have saved Petey's life!' Claire screamed at Ip. Fresnay pulled her back down on the cot, she was so close to assaulting the frail Chinese.

Ip raised and lowered his thin shoulders as if to admit the weight of guilt they carried.

'Yes. We must come to my responsibility. You see, if you have not already guessed, that I am not a gardener and not a hobbyist growing herbs for my amusement. I was a traditional doctor of Chinese practice in Kowloon. Before the war, I studied in Shanghai—medicine, English, western philosophy—with the best teachers and for a few years, I practiced very successfully in Beijing. I treated many famous members of the pre-Liberation Republican government. I ran here with all the others, fleeing the Communists in 1951. I set up a clinic in North Point in the Shanghai refugee section. Then I got even more patients and moved to a big shop on Nathan Road. It was easy to get new patients and soon I had too many.' He bit his lip. 'One too many.'

'Who was that, Mr Ip?' Fresnay leaned toward the man gently. Ip was no longer looking at his visitors. He was staring back in time at a face only he could see.

'She was a lovely young girl, a *guay-po* locally born. She spoke beautiful, fluent Cantonese, better than most of the local European children. Her parents were English. Her father was a *dai lo* in the government, a very big boss. She came to me one day without any appointment or introduction, just off the street. She told me she was pregnant by a Chinese boy. She knew her father would accept it, but she was afraid it would kill her mother's love for her and all her expectations for the girl's bright future back in England.'

Claire felt a chill going up her spine. There was something familiar here, something too close.

'It's an old story,' Ip continued. 'I gave her the herbs she needed, but they didn't work. That can happen. Under my care, she could have tried again, but always with careful supervision. But instead of coming back to me, she didn't trust me any more. She went to another doctor, a Chiu Chow working in Mongkok. Then she took all the drugs we gave her—all the medicine I gave her and all the medicine this Chiu Chow gave her—all the herbs in a single tonic.'

Ip shook his head and carefully folded his hands in his lap. 'Of course, that dose killed her baby.'

There was an awful silence.

'It killed her too.' Fresnay had to finish the story for him.

Outside, the cicadas droned their reverberating humming. Claire felt the ghost of the girl pass through the room. It was as if she knew the terrible, awful detail yet to come. Outside, she heard the Peak Tram rumble upwards, and suddenly, the image that she had lost sprang back before her. The kidnapper had escaped with her baby down the Peak on the tram. That's why none of the drivers had seen Caspar. The tram driver's back was to the passengers behind a partition. There was usually a ticket-taker too, but someone the kidnapper had managed to slip the baby past him.

But Ip was speaking again.

'This girl's father, a big government man, found the herb packets with the name and address of my clinic in her room. He knows Chinese very well, and he hunted me down in my office in Kowloon. He didn't want a scandal. He too, didn't want to upset the mother more by making everybody in the whole city talking about his family. The mother told the newspaper a story about an accidental drowning.'

Claire's fears were right.

'I thought about running across the border, but I figured they would be more likely to find me there with the cooperation of the mainland police than if I disappeared right here in Hong Kong. But where?'

Ip shook his head. 'It wasn't that difficult. You know Hong Kong— very small place but a very crowded city. I never returned to my office on Nathan Road. Not once. I avoided crossing the harbor ever again, in case somebody from the old neighborhood recognized me. I hid in North Point around the old Shanghai neighborhood for a while, working as a cleaner or a watchman. Then I bought this shack from a distant cousin and moved here. I became a simple gardener with a simple hobby.'

Without warning, Ip's face turned to them, indignant and proud. 'Now you think I am going to go to the police and admit I was practicing illegally on an epileptic boy, and that sometimes my tonic works and sometimes it's too late because of some idiotic Filipina playing witch? I will go to jail for the rest of my life because of some ignorant *amah*!'

'We understand.' Fresnay gently put his hand on the gardener's bony knee. Ip looked up in a sort of shock at the kindly touch of the Jesuit.

Claire spoke in her clear, workmanlike Mandarin. 'We still don't know where my baby is. Where is Leo Franklin? What has happened to them?'

Ip looked intently at Claire and spoke carefully in English, not sure how much of his Chinese she could follow. 'I told you already. I didn't know anything about the two little boys missing until the police took me to their headquarters today. There is no connection.'

Her courage started crumbling away.

'No, don't tell me that.' She started weeping and felt the priest's arm comforting her, holding her up as they left the gardener's hut.

'He explained so much, about the tape, the poison, even about Viola Evans-Smith. Now we know why no one heard any details about her death. That must be the way Alistair wanted it. But now to think that there is no link between Petey and Caspar. I assumed, I hoped, I—'

Now all she could do was cry her guts out, dreading the return to the apartment to relate everything to Xavier and seeing the disappointment and frustration in his eyes when he realized there was still no good news. She passed the police van at the entrance to the building in a daze. The energy drained out of her legs. She would not sleep, she would never sleep again, and she saw no end to the horror. She was afraid of seeing Caspar's face in her imagination, so she pushed out all happy memories of his touch and smell. The harder she pushed them away, the faster they flooded her with a longing more intense than any sexual or other physical sensation she had ever had.

Fresnay explained most of their story to Xavier in the living room, while Claire gave way to all restraint and went into the nursery and sobbed. The building was a deathly silent sleeping tomb. She felt exhausted and scarcely heard Fresnay, when he explained he would talk to the night officer on duty and request that Slaughter come to talk to them as soon as possible in the morning. He would spend the night in the apartment and wait for that dawn meeting.

'But why? We know Ip couldn't tell us any more than he did.'

'Maybe there is a connection, one that Ip didn't see, because Ip doesn't know the whole story. It's in our hands. Now we must put it together until it makes sense. We thought the key to this story was Crowley, then we thought it was Ip, and now we find out the central figure was a little boy who died years ago, a little boy named Ramon. You said yourself, Claire, Manny told you the meaning of the mystery herself the first day—you just didn't understand the importance of her words. You get some rest, if you can. As soon as the sun comes up, we're going to follow any trail we've got, and God willing, Claire, it is going to lead us to Caspar.'

Claire looked at Xavier and he held her tightly, and helping her to lean on him, he took her to their bed to wait for the next dreadful day to dawn.

chapter fifteen

—Tuesday night—

'Claire, here, swallow these. Doctor Sui left them to help you keep calm,' Xavier said gently when he had closed their bedroom door. He held out four small blue pills. Claire turned away shaking her head. No one had drawn the curtains, and looking down the slope toward Central, she saw the streetlights of Tregunter Path shining their futile vigil. She looked back up at Xavier through swollen eyes that felt like two stone weights. The energy and determination of the previous few hours had drained away.

'It's not going to help. It only makes me useless to everyone. Especially to you.'

He took both her hands in his. 'Don't give up now. Tonight you learned the truth about Petey's death. We might be only hours away from finding out the rest of the story. You might have Caspar in your arms in a matter of hours.'

'Don't, Xavier. Don't raise my hopes! I've read so many stories like this, stories about kids who disappeared with no explanation and their parents live in an awful limbo ever after, always wondering whether they're alive or dead, filling their lives with good works and campaigns to protect other kids because their own kids will never come back. Those are the kids whose faces stare up at you from posters and milk cartons for years, and they just never, never come back. I never imagined it would happen here in Hong Kong, or happen to me. '

Xavier sighed, put his arms around her, but it couldn't stop the rage pouring out of her.

'You get this false feeling of security here, nothing touches you because you're not Chinese, you're not a local, you're living this privileged colonial life on a street paid for with overseas housing allowances, guarded twenty-four hours a day by goddamn 'Royal' policemen like Antony Crowley!'

Xavier's expression was grim. 'They stopped being "royal" last year, remember? Take these, Claire. We're going to make it through tonight and tomorrow and the day after that, and whatever happens after that together, but I need you to be as calm as possible. Please.'

He went into the bathroom to fetch a glass of water.

But Claire was adamant, almost yelling at his retreating, unyielding back. 'I would take the pills if I thought they would bring Caspar back faster, but they only make me stupid and numb. What I realize now is that the police were wrong, totally wrong. Fresnay is wrong. Ip is right. There's no connection between Petey's death caused by Manny's stupid séances and the disappearance of Leo and Caspar. That's the first thing that hit me while I was listening to Ip. I know Fresnay wants to find some kind of connection—that's his logical, goddamn Jesuitical mind at work. He can't accept the possibility of coincidence. But there's no connection at all. Some sick weirdo snatched our baby, and the misery we feel is nothing to what has happened to him.'

Xavier grasped her by both arms, his fists digging into her muscles almost painfully rousing her from despair. 'That's the point! We don't know yet what has happened to him. We can't give up or think the worst until he's found.'

She rolled over to him and let herself collapse in his arms, her voice no longer her own, but a new voice, like the deads'—waxen, emotionless.

'But they never found Leo, did they? He's been gone exactly seven days now, there are no clues at all, no fingerprints, and no one in this whole colony reported seeing him. You know what that means, don't you? You know as well as I do. He's rotting in some rice paddy in the New Territories.'

Even as she was muttering this, muffled by his firm embrace, she wondered at how selfishly she was allowed by everyone to fear and grieve, while Xavier was expected to stay on his two feet fighting for information and alert to signs of hope. They both knew, but hadn't dared to say to the other until now that every hour that passed without Caspar made it more likely their baby was dead.

***

It must have been a few hours later that Claire awoke. She realized that in her exhaustion, she'd dozed off. She found Xavier sitting on the balcony with Fresnay. The lights from the living room reflected the grave concentration of Fresnay, smoking his pipe, leaning his elbows on his knees in the semi-darkness.

Strain lines gripped Xavier's mouth, and his normally ruddy skin had turned putty-colored. Even so, Claire suddenly saw a startling likeness between Xavier and Caspar, a likeness that had never hit her so hard. What must this loss mean to him? How many chances did a man in his late forties have to start a family? What must he be thinking? Everyone had made such a fuss about the red hair Claire had passed to her baby. Hadn't anyone noticed the chin, the mouth, and probably one day, the nose, were the father's?

One day? She mustn't give up hope. She must push herself through one full day of hope before she surrendered to the nightmarish possibility that Caspar was dead. Fresnay discreetly excused himself, saying he wanted to lie down on the sofa for a while.

'I heard you and Fabienne,' she said to Xavier, not daring to look him in the face. He didn't reply at first, but pulled away from her a bit. He wasn't ready for this conversation.

'It's an old story. It's over. I told you that from the start. OK, I realize I didn't know all the details of her side of it until last night. I didn't realize what she'd done.'

'But now you do know. For her, the relationship wasn't completely over until she'd told you. She wanted you to feel some pity or regret or responsibility, or something.

'It's more than that. After all, she could have stayed in Geneva and written it all down in a letter. Yesterday I saw something in her face that she'd hidden before. Now that she has seen you and the baby, she hates me as much as she ever loved me. Maybe because I denied her the kind of love she wanted, she wasn't really a friend. She was addicted to the challenge of changing me while pretending to be my perfect partner, to being more me than I was myself.'

Xavier's expression changed, almost cruelly. 'And she conveniently forgot that, at least in the old days, she also said she didn't want any children, that she had to be a free agent, ready to go or do anything. She was afraid of being tied down, or so she said then. Now she blames me for everything, but I certainly don't remember it the way she does.'

He rubbed the exhaustion lines across his forehead, as if trying to erase the years themselves. 'I can't help her bitterness.'

'I wasn't sure about children either,' said Claire. 'You know Caspar just landed in our laps. But you didn't suggest an abortion to me, or was I so bewildered and thrilled and,' she fought for the words to describe those heady, frightening weeks, 'so overwhelmed that I missed your hints?'

'You missed nothing, nothing,' Xavier said vehemently.

He reached over and took her firmly the shoulders and held her close. 'I could see the change in your face, in your body and the sheer joy of it all. And I wanted you that way, I admit, much more than I had wanted you before. Suddenly there was more of you there to love, and I don't mean the baby inside you. I saw all the love that was promised to me and to us together by that sudden change in you.

His voice dropped even deeper than usual. 'And I never saw that in Fabienne, even when she claims she got pregnant, so how could I have known she wanted children? She won't admit it now, but she didn't change with that joy because she didn't feel it. She didn't want to allow something she couldn't control into her life, into her own body. It's not that I want to marry you now because of the baby. It's not the baby that I'm marrying—it's you, because of who you are becoming, and how it came out from under that lonely reporter's shell you were hiding in.'

For Claire, words had always flowed rapidly and fluently out of her fingertips, into the keyboard and onto the page. But the word she said next, that simple word 'yes' came out as if its only syllable contained a book of meaning to them both.

Coffee was brewing in the kitchen. Fresnay returned to the balcony with three mugs. The priest offered them the drinks with a stalwart smile.

'I tried to rest, but my mind won't relax. Now I realize what that confession on Christmas Day was all about. One of the *amahs* who attended Manny's séances knew how Manny had caused Petey's attack and death. Remember? "Everyone thinks that the Devil looks like a man, but he can look like a woman, too," she said. She confessed her dealings with the Devil killing children on Tregunter Path.'

'I thought she meant Crowley, who dresses up as a woman,' admitted Claire.

Fresnay shook his head. 'I don't think our mysterious confessor meant him at all. She knew we were looking for a man after Leo was snatched. She might even have been making an unconscious allusion to Manny's name. You see, I'm convinced that the confessor thought she herself had more to fear from Manny but all the same, she wanted Manny stopped.'

Claire sighed. 'Robert, it's just as likely now that Manny and Petey had nothing to do with Leo and Caspar's disappearance.'

'I don't agree, Claire! This Filipina who spoke anonymously to me in the protection of the Confessional connected the death of Petey with the disappearance of Leo. But who was she? What did she fear from Manny? Was she trying to lead us to Manny in order to prevent something worse?'

Fresnay rubbed his stubbly chin. There were dark circles beneath his eyes and Claire realized his frame stretched well beyond the dimensions of the cheap rattan sofa he had tried to rest on.

He went on, 'Quek told me there were no unusual fingerprints. How do you avoid leaving fingerprints? Wearing gloves. Who wears gloves in a semi-tropical climate without raising an eyebrow? People cleaning, digging, working with their hands like gardeners, pool men, delivery men, *amahs*.'

'Police,' said Claire.

'All right, also the police. Then, how do you get into the servant's entrance of an apartment, without arousing suspicion? You see, I think,' he leaned forward with excitement, 'the latchkey is our only real starting point. Who had a key?' he insisted.

'Only the amah and us, just like Xavier told John Slaughter's men earlier tonight,' Claire shrugged.'

Xavier added, 'And Fabienne had Dovie's key. I saw it last night on the cookbook shelf where Fabienne told me she returned it.'

'But you have two *amahs*,' Fresnay said, puzzled.

'No, just one.'

'But when I stopped by Christmas evening to tell you that I had heard that strange confession and wanted to talk to your *amahs*, didn't you mention two Filipina names?'

'Connie!' exclaimed Claire. 'What happened to Connie's key when we dismissed her? Dovie!' She raced to the kitchen where Dovie had fallen asleep with her head on the table. They wakened her as gently as they could. She was still dressed in her Sunday church dress, worn for the Immigration department.

'Dovie, when Connie left here Thursday morning, what happened to her keys?'

'She gave me the front door key, ma'am.'

'And the servants' entrance keys?'

Dovie paused, taking in the implication of Claire's frantic questions. 'I don't know, ma'am. I assumed you asked for her to return her set of keys.'

'No, Dovie,' Claire replied, turning to the two men. 'She didn't give them to me. I thought Connie gave all her keys to Dovie.'

'No, ma'am,' Dovie protested. 'I copied the servants' key to the elevator entrance and our back door from Connie's keys. She gave me the front door key, so one of us would have it, but for a few days while we overlapped, we both needed to come and go through the back door at different times.'

'Xavier, we must find Connie and ask her what she did with those spare keys.'

Claire now regretted the haste with which she had dismissed Connie.

Xavier asked, 'Dovie, do you know Connie's new phone number?'

'No, sir. We weren't on good terms when she left so suddenly. She was still angry at me for telling you about the candle wax.'

'I'm going to call the Sandfords for Connie's number,' Xavier said.

Fresnay turned to Claire. 'In the meantime, Claire, try to recall the story of Ramon once again, exactly as Manny told it to you that day at the picnic site,' Fresnay reached into his back pocket and filled his battered pipe with tobacco from a pouch.

'It's so hard to think straight, Robert. I just want Caspar back.'

'I know, my dear, just humor me. Try to remember what Manny said about Ramon.'

Claire took a deep breath, thinking back to the sun-bleached scene of the of the Charismatic group—the primitive strumming of the same three guitar chords, the writhing, babbling and swaying figures of the amahs in the clearing. She told Fresnay how she had watched them from a distance and waited for a chance to talk to Manny about Petey, not expecting the subject of Ramon would come up again, just as it had cropped up during Crowley's interview.

'She said he died of pneumonia. When she asked the Sandfords for permission to go home to the Philippines, Ian assured her it wasn't necessary, that all Ramon needed was a dose of good antibiotics and medical supervision. So he didn't let her go, but he promised that he'd give her a lot of money to send to her mother for Ramon's treatment. She was afraid of getting some cheap generic drug, and he promised he'd give her enough for brand name antibiotics. She gave the money to another amah to carry back to their village.'

'What was that friend's name, the other *amah*?'

'I didn't ask,' Claire realized, as much to herself as to the priest.

'That could be important.'

Claire nodded. 'Especially because of what happened; that *amah* spent the hundreds of dollars she was carrying on clothes and makeup, which left only a little for cheap herbal medicines for the sick boy.'

'And by then it was too late.'

'Yes. Manny's mother caught up with the ruse and Manny hustled more money together, but then you know the ending.'

'Not really. What happened then?'

'Her story kind of petered out. Your colleagues in collars down at the Catholic Centre told her to pray, forgive, and forget,' Claire couldn't hide her growing frustration with the conversation and at the impotence of her own situation.

Fresnay sighed and leaned back in his chair, perversely exuding an air of satisfaction. 'I'm beginning to understand, I think. And in her grief, Manny resorted to spiritualism instead of faith. She twisted religion around on its head. Used Petey to "talk" to Ramon, she thought. But she didn't find peace. And the *amah* who betrayed her and her child—now I really wish I knew who she was—because I think that was the *amah* who came to me in the confessional. Who feared Manny's revenge.'

Suddenly Fresnay blurted, 'Claire, where does Manny's family live?'

'Bantac? Bantoc? I think she said.'

'Bontoc. That's in the north of the Luzon,' Fresnay pondered. 'Who were the other *amahs* with her that day?'

'Regina was one. Vicky knows her as a good friend of Manny's. I knew the face of the third one, but I'd never seen the fourth one before. Anyway, you've got to remember we haven't lived in this neighborhood more than a few months.'

'I know, I know.'

Xavier was dialing the telephone again and explaining carefully to Connie's new 'master' Mr. Bridgeway why he was telephoning in the middle of the night to speak to his new servant. As he waited for Connie to come to the phone, he asked Fresnay, 'Do we want her to come here?'

'That depends on her answer, I suppose, and the police,' the priest said.

In a few seconds Xavier turned to them again. 'She gave the keys to Narcisa.'

'It's what I suspected. Hang on just a bit longer, Claire,' Fresnay murmured.

'Narcisa's just next door,' Claire said, trying to take in the speed of events.

'Come on,' Fresnay said, and he led Xavier through the kitchen, followed closely by the two women. They crossed the back landing and facing the back of the Franklin's apartment, pounded on the servant's door, shouting in Tagalog for Narcisa to answer. There was no answer.

'She might have snuck out to be with her boyfriend,' Claire said. 'Especially since Lily Franklin is living downtown these days.'

'But Giles must be there,' said Xavier. He led them quickly back through the apartment and across the carpeted front landing to the Franklins' front door.

Giles Franklin answered the door, his naked body wrapped only in a sarong, the beer belly hanging over the knot he was gathering at the front with meaty hands. He looked in a foul temper at being wakened. His expression changed when he saw Xavier.

'Hullo. I wanted to come over this morning and offer my help as soon as it was a decent hour,' he said simply. 'Although I'm sure the last thing you want is what I've been through for the last week with Lily.'

'Could we talk to Narcisa?' Fresnay pressed him. 'We think she has the keys to their back entrance or passed them to someone.'

'Go right ahead,' Giles said sourly. 'Don't think you'll get anything out of that one. She went to bed straight after serving me dinner last night. A few more days and we'll be well rid of her. Maybe then Lily will come home. I swear we'll never hire another maid again, and I don't care what Lily says.'

But he was already trailing the others moving through his apartment at double speed. He looked bewildered and pathetic and Claire could see why Lily Franklin packed up her grief and confusion for the sanity of her mother's apartment across the harbor. The Franklin apartment was overlaid with the dust of a week's trauma, the wastebaskets were overflowing and the flower vases stood empty.

Fresnay had already pushed open the insulated swinging doors separating the dining room and the "master's quarters" from the kitchen and the servants' corridor. A postcard from Bontoc was tacked crookedly on Narcisa's door. The priest started knocking loudly, but Xavier grabbed his arm and pointed downwards, and said in a strangely careful version of his usually fluent English, 'Robert. Please look down at your feet.'

From under the Filipina's door a sticky pool of thick dark blood was creeping towards their shoes.

chapter sixteen

Narcisa's body sprawled face up on her narrow bed. Someone had stabbed a broad-bladed Chinese cleaver into her chest. Her eyes stared with a wild expression, but apart from the vicious wounds across her lower face and wounds to her hands used to fend off the attacker, the beauty that had tempted Giles Franklin was more striking then ever. Her long smooth brown arms, her soft black hair, and her flawless legs ending in a pathetic pair of rubber slip-on's—this was all that was left of the simple-minded, hard-working girl.

They sat in the Franklins' living room while the police guarded the entrances and the Scene of Crimes team worked around Narcisa's corpse in the back of the apartment. Photographs were taken of each wall and each angle of the body. A constable Lim asked them to wait quietly in the living room until he had a chance to talk to them, but no one could put Fresnay on hold. He spoke to Claire, Xavier and Giles Franklin quietly and deliberately.

'One wonders every Sunday, staring out at all those women—those patient, tireless, devoted women—what they might have been or what they could have done with more luck in their lives,' he sighed. 'And you can feel the rivalries, the alliances, and the disappointments seething among them, but there's nothing you can do.'

'Well,' he continued, looking up at Claire, 'That is Manny's drama—the mix of her conscience, her intelligence and her maddening grief. Petey's death was a sort of accident, but Manny is a well-educated Catholic woman by Filipino standards. She hadn't intended to kill Petey with her séances, but morally, she knew her experiments made her responsible for his death. Just as she blamed Narcisa's vanity for Ramon's death. Even when there was no hint she would be found out this week, Manny must have been laying plans to get out of the territory. All she needed to escape from Hong Kong was to distract and confuse the investigation to buy herself the time she needed—for revenge on Narcisa and then escape.'

'If she has escaped; we can't be sure where she is.' Xavier didn't add, 'and if she left Caspar or Leo alive when she fled.'

Claire listened to Fresnay's narrative, but she sat quietly, her thoughts turned inwards, distracted only when an officer walked through the room carrying an open cardboard box contained the cleaver caked with blood and skin. A rosary stuffed into a clear plastic bag left the apartment in the hands of a policeman. And finally, the body in a black rubber bag, carried out by the forensics team. And with each object ceremoniously carted off to the forensics van, her stunned mind took her back to a snapshot, a fleeting glimpse of Narcisa's face and body. Manny, who had every evening so matter-of-factly sliced meat into inch-wide strips for stir-frying in the Sandfords' wok, had slashed Narcisa's beauty into strips of pain—again and again—using the same commonplace cleaver.

The steel blade had lay grinning up at them in the garish light of the corridor's bare bulb. Narcisa's right hand, nearly severed, clutched at the lethal razor-sharp edge, while the other hand held a black-beaded rosary.

In her dulled ears, Fresnay's voice sounded both familiar and strangely distant at the same time. 'Petey died a week ago Sunday. Imagine that for the last eight days, Manny has lived in suspended terror, first over what Inspector Crowley might have seen—something odd, or incongruous—at the scene of Petey's death, and then over Narcisa, with whom she shared a tragic and bitter history. And although Manny was a calculating woman, she was probably in a state of cumulative shock. She hadn't recovered from the loss of Ramon, she'd lost Petey in the process of trying to communicate with Ramon, and all she knew every waking day was that she wanted her son back.'

Xavier looked at him. 'Or perhaps anybody's son?'

Fresnay admitted, 'I can't fully understand the psychology of such a profound loss, or a kidnapping. But in the case of Leo, it was a practical, vengeful precaution—as well as easy. She knew about the back door left unlocked, as well as the appointment with Jun, the gardener, because the silly twit Narcisa had told all her girlfriends. So we can imagine Manny did her duties at the Sandfords'—minimal because she was so discreet in the face of Mrs Sandford's grief, and she watched, she waited, and she took Leo from Narcisa the very next night to distract the investigation from Peter's asthma and to involve her old rival in the crime. I'm guessing Leo was to be her hostage until she could get out of Hong Kong. She took his passport too, just in case. Keep in mind that it might be easier for her to smuggle Leo out of the neighborhood and hide him somewhere downtown—'

'Where?'

'Possibly one of the apartments unemployed *amahs* share by the dozens when they hide from the Labor Bureau after their visa runs out—'

'Easy, because Leo is Eurasian.'

'We have to hope, Claire, because otherwise, the awful question is what did she do with him?'

Giles interrupted, 'You're saying our *amah*, Narcisa, knew all along that Manny caused Petey Sandford's death?'

'When the Sandfords didn't let Manny go back to the Philippines, she gave the money for his antibiotics to Narcisa who had holidays due. Narcisa was the *amah* who spent the money on make-up to impress her boyfriend instead, and didn't take it up north to Manny's mother,' Claire explained.

'Exactly.' Fresnay drew his finger in a line along the dusty coffee table starting from the ashtray. 'This is Manila and' he traced his forefinger towards Xavier opposite him, 'Northwards, this is Narcisa's hometown, Banaue, that she mentioned to Claire in passing the very morning after Leo disappeared. This, almost half a day's bus ride farther northwards, is Manny's home in Bontoc.'

'You see, the Ramon story might have told us everything we needed to know the same day Petey died, but Crowley, and you Claire, Vicky, the other priests and I—*we just didn't listen*. She was talking about staying close to her son through Petey's seizures when she said to you she couldn't talk to him anymore, but she was also going to tell us more if Crowley hadn't been so impatient—a tale of anger and jealousy for the beautiful, young Narcisa that she could not bury—no matter how much she led the prayers for herself and for others.'

Claire looked at Fresnay, concentrating her thoughts away from the bloodshed still behind the kitchen.

'Manny has known all week that Narcisa was the one that would have the guts, or enough fear, to betray her to the Sandfords or the Franklins or the police, because, after all, Narcisa had already betrayed her once,' she said.

Fresnay nodded. 'Narcisa had to protect her family back home in the Philippines from Manny and her relatives who, I assure you, have not forgotten their loss. If she came straight out with the truth about Petey, there would be hell to pay back home for generations to come. She tried to clue me in with her Christmas confession last Friday. She was, no doubt, the girl who went to talk to Ip about the séances. He'll be able to confirm that. But Ip did nothing about it.'

'So, it was Narcisa who planted the tape and the Grover toy for me to find on my walk that day? I had the impression I was followed.'

'Yes, I think Narcisa was watching to make sure you picked it up. If you'd missed it, she probably would have tried again and again to place it in someone's path until it was brought back to Mrs Sandford. It was the biggest clue she had to plant that Petey's fatal seizure was intentionally triggered.'

Claire counted back the days. 'I found it last Wednesday and I'm sure Connie saw me come home with it.' Claire said. 'And it was that very same afternoon while I was at the office that Connie started burning candles and praying over Caspar to protect him.'

Fresnay thought for a moment. 'I'm not defending the candle ceremony over your son's extremities, but maybe Connie knew what Dovie couldn't have known—'

'—We'd just hired Dovie. She was too new in the neighborhood to have joined the Charismatics group.'

'But when Connie saw the tape and the Grover toy, she must have incorrectly jumped to the conclusion that you knew the implication of the music and the seizures already, which put Caspar in danger. She was trying to protect him from Manny.'

'I didn't understand until Saturday when I gave the toys back to Vicky. Even then we didn't really understand.'

Fresnay continued, 'I think all the *amahs* along Tregunter Path fear Manny. Obviously she's capable of anything. You remember my sermon a week ago about witches? I knew something as evil as this was going on, but none of them would tell us priests the name of this the witch. It turns out Narcisa was different. She feared Manny for a very specific and perfectly rational reason. Maybe Narcisa even felt she deserved Manny's revenge, that she'd murdered Ramon, in a way. She wouldn't really feel safe until Manny was gone from Hong Kong.'

'Bloody hell, and I thought she was hiding from me all these days in her room,' Franklin muttered.

'But all that talk about a *guay-lo* lurking around Tregunter Path?' Claire interrupted him.

'It might have been just any *amah* mistaking a plains clothes officer on duty, or maybe the rumor was intentionally started by Manny herself after watching too many serial killer movies on television.'

'Crowley,' sighed Claire. 'I was sure it was Crowley, especially after Cecilia talked to the toy boys down at Repulse Bay, but then I was confused about the poison and Ip. But Ip was only trying to help Petey.'

Fresnay nodded, 'I was wrong earlier this evening on that point. Ip didn't know anything about Ramon or the hatred festering between Narcisa and Manny. He could only take us part of the way.'

Giles Franklin pulled himself together and demanded their attention. 'Then what happened yesterday? Where's Leo? Where's your child?'

'I should have known it was a woman who took Caspar. Only a woman would remember to take the breast milk from the refrigerator,' Claire murmured.

She felt Xavier's arm tightening around her. She saw him look soberly at Fresnay, warning him with his eyes to slow down. Giles Franklin was sitting behind them, and as they turned, he put his head in his hands and they realized suddenly that he was quietly crying. Fresnay went to comfort him and at the priest's touch, the huge Australian started to openly sob, his sweating chest heaving with the strain of the nightmarish week, saying over and over again, 'I need Lily, I need Lily. I don't care what time it is. Call Lily, please. Tell her I need her now, here at home.'

Constable Lim came into the room, bringing with him the small but now familiar sounds of authority; the brisk walk, the static of his walkie-talkie, the murmured Cantonese asides to his assistants.

'Father, could you lead your group to our cars now?'

Xavier looked up, 'At least, couldn't my wife rest before she has to make a statement?'

My wife, he said, my wife . . .

'I'm sorry, sir, it's urgent. We're not going to Arsenal Street. We're going to join Chief Inspector Slaughter at Kai Tak airport. The *amah*,' he checked his notes, 'Manuela Gacad, has just tried to board the first flight to Manila by Cathay. Would you mind coming right away? Please.'

'Has she got Caspar with her?' Claire blurted at Lim. Xavier held Claire's hand tightly, as if to hold her back.

'No, ma'am. But we believe she has the Franklin boy with her. She's trying to pass on a little boy as her illegitimate son.'

'Oh, thank God,' Giles Franklin was sinking under the relief, and Fresnay caught his bulk and helped him towards the corridor. 'I'll be fine now, I'll be fine now, just let me get my trousers,' Franklin blurted, stumbling back toward the bedroom.

Xavier's arm stayed tightly around Claire. She stared. She took a deep breath. She tried to speak. But Lim was already walking away from her and had disappeared back through the kitchen to give instructions to his team. She could not breathe. He had said nothing, nothing more, nothing about a redheaded newborn, not a word about Caspar.

It would not take long to reach Kai Tak before the early morning commuters started crisscrossing the harbor by ferry, by car, by high-speed underground rail, to Mongkok, to Hung Hom, to Kowloon City, to Kun Tong, to Central, to Wan Chai, Kennedy Town, North Point, and beyond the border to the north, to Shenzhen, Panyu, Foshan, Zhuhai and all the destinations of cement blocks, old and new, that made up southern China's success story. But now Claire saw only the empty streets at dawn, soon to be given back, relinquished in six months' time to the tune of a band and the change of a banner.

She kept her slender hand with its long freckled fingers and short musician's nails in Xavier's wide, strong, fist as they rode behind Lim and his driver. 'My wife,' he'd said to Lim. They were going to hold on to each other and come out the other end. They were indissolubly joined, now, she realized, not by joy, but by tragedy, but married they were—even if from now on it would be in a sense she had never desired.

What had happened to Caspar? He was gone. She had the sensation that someone had gripped her throat, his fingers digging deep into her clavicle. She couldn't look Xavier in the eyes, she was so awed by his strength. She wondered at herself, dazedly asking deeply within why she had feared he was too frivolous or too unsteady to partner her? How cruelly she had typed him as unreliable, underestimating the depth of his reserves. She'd worried so much about his past love affairs, her fears had eclipsed from her his true character and masked his potential and hidden his needs.

Lim was talking to Xavier now. ' . . . An escort will pick us up as we turn past the offices of Hong Kong Aircraft Engineering and run us to the side gate.'

But something was wrong. Claire saw it in Xavier's eyes and the recognition of alarm in Fresnay's expression. Something had been said between the two men.

'Xavier, has Manny said anything to the police about Caspar? What did she do with him? Did Lim tell you something?'

Xavier looked at her as if to judge her state of mind. 'Manny isn't talking to the police. They don't have her in custody. She's holding Leo as a hostage until she gets on the plane. They didn't want to tell Giles if they don't have to. They just want to get us all there.'

'Hostage? How?'

Her question was answered within a few minutes.

As they drove through the security entrance at the side of the airport, Claire remembered an occasion in the 1980's when she had stood along with the rest of the press corps, presenting passes, to be allowed into the VIP waiting room. Who had she been waiting to interview? She couldn't remember, probably some politician from the US in transit or a secondary member of the royal family. She'd done so many stories in Hong Kong, her memories of the individual assignments, the years, even the editors they were written for, were beginning to merge in her mind. She'd loved this city so much. It held her youth, her energy, and her freedom. Now, all around her, she saw the end of everything in that pool of darkening blood.

The airport tarmac stretched beyond the parked police van. The runway lay directly in front of them, its end dropping abruptly off in the brown-gray waters off Hung Hom, one of the most notoriously tricky landing strips to navigate in the world.

A flight was taking off, speeding in the direction of Taiwan. Half a dozen police cars and airport security vans stood in front of them, and beyond, Claire saw as she jumped out of the van behind Xavier, a huge Cathay Pacific 747, its engines running.

Nothing could be heard over the engines' roar. A passenger bus stood thirty feet away, emptied of its clusters of travellers who'd innocently stepped onto the tarmac, and then been heedlessly elbowed aside by the frantic *amah* dragging a confused and unwashed toddler by one hand. Leo was crying and trying to protect his ears from the deafening plane noise.

On the tarmac between the bus and the plane, someone had abandoned the kind of cheap red-and-blue striped plastic carrier bag used by half of Asia as a temporary suitcase for gifts and goods needed by relatives back home. The panicked *amah* hadn't made it into the plane yet and for a reason that was horribly clear, their flight was being delayed.

Manny had reached the boarding steps but she and the boy had been denied entry to the plane. She was now screaming at the police who stood at attention, waiting for a command. Claire started to feel she was going to throw up again when she saw the *amah* was holding a short knife with her right hand. With her other arm, she clasped Leo around the stomach. They were witnessing a crazy standoff, with passengers poised to grab the boy if Manny dropped her guard, and police pistols trained on her every move. Every few feet Manny reached back to drag forward the carrier bag, which was filled to bulging with all her worldly goods. But she never released her grip on Leo or took her eyes off the row of security men inching forward.

For a moment, Claire realized, Giles Franklin stood beside her, taking in the extraordinary predicament of his son. Leo's dirty curls were flying in all directions with the wind of the engines. Suddenly he spotted his father near the van. Where the Cantonese and Brits had stood frozen by Manny's threats, the Aussie father didn't hesitate. Giles Franklin lumbered forward so fast, Manny's shouted threats went unheard under the roar of the Cathay engines. As he lurched forward, Manny pressed the knife right into Leo's throat. She drew blood. Leo screamed.

Giles' bulk moved across the tarmac with unbelievable speed, but he wasn't as fast as Manny who had turned Leo into a better position for her final, lethal stroke of the knife in a desperate attempt to halt the onslaught of Chinese security dashing right behind the Australian. Whether the uniformed men wanted to stop Giles or to assist him an attacking Manny was impossible within those seconds to guess.

Claire saw in a second what was about to happen and felt faint. Xavier was behind her, half supporting her. For a second, it seemed Giles would reach his son in time, then beyond him, Claire saw Manny's arm lift again to strike. The enormous Australian reached the Filipina, grabbed the knife and savagely kicked Manny to the ground. With superhuman energy, she scrambled back up and insanely yanking her carrier bag into her arms, scrambled and stumbled up the boarding stairs. People already inside the plane were silently screaming and pointing out the windows, Claire realized, some gesturing wildly inside to the crew.

A stewardess stood at the top of the stairway. She saw Manny wildly struggling with the over-packed carrier, lugging it up a few steps at a time. The stewardess started to jerk at the door of the plane, which— on the command from the police relayed through the tower—now started to back away from the boarding steps.

Seeing the plane sliding away from the top step, Manny finally let go of the carrier bag. She dashed up the last steps pursued by Slaughter and his men.

For a second, Claire saw with disbelief the amah gauge the widening gap between the plane, the closing door and the boarding steps. She leaned forward and grabbed at the door, her body stretched across the space twenty feet above the tarmac. She took one final leap and stumbled forward just as the airplane door swung closed—on her neck.

Her body hung horrifically from the side of airplane. Her legs and arms pounded and kicked, then twitched.

The door was pushed back open by the terrified stewardess within a second, but too late, knocking Manny brutally off the side of the plane and directly down onto the tarmac. The confused pilot and co-pilot could be seen conferring with each other and the tower. They started backing up the plane now to return it to its original position.

In the next moment, the plane's front wheels were moving again, but directly towards Manny's broken, unconscious body. Claire screamed out her own private disbelief in a cacophony of confused shouts.

The engines finally died. As Slaughter and the airport team rushed underneath the plane, the sounds of construction, of ferry horns, of any morning in Hong Kong went on all around them.

Another plane took off in the direction of Guangdong Province.

Minutes passed as Xavier held Claire. Her eyes filled with tears. Another plane smoothly lifted off in an indifferent roar. Sirens screamed all around them.

Fresnay stood at their side. He spoke to himself, more than to his two friends. 'Like the *magtatangals* who appeared headless by night. Or the *asuang* who could fly. But she couldn't fly fast enough.'

The three of them stood together for many, many minutes. Everyone else seemed to have so much to do. The scene filled with more trucks, cars, police and airport officials. Claire saw an ambulance carry off Leo and his father to Queen Elizabeth Hospital. No one spoke to them, and Claire realized there was no time for the three *guay-los* standing at the edge of the tarmac, staring at the dismayed and confused passengers rounded up and taken away from the shuttle bus for another flight.

Fresnay suddenly remembered himself and crossed the tarmac to Manny's body, even as her remains were being photographed by the police. They shouted at him to clear off, but heedless of their orders, the priest knelt next to her broken neck and recited prayers for her soul in a fiercely defiant act of concentration.

Claire and Xavier could not look each other in the face, but stood watching dumbly. Off in the distance, the Manila airline crew was driven back to the airport building.

Fresnay stood up and left Manny to the police force.

It was time to leave. They watched as the police picked up Manny's body. One of the airport's service truck drivers signaled to the policeman Lim. In response, Lim ordered a subordinate to cross the tarmac and collect Manny's bulky carrier bag off the stairway as evidence. He gestured for the junior officer to load it into one of the police vans headed back to the airport police station.

Off in the distance, Claire saw the younger policeman yank at the heavy bag and heave it over his back to carry out the order.

Suddenly, from inside the carrier bag, came a baby's desperate squalling.

epilogue

'So, in the end,' Robert looked down at Xavier and Claire standing in front of him, 'we can rejoice that God has included the possibility of marriage and family, among all the different kinds of relationships or paths of spiritual growth offered to us. For each one of us, married and unmarried, beloved or lonely, benefits from the promises made before us today. We hope for a stable partnership between two people in love, but more than that. Let us, as witnesses, not just friends, pray together for a partnership that says love is not an accident, it is not a hit and run vehicle, it is not infatuation—what a great word for that!—no, let us pray for a partnership that says this; love, real love, best grows out of the active decision, the firmest commitment, the opening up of the will to feed that devotion and support it to the best of our human ability.'

'A partnership that carries these overwhelming vows, until death,' Fresnay widened his eyes dramatically,'—this promise before friends and families transcends the fact of love that exists in us today, and says it will be nurtured, it will be protected and it will be recognized not only by this couple, but by all around us.'

'Merely a social contract? Yes, Yes! It is a public declaration that says, 'We will make love!'

Fresnay raised his arms and threw up the long sleeves of his plain vestments in a happy gesture of abandonment, getting a good laugh from his small audience. He dropped his voice and said slowly again, 'But it is also a gift to all of us here today, one in which we all share. It is a declaration from this couple, who are saying, we will not just enjoy our love, we will make, we will create, love!'

Soon it was Caspar's turn. Fresnay baptized him with all the pomp one could give a restless baby whose head had been shaved clean of all red fuzz for his journey to Manila, and whose left shoulder was still sore from bruising. Manny's desperate attempt to smuggle him home to Bontoc had included removing his telltale hair with a dull razor.

Without no passport for Caspar, Manny had drugged him with her own sleeping pills and then cushioned him on top of her clothing in the huge striped carrier with newspaper crumpled lightly over his face while she stood in line at the ticketing counter. Then she had held him in her arms while the carrier bag was X-rayed, but smuggled him back into the bag again through check-in at the gate and into the passenger bus for boarding the plane.

She had wanted a little boy of her own again. She had tried to kidnap two in the bargain.

A sun cap hid the Band Aids covering the bruises on Caspar's skull, until Robert lifted it off to pour holy water on his forehead. Predictably, this triggered up a miserable wail and the rest of the ceremony turned into a high-speed wrap-up and race to the luncheon banquet spread on a table next door on Ah Fok's terrace.

Ah Fok's two grown sons had grumbled on foot all the way into Tai Long Bay with crates of champagne and red wine strapped to their sturdy backs. Dovie had enlisted her daughter to help her carry the ingredients for baking the cake, which was beyond Ah Fok's repertoire. Berkeley still lingered in Claire's core and she'd asked Dovie for a banana cake full with walnuts, large enough to feed a crowd. It had been cooked in three sections in Father Fresnay's counter-top oven and then assembled and frosted on the terrace an hour before the wedding began in the chapel.

Claire had been brought close to tears of appreciation to see the arrivals straggling down that final slope towards Fresnay's house in their hiking clothes. Alistair Evans-Smith hiked in with the Forsythes, chatting the entire time with Miriam and Gordon about developments in the New Territories, the choice of the Chief Executive to replace the Governor, the likely lineup of his future cabinet—and making it clear as they marched gaily down the path and into the shade of the cemented terrace, that all the three old colonial civil servants needed was an impromptu branch as a walking stick and they could make light work of a two-hour hike through the sun.

Vicky had bowed out at the last minute, on the excuse of her pregnancy, but her husband Ian, said Gordon, 'was toddling along' behind. Sure enough, Vicky's husband arrived a full ten minutes after his in-laws. He was breathless, red, sweaty, and clearly unfit from a life of long hours in the cockpit.

Though many of the other guests had lived in Hong Kong all their working lives, some had never visited Ham Tin village before, particularly Claire's fellow foreign correspondents who used the city more as a regional hub than a home. But Lornia was quite at home, and was her bright self again, joking with Claire that 'Every girl in the office is sorry to see the boss get married.'

Cecilia had hiked the Sai Kung hills all her life. She came with her brother Winston Chau whose backpack was armed with congratulatory E-mails from all the editors in New York and correspondents around the region. They were filled with rude jokes about the order of events, like 'We hear this story carried an interested side-bar in diapers,' or 'Are you sure you didn't get your deadlines mixed up?' which drew predictable chuckles and toasts.

There were Chinese friends Claire and Xavier had made during their weekends with Fresnay in the village, sitting together along a wooden bench on one side of the terrace eating already and telling Cantonese marriage jokes. There was a businessman Claire had worked closely with on a story a few years back, and curiously, both Barrie and Fiona Reynolds. Claire hardly knew them, but they had heard of the wedding from the Sandfords and invited themselves without hesitation. Fiona formally wished Claire well, and helped herself to more than a drink or two. They had ploughed up to Sai Kung from Queen's Pier on a speedboat and had their 'boat boy' ferry them through the rough surf in a dinghy. Fiona's gold-laced boat sneakers were drenched with saltwater and dry dirt from the clamber up from the beach, but she seemed in good spirits.

'Sorry about your car,' Claire said to Barrie, more as conversational filler than anything else.'

'Turned up in Canton in a round-up of stolen vehicles, dragged out of the harbor in an airtight cover and then driven north,' chuckled Barrie, his mouth full of Ah Fok's shrimp dim sum.

'You mean another Benz-in-a-Bag scam?' asked Claire.

He nodded, 'Bloody clever. The cars don't surface 'til they're out of Hong Kong waters, and frankly, I won't be in a hurry to get it driven back down here. I think we all had a lot more peace of mind after it was nicked and Fiona had to be driven everywhere.' He looked at her, eyebrows raised, 'Rather like the feeling of relief you got at the end of *Jaws* when they killed the shark.' He was chuckling to himself strangely.

'You personally arranged to have it stolen!' Claire joked and was startled when Barrie slowly turned full face to her, winked slowly, and then dodged off to talk 'government' with Gordon.

Claire got the feeling that she should spend time with Alistair, but didn't know whether or how to tell him she had discovered the true tragedy of Viola's death. When she sat down to eat her cake with him, he surprised her. 'You know, your favorite police officer announced a major life change.'

'Not a sex-change operation!'

'No!' he laughed. 'God, woman! You're a bloody Victorian with all your little sexual nightmares! No!' he caught his breath again and stopped laughing finally, 'He's seen his main chance is clearly not in the police force. So, he's quit the force to start a Balinese restaurant with an Indonesian partner. He's in love, quite happily, with someone his own age. Or at least that's what he told his immediate superior last week.'

'So I wronged an innocent man.'

'With a closet full of child pornography,' said Evans-Smith dryly. 'Yes.'

'Well, good luck to him. I trust he'll be performing something on his own stage.'

'Apparently he sings straight songs quite well. His mother was, as it turns out, a pretty popular cabaret artiste from Leicester in her day. Worked the cruise lines to Marbella, that sort of thing.'

'So that's what she did to support him. He certainly admired her for raising him on her own.'

Evans-Smith drew himself up proudly and announced, 'Attention, attention! More news! After ten weeks with the 'Evans-Below, Althea already loathes England, can't get good help, finds her friends have all withered up into boring old sticks so she has decided to come back here, effective as of yesterday. If I know her, she'll be completely unpacked and back to giving orders at the Kung Tong Women's Health Advisory Coalition by, um, let's say, next Thursday.'

'Then, you're not leaving!'

The sunlight caught the top of his white hair as he turned to Claire; 'I'm not leaving!' he mocked her. 'Not only that, I'm going to work for the enemy!'

'You're going to stay on in government? I thought Beijing wouldn't allow it. Everyone they fingered for the future "elected" legislature is going to be like some toadie or well, you know, no offense, but certainly not you!'

'No, not in the government itself, of course. Beijing wouldn't stand for that. But some of my old Chinese friends out in the Territories here have hired me as a consultant to act as a liaison of information and support system to London as things here along the border undergo what you Americans call melt-down.'

'I hope you know what you're doing. You know, the old staying-on syndrome. Didn't Paul Scott write a sad short story about it, some old couple laying down to die in India, laughed at by all the locals?'

Alistair rolled his eyes. 'Do I act like the Raj type, molting underneath some mosquito net? I want to be useful, keep my hand in, watch the deluge, if you insist.'

There was an extraordinary youthful glow on his face and he danced up to refresh his drink. He was not renouncing 'home,' she realized as she heard him correct Ah Fok's elder boy on the proper drinks proportion in Cantonese dialect. He was already home. And Claire envied him, knowing that protecting Hong Kong in his own way against Beijing's detailed planning and vast manpower would be his greatest, if ultimately futile, challenge yet.

Fabienne had not been invited to the wedding, nor did she send a gift. Claire realized as Xavier's silence about Fabienne stretched for hours into days and weeks that this was Xavier's choice. Fabienne would always be to Claire like a parallel line running within Xavier's reach, but not crossing, as the three of them moved into the future. Claire digested the understanding that she would never know what their last words had been, whether on the phone or by letter, or even if they had resolved their anger at all.

But she had decided to risk more, to risk all, with him, anyway.

Xavier stood with Fresnay directly across the terrace from her, the two men intently discussing something. She enjoyed watching Xavier from a distance, so clearly comfortable now with her friends, new and old, confident as never before in his place in her life. He was laughing at something, then listening intently and nodding. She had never seen him look so youthful and she was pleased when without warning, he looked up for her and found her eyes across the crowded space.

She wondered briefly what point it was that Robert was trying to make to Xavier, what subject so amused and concerned her lover and her friend. Although her better sense told her otherwise, she hoped in her vanity they were gossiping about her.

After all, she had already become the wife and mother, but it was her one and only day as the bride.

The End

acknowledgments

The Christianization of the Philippines: Problems and Perspectives, Miguel A. Bernad, S.J., The Filipiniana Book Guild, 1972

Martina Burns Bertoni of Grosse Pointe, Michigan, for accounts of epilepsy triggers and symptoms as well as for passing on:

Seizures and Epilepsy in Childhood: A Guide for Parents, John M. Freeman, M.D., Eileen P.G. Vining, M.D., and Diana J. Pillas, John Hopkins Medical Institutions

Another book that was quite useful was:
Seizures, Epilepsy and Your Child, Jorge C. Lagos, Md. 1974

'I Wonder Where My Easy Rider's Gone,' Mae West, from the film, *She Done Him Wrong*

The poem by Charles Baudelaire, one of Father Fresnay's favorite poets, translated by William Rees in *The Penguin Book of French Poetry, 1820-1950*, (Penguin Group, 1992 edition,) as follows:
'Languorous Asia and burning Africa, an entire distant world, absent, almost extinct, lives in your depths, aromatic forest! As other spirits sail on music, mine, O my love, swims on your perfume.
I will go there, where trees and men, full of sap, swoon in a long slow trance in the burning heat of the climate; strong tresses, be the sea swell that carries me away! You enfold, ebony ocean, a dazzling dream of sails, of rowers, of pennants and of masts . . . '

Information on herbal poisons and medicines were gathered primarily from the following sources:

Herbal Pharmacology in the People's Republic of China, from the National Academy of Sciences 1974

Legendary Chinese Healing Herbs, Henry C. Lu, Sterling Publishing Co., Inc. New York 1991

The Illustrated Dictionary of Chinese Medicinal Herbs, Wee Yeow Chin and Hsuan Keng, CRCS Publications 1992 (originally from Times Editions 1990 from Singapore)

And last, but not least, thanks to the Mystery Writers of America's "Mentor Program"—in particular, the prolific veteran mystery author Justin Scott who served as an MWA mentor.

D. L. Kung
2011

D. L. Kung worked in Asia for over twenty years, writing for a number of publications, including *The Economist* and later *Business Week*, *The International Herald Tribune*, *National Public Radio*, *The Washington Post* and *The South China Morning Post*. Kung won The Overseas Press Club's award for Best Human Rights Reporting in 1991 for an exposé on China's prison labor exports, and Kung's play based on Chinese writer-in-detention He Depu, *Dear Mr Rogge*, won a commendation from the BBC World Service/British Council's biennial International Playwriting Contest in 2009.